On Laughton Moor

Lisa Hartley

For my family, and in memory of Wack Woollas (1927-2009)

1

The victim lay on his back, arms spread wide as if pleading. His face showed traces of blood, though his injuries seemed to be at the back of his head where the liquid had pooled. A crime scene tent had been erected around him and Knight stood inside it, considering the dead man. Young, probably late twenties, and athletic looking, the sort of bloke you might think would be able to look after himself in a street fight. Knight didn't think that a street fight was what had happened though. There was no bruising on the man's face or hands. This incident may have started in a pub but it had ended out here, in an alley that ran parallel to one of the main tourist stretches in Northolme. The town had its fair share of visitors, nothing like the numbers that flocked to York or nearby Lincoln, but enough to keep the tea rooms and souvenir shops in business. Knight doubted many tourists had realised the alley was there; it seemed mainly to be a place where the nearby shops kept their dustbins, so not exactly a sight worth seeing. No doubt the place would be full of gawping bystanders if they were being allowed near but both the alley and the surrounding area had been emptied of people and cordoned off, much to the outrage of the local shopkeepers.

Emerging from the tent, Knight glanced around the alley. Heavy rain fell steadily. Knight made his way through to the cobbled street beyond before removing the protective clothing he'd put on to view the body. The photographer had done his work and a video recording had also been made. Scene of crime officers were busy, always reminding Knight of worker bees as they moved around the area. A short, stout man strode over.

'You're DI Knight? I'm Beckett, the pathologist.' He gestured towards the alley. 'Not a good way to end your night out.'

Knight frowned.

'By being killed, you mean?'

The doctor grimaced.

'You've got to admit, it's a strange one. Such a public place.'

'Shops though, not houses. No pubs or restaurants on this street, not much risk of passers by. I'm presuming he was killed last night?'

Beckett nodded.

'Without really committing myself, I'd say between midnight and five am. Of course, he's been out in the rain and cold all night so . . . There'll be more to say after the post mortem, but the cause of death seems pretty clear. He's taken a good few blows to the back of his head.'

'With?'

'Blunt instrument.'

'Right.' said Knight, with a sigh.

Beckett was shuffling his feet, obviously keen to be on his way.

'No sign that he fought back, he seems to have been taken by surprise.'

'He'd probably had a few.'

'And his jeans were undone.'

'Any sign of sexual activity or assault?'

'Not so far, but again, I couldn't say for certain until after the post mortem. Maybe he'd just stopped for a pee.'

'That's what I was thinking. Thanks, Doctor.'

In the station canteen, Detective Sergeant Catherine Bishop waited impatiently behind an indecisive DC who was dithering over crisps, seemingly unable to make up his mind between cheese and onion and salt and vinegar. She prodded him in the back.

'Hey Chris, why don't you just have ready salted? Takes the pain out of choosing.'

He started and span around.

'Very funny. What's up with you?'

Bishop shrugged, then spread her arms wide.

'Just another day in paradise isn't it?'

The DC grunted, turned back to the crisps and took a bag of cheese and onion. Bishop pushed past him, paid for a cappuccino and went to sit down. Chris Rogers followed and sat in the chair opposite her.

'So what's made you so cheerful?' Rogers tore his crisps open and offered them to Bishop. She crunched a couple loudly before replying.

'Nothing, time of year maybe. Dark when you get up, dark when you get home. It's miserable.'

'Suppose so. Still, Christmas is coming.'

Bishop sighed. 'And?'

Rogers shook his head then tipped it back, shaking the last of the crisps into his mouth.

'I see Inspector Wallpaper's back in.'

'Back this morning.' Bishop nodded. 'Not much of a tan to say he's been away for a week.'

'Depends where he's been though. Not everywhere's that hot at this time of year.'

Sitting back in her chair, Bishop folded her arms.

'What's the point then? If I'm going to spend a day travelling on a plane and buses I want it to at least be hot when I get there.'

'Me too, but who knows with him? We went away with the in laws this summer – bloody nightmare.'

'Really? I thought you got on with them?'

'I do for a few hours, not for a week.'

She grinned at him.

'Don't let your wife hear you say that.'

Getting to his feet, Rogers said with a mock shudder,

'Don't worry, I won't. See you later.'

Bishop sipped her coffee, thinking about Inspector Wallpaper, as he'd come to be known since his arrival from the Met the month before. Detective Inspector Jonathan Knight. He was supposed to be a sound detective, but no one knew any more than that. She couldn't understand what he was doing here; why would a good detective leave London with all its opportunity to transfer to Lincolnshire? All right, the job still needed to be done, but talk about strange decisions. Of course, it may not have been his choice, maybe he wasn't a "good" detective after all. Perhaps he'd been a naughty boy and been sent somewhere he was well out of the way. No one knew, and Knight wasn't telling. He'd been polite and pleasant when she'd had cause to speak to him but also reserved, or as reserved as his rank allowed him to be anyway. Time would tell. Bishop glanced at her watch, drained the last of her cappuccino and stood. Back to it.

As she returned to her desk, Simon Sullivan, another of the DCs, called to her.

'DI Knight's just gone out at a hundred miles an hour Sarge, said to tell you to ring him as soon as possible.'

'Right, thanks.'

Bishop sat down and reached for the phone on her desk. Why hadn't Knight sent Sullivan to find her? There weren't that many places she might be, only the canteen or the toilets. She shook her head as she dialled Knight's mobile. He answered after the first ring.

'DC Sullivan said you wanted me, sir?'

'That's right, I need you to come down to the town centre, a body's been found. Bring DC Sullivan too.'

He gave the location and Bishop was up and out of her chair.

As Beckett scurried away, trying to avoid the puddles, Knight made his way over to the head of the scene of crime officers, Mick Caffery.

'What have you got so far?'

'Well, there's no wallet on him which seems strange, especially if he was on a night out. No mobile phone and no sign of the weapon so far either.'

Knight glanced back towards the alley. He'd noticed the victim wore black shoes rather than trainers and his jeans were smart and expensive looking, as was his designer T shirt.

'The majority of the blood is obviously around his head but we've found other traces in the area, probably deposited as the weapon was swung back and forth.'

'Any urine?'

'In that area, there's probably gallons of it. We'll see what we can get, the rain's not helping. You're meaning because of his trousers being undone? Caught short, as it were?'

'Something along those lines.'

Caffery nodded and stepped away. Knight took a deep breath, then blew onto his hands. He was beginning to feel the cold, though not as much as the unfortunate young man who had found the body. He had started a fortnight's work experience in one of the local shops that day and had stumbled on the body, almost literally it seemed, when taking some rubbish out into the alley. Knight had almost smiled when he'd heard that. It made a change from a jogger finding it, or someone walking their dog. Still, it wasn't something the boy sitting hunched in the back of Knight's car would forget in a hurry.

'Sir?'

Knight looked up. DS Bishop and DC Sullivan had arrived. He quickly explained the situation to them, then when they'd put on their protective clothing, led them towards the alleyway. Bishop and Sullivan approached the victim carefully. A suspicious death in Northolme was a rare occurrence.

'Bloody hell.' exclaimed Sullivan.

'It's Craig Pollard.' Bishop whispered.

2

DCI Keith Kendrick sat back in his chair, resting his hands on his considerable belly. Knight, sitting across the conference table from Kendrick, waited as his boss organised his thoughts.

'So Bishop and Sullivan both recognised the dead man?'

'Yes, and according to them, most of our uniforms would recognise him too. Craig Pollard was well known around town. Fights in pubs, drunk and disorderly, disturbing the peace . . . '

'The sort of person who could get himself killed in a bar room brawl and no one would raise an eyebrow then?' said Kendrick.

'If it had been a bar room brawl but this wasn't. Doesn't look like it anyway, unless he was followed.'

The phone on the table between them began to ring, and Kendrick reached out a hairy hand to grab the receiver. Knight watched Kendrick's expression change from mild irritation at the interruption to confusion, then to disbelief.

'And you found this in his pocket? Why the hell didn't you tell Knight this at the scene? Rain? What do you mean, it was raining? Christ, Beckett, you won't melt, you're not a bloody jelly baby . . . Email it then, email a copy, I want to see it now. Yes, now. Thanks.' Kendrick, shaking his head vigorously, replaced the receiver. 'You'll never believe this – Beckett's found a photo in the victim's pocket, which he should have done at the scene, of course, but apparently he was getting wet.' Kendrick's face twisted in disgust. 'Idiot. Anyway, this photo is of - and it's like the plot of a crappy TV programme – our lovely police station.'

Knight stared at him, brow wrinkled. 'I don't follow. Why would . . . '

'I've no idea why,' Kendrick interrupted, 'but the fact is, that's what was there. Beckett's emailing me a copy of the picture over. It's bloody weird, if you ask me.'

There was a pause as both men puzzled over what Beckett had said. After a couple of minutes there was a ping from Kendrick's mobile and he hauled it from his jacket pocket.

'Right, let's have a look, let the dog see the rabbit.' he said, chunky fingers prodding at the screen. 'Yes, he's right. There's the building, looking as depressing as ever, and a figure going in through the door . . . looks like . . .' He held the phone out to Knight.

'Catherine Bishop.' Knight said, peering at the screen.

'I don't like it.' Kendrick said, after another pause. 'Did DS Bishop say anything else about Pollard?'

'No, she just knew who he was when she saw him, but then Sullivan did too.' Keith Kendrick stood, stuck his head through the door and spoke to the nearest officer. He collected a fresh jug of water from the dispenser and three plastic cups on his way back to his seat. Knight gratefully filled a cup with water, drank, and refilled the cup. There was a light knock on the door, and Catherine Bishop appeared.

'You wanted to see me, guv?'

'Sit down, Catherine,' Kendrick said, pulling out a chair. Knight poured a cup of water and slid it over the table towards her. She gave him a quick smile of thanks, not quite meeting his eyes. 'Now then Sergeant, something a bit odd's turned up and I wanted a quick chat about it.' Kendrick said.

Bishop looked questioningly from one man to the other.

'Odd? What do you mean?'

'Doctor Beckett did a proper search of Pollard's body - eventually,' Kendrick raised his eyebrows. 'And in Pollard's pocket, he found this.'

He held the phone out to Bishop, who squinted at it.

'In Pollard's pocket? Looks like me coming into work – but why?'

Kendrick set his phone on the table.

'Like I said, Catherine – it's odd.'

'Creepy is what it is.' Bishop shuddered, taking a sip of water. 'Makes no sense.'

'Is there anything else you can tell us about Craig Pollard?'

'No, guv. I mean, as soon as I saw the body I knew it was him but I think every other person in town would have been able to tell you that, definitely every copper. He's been in trouble one way or another for as long as I've been on the force. I've never arrested him, and I certainly had nothing to do with his death, so . . . '

Kendrick met her eyes.

'No one's saying you had, we just need to try to make sense of it. It looks like Pollard upset someone in a pub or club or wherever he'd been, who followed him and hit him a bit harder than they meant to.'

Bishop glanced at Knight, who said:

'But does it? He was hit on the back of the head several times, according to the doctor. It didn't look like he'd been punched or kicked or glassed. Of course, we'll have to wait until we get the post mortem report, but . . . '

Kendrick pinched his lower lip between his thumb and forefinger, frowning hard.

'Point taken, but it could still be some bloke he'd upset before who saw their chance, gave him a crack over the head and got carried away.'

Knight nodded.

'Could be. But what did they find along the way to hit him with, and where's the weapon?'

'Until we get the full reports from Caffery and the pathologist, we can't make up our minds about anything. We need to get Pollard formally indentified and start sniffing around his friends, see if anyone will give us anything we can use.'

'Assuming he had any friends.' muttered Bishop.

'Blokes like Pollard usually know a lot of people, Sergeant,' said Kendrick. 'Whether any of them will care enough that he's dead to tell us anything is another matter, and as for the photo . . . '

Catherine Bishop gave another shudder.

3

I did it. I can't quite believe it. When it was over, I waited. I didn't think he was breathing. There was nothing left of him in his face, none of the arrogance and cruelty I'd seen there, none of the boastfulness he'd displayed in the pub or the confidence that radiated from him as he chatted to women in clubs. He was gone, I was sure of it. The back of his head was a mess. I held the mirror over his mouth, and although it was streaked with rain, there was no misting, no breath was left in him, no life. I stared down at him. There was blood but not as much as I'd expected, not that I'd really had any idea how it would be. There isn't any way you can rehearse this, to have a practice or dry run. As soon as the first blow had connected I knew I could do it, knew I would. Such a strange sound, not like the crack of hitting a cricket ball, more of a solid sort of thump. I left him lying there. I'll have to find somewhere to burn the clothes I wore soon.

One down.

4

'All right, all right, let's have a bit of hush, shall we?' Kendrick bellowed over the racket as he barged into the briefing room, clutching a sheaf of paper in his hand. Placing the sheets on the desk in front of him, he rounded on his audience, set both hands on the surface of the desk and leaned forward. The noise abated briefly, then stopped altogether as Kendrick glared at the assembled officers.

'Better,' he said. 'You're like a gaggle of school kids sometimes. Now. The PM on our victim, Craig Pollard was conducted this afternoon. I know that Pollard was a familiar face to many of you,' Kendrick raised his eyebrows at a uniformed constable who had given a snort of derision at that. The constable shut up. 'The report confirms that Pollard died sometime after midnight, but before four am. He was killed where he was found - the body hadn't been moved.' Kendrick consulted his notes. 'The alcohol level in his blood indicated that his reactions would have been slowed by the amount he had drunk; in fact, Doctor Beckett was quite surprised that Pollard had been able to stumble along at all.' Again, Kendrick was interrupted, this time by someone muttering, 'Typical.' not quite under their breath. Kendrick folded his arms and rocked back on his heels. When he spoke again, his voice was soft, dangerous. 'Can I remind you that whatever dealings you've had with Craig Pollard in the past, he's now our victim?' He left a deliberate pause, just long enough to make his audience, especially those on the front row, right under the DCI's nose, squirm a little. Eventually, Kendrick resumed his summing up, his voice businesslike again. 'The report also states that several of the blows inflicted on the back of Pollard's head could have been the one to actually kill him, such was the severity of the damage they had done.' There were a few winces at this. 'The person inflicting the blows was right handed and seemingly shorter than Pollard. However, as Pollard was over six feet tall, that doesn't exclude too many people.' Kendrick spread his hands. 'So. That's where we are. The PM hasn't really told us much that we didn't know before. Doc Beckett did find a photo in Craig Pollard's pocket, which was of our beloved police station.' Kendrick gestured behind him with a sharp movement of his thumb. One of the constables on the front row raised his hand doubtfully.

'A photo of this place, sir? Why?'

'I don't know.' Kendrick said. 'DI Knight, will you summarise what our friends in uniform have been able to find out please?'

Knight rose slowly from his chair and made his way to the front of the room. A couple of jokers on the back row nudged each other as Knight cleared his throat and took his time before beginning to speak.

'Unfortunately, again, not much has come to light. We've collected all of the CCTV footage from the pubs in the area, and the streets Pollard may have walked down on his way to the place he met his death, but the officers who had been working on the film haven't had any luck yet.'

Kendrick blew out his cheeks. 'And that's it?'

Knight nodded. 'The local shop owners couldn't help either, since Pollard died overnight and none of them were around. We're going back later to the pubs, talking to people who may have been there drinking last night, but there's very little to go on at the moment.'

With a shrug, Knight went back to his seat.

'Our own Sherlock Holmes.' a voice said softly. Bishop, seated in the front row, turned and glared over her shoulder. Innocent faces smiled back at her. Bishop shook her head, turned around. Knight didn't help himself sometimes, she had to admit. She focused back on Kendrick.

'DS Bishop? You and DC Sullivan went to find out Pollard's movements last night?'

Bishop stood, then turned and faced her colleagues. She had worked with most of them for a number of years now, and knew they were generally a good bunch. In death, Craig Pollard seemed to be generating about as much sympathy as he had in life – none. Still, his life had been cut short, and he hadn't deserved that, no matter how much trouble he had been. Bishop flipped open the cover of her notebook.

'We spoke to Craig Pollard's brother, Mike, who was able to tell us which pub where Craig usually started his nights out in, so we went there first. It turns out that Pollard actually spent the whole night in that same pub. The bar man we talked to was working last night and he was able to confirm that Pollard had arrived there around nine pm, drank steadily until around twelve thirty, then stumbled out of the door. He spoke to a few people, but not for more than a couple of minutes. He left alone.'

'Sounds like this bar man had nothing better to do than watch customers all night.' said Kendrick. 'Quiet, was it?'

Bishop nodded.

'Seems so, although Sunday nights usually are apparently. Pollard was one of the few Sunday night regulars. Friday and Saturday he'd just call in for a few drinks then go off elsewhere, but his Sunday routine was just to sit at the bar and drink himself silly.'

'And always by himself?' asked Kendrick.

'Usually. Occasionally his brother or someone else joined him for a couple of pints, but not very often. The bar man said Pollard seemed to be in a world of his own, just interested in staring at the bottom of a glass. Pollard wouldn't enter into conversation, even if someone spoke to him.'

'Interesting.' said Kendrick. 'Worrying about something?'

'Doesn't sound like Pollard.' Bishop replied, and there were nods of agreement all over the room.

'And only on Sunday nights, from what you've said.' added Knight.

Bishop nodded, then glanced down at her notebook.

'Pollard's brother Mike said as far as he knew, Craig had no worries, no problems. Pollard's a complete saint according to his mum and dad too.'

Kendrick snorted.

'Hmm, a hint of rose tinted spectacles there, I think. What did his girlfriend have to say, Jonathan?'

Knight smiled faintly.

'She didn't agree.'

Kendrick waved him forward again.

'Let's hear it, then.'

He'd gone himself with one of the uniformed officers, PC Emily Lawrence, to speak to Kelly Whitcham, expecting her to be grief stricken and tearful. The address wasn't officially Pollard's, but according to his family, this was where he often slept. The house was in the middle of a terrace, one of the streets on the outskirts of town where the local council had bought many of the houses and rented them to tenants. It wasn't run down exactly, but there were better places to live. Whitcham's house had vertical blinds and a broken upstairs window. Further down the street, two small boys bounced a football across the road to each other. Knight knocked on the door, eventually seeing movement behind the frosted glass panels. Fingers appeared, holding the metal letterbox open from the inside.

'Who is it?'

Knight glanced at Lawrence, feeling a little silly, then squatted slightly and leant closer to the door.

'I'm Detective Inspector Knight.'

'Oh, right. Police? I can't open the door.'

'You can't? Why not?'

'Because Craig kept us locked in here and I haven't got a key, that's why not.'

Knight frowned. 'You mean you can't get out?'

'We can't get out and you can't get in, unless you want me to smash a window and I'm not doing that with my kids inside.'

Knight shook his head in disbelief.

'You can't stay in there forever. Would you have any objection to me calling some colleagues and asking them to break the door open?'

There was a pause. Eventually, Whitcham said, 'And how would I explain that to the landlord?'

'We'd sort that out, don't worry.' Knight reassured her.

'All right then.'

Sighing, Knight took out his phone and called the DCI. There was some muttering and complaining, but Kendrick agreed to send some officers over. Knight told Kelly Whitcham what was happening, then he and PC Lawrence went to wait in the car. Knight started the engine and turned the heater on full. After ten minutes or so, a marked police van drew up and two grinning uniformed officers climbed out. Knight went over to meet them, Lawrence not far behind.

'Afternoon, sir.' said one, opening the back doors of the van.

'Having a bit of trouble?' the other asked.

'Something like that.' Knight agreed.

'No problem, we'll soon be in with this little lovely.'

The officer lifted the Big Red Key from the back of the van. It was a battering ram, constructed from steel, painted red. The officer approached the door, Knight trailing behind him.

'Stand away from the door, Miss Whitcham.' Knight called.

Gripping the handles on the Big Red Key with both gloved hands, the officer swung it towards the door. There was a thud, and the door was open.

'Pah,' the officer said, disappointed. 'An easy one.'

Knight grinned at him. 'Thanks very much.'

'Anytime.' he replied, and strode away.

Knight turned back to the open door. The girl who stood there seemed to be only in her late teens, but he knew Kelly Whitcham was twenty four. Thin, with light brown hair and tired eyes, she wore grey jogging bottoms, a light blue hooded sweatshirt and what Knight's mother would have called bed socks. They might once have been white and fluffy, but were now grey, thin and in need of a wash.

'Miss Whitcham good afternoon. I'm sorry about Craig's death.' said Knight awkwardly.

'I'm not.' said Whitcham. 'You'd better come in, now you can.'

They followed her through a short hallway, carpeted in a dingy brown, to the living room. It was almost completely empty. Two small children sat on a double mattress in front of a huge flat screen TV that was fixed to the wall above their heads. They wore pyjamas, though it was mid afternoon, clean but faded and creased. They turned as Knight and Lawrence followed their mother into the room and looked at them with interest. A boy and a girl around three years old, the boy fair, the girl with long, curly dark hair. They were sharing a bag of crisps, the space between them on the mattress and a second bag of crisps showed where Whitcham had been sitting when Knight knocked on the door.

'Connor, Jessica, stand up so these people can sit down please.'

Whitcham bent over the mattress, sweeping crisp crumbs from it.

'No, please, it's fine. We'll stand. Could we talk in the kitchen?'

With a strained smile, Whitcham said, 'It's okay, they know about Craig. His brother Mike came to tell me, shouted it through the letterbox. It was ridiculous really, didn't feel real. What do you want to know?'

Knight hesitated.

'All right, we'll talk in the kitchen. I'll warn you though, it's not up to much.'

She led the way across the thin carpet.

The kitchen was also almost empty of furniture. There was only the unit that held the sink and a kettle and microwave on a low pine table. Mismatched plates and cups were stacked on a tray that sat on the floor nearby. A cardboard box held bags of crisps, cereal bars and sachets of soup. There were a few tins of baked beans, a half empty jar of coffee, a bag of broken biscuits. Kelly Whitcham gave a bitter laugh.

'You can see why I'm thin.' she said. 'Whatever you've been told about Craig, you can see what sort of person he was from this house. We've no furniture, but we've got a top of the range TV. The kids have a couple of second hand outfits each and some pyjamas, but everything of Craig's is designer. I have to do our washing in the sink, try to clean the carpets with a dustpan and brush and feed us with a microwave, a kettle, and whatever food Craig's managed to remember to bring from the corner shop. You're lucky you're here when the electricity's on.' Her voice broke and she put her hands to her face, turning away from them. She spoke from behind her hands, her voice choked with tears.

'If you're expecting me to be heartbroken because Craig's gone, you're in for a disappointment.'
She told them how Pollard had controlled everything, keeping all of the money, even the family allowance that she wanted to spend on the children, bringing home a minimum of food and discouraging her from seeing friends or family.

'My mum lives miles away, I've no money for a bus, no mobile to ring her. Craig let me use his phone to text her now and again so she knew we were okay, but he always read the message before he sent it. I had to keep making excuses when she replied and asked to come around. I don't know anyone round here to ask them for help, my friends are all near home.'

Knight gently asked if Pollard was violent, but she said no, never, not to her or the children. He didn't bother with them much at all really, she said, though he had come home with a football and a teddy one day around Christmas. She didn't know what Pollard did with the money. She'd met Craig around three years earlier, becoming pregnant soon after. She'd lived with her mum for a couple of years after the birth of the twins with Craig just as an occasional visitor, until he'd persuaded her that they should live together as a family. He'd brought her to this house in a borrowed van. Smiling sadly, she said it had a full kitchen then. Seemingly, Pollard had sold the kitchen units and anything else he could, including the downstairs interior doors and the shed that had been in the back garden. She couldn't tell them much about Pollard's friends or family as she'd never met any of them. Pollard's brother had come to the door a few times, but he'd not been inside the house. Craig had taken the children to meet his parents a couple of times but again, they'd never visited.

'It's like he was ashamed of this place,' she said. 'Not surprising really, I'm not proud of it myself. Not really what I planned when I stayed on to do my A levels.'

Knight took out his own mobile.

'Do you know your mum's number?' he asked. When Whitcham nodded, he handed her the phone and left the room as she pressed the keys, thanking him. Lawrence raised her eyebrows but said nothing. They went back into the living room, where the children were still watching cartoons. The girl stood and walked over to them.

'What's your name?' she asked Knight, looking up at him, hands on hips.

'My name's Jonathan.' he replied. 'What's yours?'

'Jessica. His name's Connor. We're three. Do you know my daddy?'

Knight shook his head.

'My mum says he can't come to see us again. He never played with us anyway.' Jessica continued. 'My mum plays shops and I spy and we play outside when Daddy lets us.'

Whitcham came through from the kitchen.

'Mum's on her way round,' she said, wiping her face with her hands. 'We'll be going back with her – lucky there's not much to pack, I suppose.'

Knight smiled awkwardly. Whitcham had to be at least considered as a suspect, but he couldn't believe she was responsible for Pollard's death. They took her mother's name and address and left the house. Outside, the boys were still playing with the football in the road.

Kendrick shook his head.

'Was she just going to stay there forever? So he left them with no furniture, no clothes, no . . . did they even have beds?'

'I didn't go upstairs. The mattress in the living room was probably the bed as well.'

'Sounds as if she was looking after the children as best she could though?' Bishop put in.

Knight nodded. He knew they'd have to see Kelly Whitcham again, and that social services could step in if necessary. It seemed to him that all Whitcham needed was control over her own life. Kendrick strode back to the front of the room. 'Right. We won't have full forensic reports for a while. The weapon used to kill Pollard hasn't been found, despite a thorough search of the area surrounding the crime scene by SOC and by our own dashing boys and girls in blue.' He waved a hand towards his audience. 'We've asked for Pollard's mobile phone records; the phone wasn't found on his body, so his killer probably has it. That might mean they were worried about being incriminated by something on the phone, or it might mean nothing. Same goes for his wallet. I think that's about it for tonight. I'll see you all in the morning.'

Kendrick turned on his heel and clumped out of the room. The noise level rose sharply again as the assembled officers got to their feet, eager to get home. Bishop remained seated for a moment, rubbing her aching temples with her fingertips, then stood and joined the crowd pushing to leave the room. She moved forward, stumbling a little as her foot caught the heel of the person in front of her.

'I'm sorry.' she said automatically.

The woman she'd stepped on bent to adjust her shoe, straightened up and turned with a smile. Bishop gazed for a second into dancing blue eyes before the woman said, 'Don't worry about it.' then disappeared into the crowd.

Knight was waiting for Bishop in the corridor, standing apart from the stream of officers now jostling their way towards the exit doors.

'Not much to go on so far.' he said 'Are you okay? About the photo, I mean?' he clarified quickly. She smiled.

'Yes thanks, sir. I'll admit, it shook me up at first, but I'm fine, honestly. What do you think about it? The DCI didn't make much of it in there.' She nodded towards the room they had just left.

'I don't really know what to think.' Knight admitted. 'It might mean nothing, just a joke or a mistake, maybe Pollard printed the wrong photo and shoved it in his pocket meaning to put it in the bin later.'

Bishop frowned. 'But why would you take a photo of a police station in the first place? It's not as if it's some sort of historical building, or even a pretty one – it's horrible, just loads of bricks, concrete and glass.'

'True and it's not as if it was taken on a night out, a load of drunken mates posing in the street. This was taken during the day and when we were working – you're proof of that.'

'It's just strange, like the DCI said.'

'I think we'll leave the photo out of the investigation for now, though the usual tests for fingerprints and so on will be run on the original.'

'Do you think there's more to it than Pollard chatting up some bloke's girlfriend, and the bloke smacking Pollard one later then? The DCI didn't seem to think so.'

Knight thought, but didn't say, that Kendrick didn't want to consider the possibility just yet, that it potentially made the situation much more complicated.

5

Knight sat back on his sofa with a plate that had contained fish, chips and mushy peas on his lap. He didn't think he had many vices, but fish and chips were one of them. He closed his eyes, relaxing for possibly the first time since Craig Pollard's body had been found. It was a strange case. Initially it had seemed fairly straightforward, but the lack of leads and witnesses, not to mention the absence of the weapon used to kill Pollard, bothered Knight. Then there was the photograph. He closed his eyes, wondering what it could mean then started, almost losing the plate from his lap as his mobile phone began to ring. He snatched it up from the cushion beside him. The display told him the caller was Catherine Bishop.

'Sir? Are you there?'

Bishop sounded strange, panicked almost.

'Catherine?'

'I'm sorry to call you but I've got a problem, I think it's related to the Pollard case.'

'What do you mean? I thought you were on your way home?'

'I am at home. The thing is, I think someone else has been here too, well I know they have. They've posted me a photo.'

'A photo? Of what?'

'It's me in my living room, taken through the window and another picture that I haven't completely figured out yet.'

Knight got to his feet, hurriedly setting the plate on the floor.

'What's your address?'

Fifteen minutes later, Knight stood in Catherine Bishop's kitchen. She lived in a semi detached house on a new estate. At the back of the property, patio doors led into a small garden; that was the window the photo had been taken through. The picture lay on the pine table, DS Bishop clearly visible, relaxing on her sofa with a paperback novel.

'It must have been a Sunday morning.' said Bishop. 'I don't normally lie around in my pyjamas like that.'

'And you live alone?' asked Knight.

'Yeah, for the last six months, since my partner moved out. Although,' she gave Knight a sideways glance 'she wouldn't have been much use with a face at the window anyway, she'd have been terrified.'

Knight's expression didn't change as he absorbed what Bishop had just revealed. He looked again at the photograph.

'I just don't see what he hopes to gain from this.'

'You think it's a he?'

'He, she, whoever. So he knows where you live . . . '

'Yes, and God knows what else I might have been doing that morning. I've been trying to think when exactly it could have been. And then there's this.' Wrapping her hands in a piece of kitchen towel, she lifted the photograph of herself from the table top to reveal another piece of paper beneath. Knight stepped forward to have a look. There were two images, the first a colour reproduction of old painting showing a pale faced woman in a brown jewelled dress, the second the black and white outline of a chess piece. Knight stared, his mind unable to take in what he was seeing. He shook his head.

'That's . . . '

'Catherine of Aragon?' Bishop replied in a monotone. 'I didn't know, but if you put the name 'Catherine' in Google, this is the first image that comes up. The chess piece is a bishop, isn't it? That gave me a clue. Catherine Bishop. They're talking about me. What is this?'
Knight shook his head, not able to make sense of what he was seeing.

'I've no idea. You're sure Pollard had no reason to have a grudge against you, or . . . '

'None, none at all. Pollard's dead, how could he be involved? I know it was probably posted yesterday, so he could have sent it. That would make sense if he'd meant it as a threat, if he'd been blackmailing me or whatever, but it's ridiculous. I've done nothing to be blackmailed about. I knew his face, I knew his name, but I've never spoken to him, had no contact with him whatsoever.' Bishop closed her eyes for a second. 'It's like a nightmare, I feel like a suspect must feel.' She gazed at Knight. 'I don't understand any of this, I swear.'

'Neither do I, but I don't like it.' Knight said, looking again at the images. 'We need to tell the DCI about this.' He took his mobile out of his pocket as Bishop sat down at the table, propping her forehead on her hands and gazing down at the pictures. Kendrick answered gruffly and Knight explained as quickly as he could.

'Bloody hell, this gets stranger.' Kendrick said. He was obviously eating. Knight heard him chew then swallow. 'And Catherine has no idea what's going on? This might sound harsh Jonathan, but do you believe her?'

Knight glanced at Bishop, remembering the fear he had heard in her voice when she had phoned him, thinking about the quick, nervous movements she'd made since he'd arrived at her home.

'Yes.' he said firmly. 'Definitely.'

'Good enough for me.' Kendrick replied, taking another bite. 'We'll talk again in the morning but in the meantime tell her to be careful, get her to book into a hotel or go to a friend or relative. If I was her, I'd be nervous. How's she holding up?'

'Okay, I think.' Knight looked again at Bishop, who gave a shaky smile.

'Typical Catherine. I'll have to let the Super know as well, I suppose.' thundered Kendrick. 'See you both tomorrow.'

Knight ended the call and pointed at the pictures.

'I know you touched these before you realised what they were, but I think we need to get all of this fingerprinted. I doubt we'll get anything from it, but you never know. How do you feel about staying here after this?'

Bishop sighed.

'To be honest I'd rather not, not tonight. I know the picture was probably taken weeks ago, but still. I was just going to say, I think I'll go to a hotel. There's one of those budget type places on the ring road, they'll probably have a room. I'll give them a call.'

Knight folded the photograph, envelope and second sheet of paper into a tea towel that Bishop had ready for the purpose, then glanced at his watch. He wouldn't normally offer, but this was an unusual situation.

'It's almost ten now. I've got a spare room, it would save you the bother of trying to organise a hotel. My bedroom has a shower room so you'd have the bathroom to yourself. I know it's not the usual thing to do but it's not as if it's going to start any gossip.' Bishop smiled. 'If it were me I wouldn't want to be in a hotel room, I'd want to know that there was at least someone else around.'

'Thank you sir, that's really good of you. It'll just be for one night. I'll pack a bag.'

She left the room and Knight frowned down at the tea towel containing the photo. The message to Bishop, though disturbing, didn't seem like a threat. It was almost as though Bishop was being recognised, pointed out. Of course, it was worrying that not only did this person obviously know where Bishop lived but had actually visited the property. This was beginning to feel like no case he'd known before.

⁘ ⁘ ⁘

In her bedroom, Catherine Bishop threw clean underwear into a bag. She took a black suit from the wardrobe and looked frantically for a shirt or top to wear under the jacket that wasn't too creased. It was going to be awkward enough staying at the DI's house without having to ask to borrow his iron in the morning. The thought suddenly occurred to her that she had no idea whether he had a wife, a partner, children . . . Perhaps the hotel would have been a better idea after all. At least he'd made it clear that she would have privacy. A few men she had worked with in the past would have been only too happy to have tried to take advantage of both the situation and of Bishop, whether they were aware of her sexuality or not. Being an overnight guest in the home of another officer, especially a senior one, was not an option Bishop would have even considered in any normal situation. This evening, however, had been anything but normal and it had shaken her more than she liked to admit. She'd always felt safe in her house, even after Louise left, but the thought of those patio doors and someone waiting outside them was too much tonight.

Knight sat at the kitchen table, hoping Bishop wouldn't be too long. Though she was attractive, it was in a fresh faced way; he doubted she'd spend all night packing make up and hair styling products. He thought about the bathroom he'd shared with Caitlin - there'd been hardly any room for his stuff and it wasn't as if he was vain. All he needed was a razor, shaving gel, shower gel, deodorant and a tiny splash of aftershave on special occasions. Caitlin had bought him moisturiser and facial scrub and had even wanted to have a go at his eyebrows with her lethal looking tweezers. She'd only asked once. Bishop called down the stairs, 'Just need my toothbrush.' Knight stood and carefully picked up the folded tea towel. Bishop reappeared at the door. 'Ready when you are.'

They'd agreed that Bishop would drive her own car and follow Knight to his house. Bishop's home was fairly close to the centre of town but Knight led her out into the countryside, down a maze of dark, quiet lanes. She was grateful for the way he was aware of her following, indicating early and not getting too far in front. Although Bishop had lived in the area all her life, she'd never been to the village that suddenly appeared over the brow of a hill, as if from nowhere. Knight drove slowly down what appeared to be the main street, past a church and tiny fish and chip shop. He indicated left and pulled into the driveway of a cottage, semi detached and built from weathered grey stone. Bishop squeezed her car in behind Knight's.

'Nice house.' she said, following him to the black painted front door.

'Thank you - it's not quite finished, but it's getting there.' Knight replied, fumbling with his keys.

The hallway floor was grey slate, the walls painted white. Knight took off his coat and draped it over the stripped wood banister, then led the way into the living room. More white walls and stripped wood, this time the floor, door and skirting board. A battered brown leather sofa stood against the wall with a plate on the floor in front of it showing traces of what looked to Bishop like mushy peas. She realised she'd not eaten since early that afternoon. Knight hurried forward and picked up the plate.

'Sorry, I'd just finished when you phoned.' he said.

'Don't worry, it's your house.' Bishop smiled faintly. 'Fish and chips?'

'Yeah, I got there just before they closed. The shop in the village does the best fish and chips I've ever had.'

'Was that why you moved here?'

Knight grinned.

'It wasn't the only reason, but definitely one of the main ones. Can I get you a drink? Tea or coffee, or I think I've got a couple of bottles of beer somewhere?

Sit down, by the way, unless you want to go straight to bed? I'll take your bag up to your room, it's on the left as you go up the stairs and the bathroom's straight in front of you.'

Bishop made herself comfortable on the sofa.

'Tea's fine thanks. Just milk, no sugar. Thank you.'

As Knight left the room, Bishop had to smile to herself, shaking her head. It was very surreal, sitting back whilst your boss took your overnight bag upstairs and made you a cup of tea. It was especially bizarre when that boss was Jonathan Knight, a man seemingly so reserved as to almost blend into the background altogether. He'd earned the name Inspector Wallpaper within two weeks of arriving in Lincolnshire and it wasn't difficult to see why. Since they'd arrived at his home, however, Knight had visibly relaxed and become friendlier, almost chatty. It was one surprise after another tonight. They'd never believe it back at the station, not that she would be telling anyone. She gazed around the room, liking what she saw, gradually relaxing. The room was cosy and comfortable, with a brick fireplace housing a log burner dominating one wall. Bishop got to her feet and made her way over to have a closer look at some framed drawings that hung on the far wall. They were pen and ink sketches, a couple seemingly drawn somewhere far more exotic than Lincolnshire, judging by the plants and buildings. Bishop turned as DI Knight came back into the room, mugs in one hand, packet of chocolate digestives in the other.

'These are amazing.' Bishop gestured at the drawings.

'Thank you, my sister drew them. I practically had to beg her to let me put them on the wall, she doesn't seem to see how talented she is. She loves drawing, always has.'

Knight handed one of the mugs and the digestives to Bishop.

'Not sure if you fancy a biscuit?'

'Thanks very much, sir.' Bishop said, struck again by the oddness of the situation. Knight had accidentally shared some information about himself. There were those amongst her colleagues who would be amazed that Knight had any family at all, that he hadn't just been hatched inside the police training college.

Knight seemed to feel awkward once he'd completed the pleasantries of tea making and biscuit sharing and sat back, cleared his throat, then sat forward again. Bishop smiled to herself through a mouthful of tea, wondering again why Knight had turned up in Lincolnshire. He obviously hadn't made DI by accident, but compared with other officers of his rank that Bishop had encountered, Knight was different. He seemed ill at ease with people, unsure and unconfident. Of course, get him in an interview with a suspect on the other side of the table and he might turn from Jekyll into Hyde. As Knight stared at the fireplace, seemingly lost in thought, Bishop had a good look at her boss. It was strange how you could work in the same place as people day after day without really seeing them. She knew from experience how difficult witnesses found it to describe the woman they'd seen, the car that had been hanging around, the man's accent. She had tested herself and doubted she would do much better in their place. The first word that came to mind when she looked at DI Knight was "average". It was no description at all, but it was true. Average height, average build, no sign yet of grey in his hair. She couldn't see him colouring it though and smiled again at the thought of Knight worrying over his roots and sneaking into the chemist to buy some manly hair dye. She doubted if he'd notice if his hair went white overnight. Clean shaven, small neat sideburns. Serious face – totally unremarkable.

'I don't understand,' Knight said suddenly, causing Bishop to start and spill tea over her hand, 'why the photo was taken, why it was sent to you. Obviously, there's a message there, especially when there was a photo of you found on Craig Pollard's body, but it's so cryptic. I just don't see the point.'
Bishop leant forward, surreptitiously wiping her hand on her trouser leg.

'I know. Ever since the DCI showed me the photo I've been trying to think what they could be trying to say, and whatever it is, why say it to me? And why Pollard? I can't believe it was just a random attack on a man so drunk he'd not be able to fight back. Pollard must have said something, done something and whoever walked away at the time hit back later. But it still doesn't make sense.'

Knight nodded, and then shrugged apologetically.

'And the worry is that the only way it will make sense is if you're contacted again.'

Kelly Whitcham lay in the bed she'd slept in as a child, staring up at the ceiling. She could hear her children's even breathing as they slept on the old inflatable mattress her mum had unearthed from the depths of the airing cupboard. They were so good, they never complained and were always cheerful. It had been such a struggle at times to keep them occupied as they grew older, to begin to educate them as best she could in a house empty of almost everything except that ridiculous television. It would have been so easy to just sit and lose herself in the mindless programmes, many of which featured people who had somehow got themselves into situations which were even more unlikely than her own. Inventing games and stories had kept her mind at least halfway busy, and whatever memories the children were going to have from their first few years, she hoped they would remember that she had done her best. Shamefaced, she'd told her mother the truth about her life with Craig. Her mum had been disbelieving at first, outraged and then puzzled, not able to comprehend why Kelly would stay. Kelly had just shaken her head helplessly. She hadn't been afraid of Craig; her mum had assumed that he'd beaten her and the children, threatened worse if she'd tried to leave, but it wasn't that. Kelly had tried to argue that she couldn't have left with both doors and windows locked, but she and her mother both knew that she could have attracted a neighbour's attention somehow, or smashed a window. Kelly had admitted to herself, if not her mum who no doubt knew anyway, that she hadn't been able to leave because she was ashamed of what her life had become. Her children weren't hungry, although their diet probably hadn't been the healthiest, they weren't abused and so she had allowed the situation to continue. She'd known that the children would need to be registered for school and Craig would have had to make changes in their lives then, they could hardly begin their education in second hand pyjamas. The authorities would soon have been called in and there was no way Craig would have allowed the truth about the life of his family to be exposed. Kelly closed her eyes. She'd failed her children and she could now admit it, at least to herself. Before she'd met Craig she'd been doing well, had good grades at GCSE and A level and a job in the offices of a local solicitor, general administration but with her eye on more qualifications, progression, a career. Settling down and having a family had been distantly visible on the horizon. She would never regret having the twins, but it never should have happened as it had. She hoped she would have the chance now to stand on her own two feet, to provide for her children. She still had those qualifications and she was only twenty four. Jessica and Connor would be at nursery soon, then school and she could work, maybe study as she'd planned.

Kelly turned on her side, promising herself that she would find out in the morning who she could speak to for some advice on what to do next. She hoped that the police officers who'd come to the house had seen that she wasn't just some brainless idiot who had no idea how to look after herself, much less two small children. They might tell Social Services how they'd found them. Maybe they would come to see her, to see the children, talk to them, examine them? They could, but they would see that the children were clean, healthy, not underweight. Their speech was good as far as she could tell - Jessica talked more than Connor, but that was just their personalities. They knew their colours from the packaging on food their father had brought in, they could recognise numbers. Let Social Services come if they wanted to. The inspector had been kind, not letting his face show what he must have thought, what anyone would think walking into that house. She should thank him, but surely you couldn't just ring up and ask to speak to a policeman, especially not an inspector. She could send a card but again, was that really the right thing to do? He might think she was trying to be friendlier than she meant to be, maybe they would think she had killed Craig and was trying to throw the inspector off the scent. It crossed her mind that because she'd used Knight's phone to ring her mother, his number should show in her mum's call log. She'd send him a quick text. No one could blame her for that, no one could say it was wrong or that she was trying to bribe him or something. She sat up slowly, moving the duvet as quietly as she could and stepped carefully around the inflatable mattress. There was just enough room to open the bedroom door and move out onto the landing. She crept downstairs and into the living room where she found her mum's mobile on the coffee table. Sure enough, the last call the phone had received was from a mobile number that afternoon. It must be his. Quickly, she typed:

Thank u. Kelly W

She pressed send immediately, not giving herself time to change her mind.

Knight was used to lying awake and had resigned himself to another sleepless night. Having DS Bishop in the house was strange too and though she had seemed the perfect house guest so far, she wasn't a relative or a friend, she was a colleague, a junior colleague at that and therefore not someone Knight would normally have offered his spare bedroom to. However, he'd seen how much the first message from the crime scene and then the pictures she'd received at home had shaken her, so what could he have done? Her sexuality at least made gossip around the station less likely if anyone should find out she had spent the night at the new DI's house. Not, thought Knight, thumping his pillow, that it was the business of anyone else, but like any workplace, police stations were abuzz with gossip. Knight's mobile, on the bedside cabinet next to him, lit up with a double beep, indicating the arrival of a text message. Knight groaned and rolled over, fumbling for the phone. Reading the short message from Kelly Whitcham, he sighed. He should have thought that allowing her to use his mobile would mean she would have access to his number. She had thanked him several times already that afternoon, and he certainly didn't want to be exchanging texts with someone who still had to be considered as a suspect in a murder enquiry. He remembered how she'd looked when she opened the door, defensive but challenging, as if almost daring him to expect her to be devastated by Pollard's death, or to comment on the place she and her children were living in. Knight knew a full statement had been taken from her - he'd read it, but he'd wanted to see her himself to gain his own impressions. Though she'd said she wasn't sorry Pollard was dead, Knight knew the first days after a violent death were a turmoil of emotion. Eventually the enormity of what had happened, or possibly what she had done, would break through the initial shock. He thought about the way she had led him through to the almost bare kitchen, pride making her matter-of-fact, her embarrassment hidden under resentment. Knight hoped she would make a new start; she was young and obviously intelligent, could be attractive too Knight admitted. He replaced his phone on the cabinet and turned over to again try to sleep. He wouldn't reply to her message.

The sound of a text message being received came faintly through the wall. Catherine Bishop wondered who would be sending DI Knight a text this late. He must surely have friends and she knew now he had a sister. Perhaps he did have a partner after all, she might be working away or visiting friends. She hadn't seen any evidence of that a woman lived in the house so far though, or a man, or anyone other than Jonathan Knight himself. He probably was single then, living alone as she and as many of the other officers she knew were. She took her own mobile phone from under the pillow and hesitantly typed out a text, choosing Louise as the recipient:

I miss u

She'd probably regret sending it, but it had been a strange day and trying to get some sleep in the house of her boss wasn't making things any more typical. Anyway, she did miss Louise and what harm could it do to tell her so? They'd kept in touch since Louise had moved out and Catherine was fairly sure Louise was still single. She hoped so anyway. She wouldn't have admitted it to Louise herself, but she still hoped they might get back together at some point. Just when that might be wasn't clear as the main reason they had split up hadn't changed. Her phone lit up almost immediately and she read Louise's reply nervously:

Maybe, but not as much as you would miss your job.

Catherine pulled a face. Louise the English teacher was the only person she knew who bothered to put grammar in her texts, although Inspector Knight probably would too, Bishop thought. She lay back on the pillow. Not a very promising reply from Louise, but then what had she expected? The situation was just the same as when they'd had all those rows about it and Louise had moved out. Catherine's work meant long, unsociable hours, stress and regular exposure to sights that most people wouldn't even want to imagine. None of that sat well with Louise. When they'd first met, Louise had been intrigued by Catherine's job, but living with the reality of it had eventually been too much. Louise went on with her teaching, marking, planning and regular hours and holidays, and Catherine was around as much as possible, which in truth wasn't that often. She supposed it was only a matter of time before the relationship ended, given that neither of them appeared to care enough about it to try to make it work. If Catherine was absolutely honest, she knew it wasn't so much Louise herself she missed but knowing that when she eventually got home at night that someone would be waiting, that when she did have time off there would be another person around to go out with, to stay in with, to moan to about work at if necessary. She did have colleagues like Chris Rogers who were happily married or had long term partners, but it seemed almost as many were single. Catherine turned over, knowing she should try to get a few hours sleep, that tomorrow and each day while the Pollard case was ongoing would be long. She wasn't hopeful of getting any rest though, not with the images of Pollard's body and those cryptic messages swimming before her eyes.

6

The body was found quickly, but then I knew it would be. I half expected the police to be hammering on the front door within minutes, but I was as careful as it was possible to be. The rain will have helped I think. There should be no traces of me on his body or clothes. I suppose their tests will take time to produce results, I'm not sure how long. They hardly mentioned it on the local news. Perhaps a murder isn't much of a news story these days, people after all are killed every day in domestic rows or drunken fights. It may be that the police still think Craig's death was the result of a pint too many. Idiot. Big mouthed, arrogant bastard. He deserved it. When he was lying there, the light leaking from his eyes, I wanted to tell him why I'd done it, why now, but there was no time. Pity. I would have liked to have seen his expression when he realised. Not so pathetic after all.

7

Bishop had politely turned down DI Knight's offer of the breakfast, preferring to arrive early at the station and picking up a bacon sandwich and tea that tasted of the cardboard cup it had been served in on her way. She sat at her desk, took a sip of tea, groaned and sat rubbing her eyes. She doubted she'd had more than a couple of hours sleep. Chris Rogers wheeled his desk chair over to her.

'Late night then, Sarge?'

'What do you think? Bet you were late home yourself.'

'About ten. Fay had pie and chips waiting for me.'

'Lucky you, wish I'd had the same.'

'Fay or the pie and chips?'

Either, preferably both. Don't think I'm Fay's type though.'

Rogers grinned.

'Maybe not, but she might know someone who's just your cup of tea.'

Bishop screwed up her nose at the cardboard cup on her desk.

'Don't mention tea, that stuff's bloody awful. What do you mean?'

'There's a woman just started working with them at the council offices – she's gay.'

Bishop forced down the last of the tea and dropped the empty cup into the bin under her desk.

'So are six percent of the population. Why are you telling me?'

'Come on Sarge, Louise has been gone over six months. Don't you think it's time you started enjoying yourself, or did really she break your heart?' He pulled an exaggeratedly miserable face then smirked. 'You've not acted like it.' She pointed a finger at him.

'You're going too far, DC Rogers.'

Rogers sat back in his chair and waited, knowing Bishop wouldn't be able to leave it at that. Eventually, she took the bait. Eyes still fixed on her computer screen, she said:

'Even if she is gay, which is probably just a rumour that's been started because one of the lads asked her out and got turned down, it's no one's business but her own and it's certainly of no interest to me. In case you've forgotten about it overnight, we've got a briefing with the DCI in ten minutes.'

Rogers wheeled himself back over to his own desk with a smile. He'd known Catherine Bishop a long time and was quietly satisfied he'd given her something to think about. She'd been moping long enough. It was time she had some fun, although knowing Bishop, she would find it outside of work. He knew her self imposed rule about not mixing business with pleasure and couldn't blame her.

Knight sat in front of the officers that were assigned to the Pollard case, his eyes travelling over their faces as DCI Kendrick spoke. There didn't seem to be too much sympathy around for Craig Pollard or his family, which was unusual in a case like this, especially with Pollard being father to two small children. The general consensus seemed to be that they would be better off without him. Kelly Whitcham certainly appeared to think so, though maybe her attitude would have changed as the shock wore off. Knight knew they would have to speak to her again today. As always in a murder enquiry, the victim's partner and immediate family were under suspicion, but Knight had a feeling this wouldn't be as simple as a family dispute gone too far. The Bishop messages didn't tie in with that. Whitcham had no real alibi, but then neither did the rest of Pollard's family. His mother and father had both said they had been at home watching the TV all night, but Knight knew the questioning would have been fairly low key since they'd just been given the news of their son's death. The family liaison officer, PC Stathos, would be with them now and one of the uniforms plus a DC would be soon on their way for more questioning. The information they had collected from witnesses and family since the discovery of the body so far seemed to tell them nothing about Pollard's life. As Knight had found out during his career, people often died as they had lived and perhaps Craig Pollard would be another example of that. They needed more information though and Knight thought he knew who could best provide it.

A wet, muddy building site wasn't Catherine Bishop's idea of a suitable place to talk to anyone, especially on a cold, windy day in mid November. She followed Knight over a rough patch of clay and gravel with a few vehicles parked on it and waited while he had a quick word with the nearest builder, who nodded towards a taller man standing alone, smoking and staring at his filthy work boots. Knight beckoned to Bishop and she began to pick her way through the mud. Knight strode up to the smoker.

'You're a difficult man to find, Mike.'

Mike Pollard's head jerked up and he glared at Knight.

'Who the f . . .'

Knight held up a hand.

'I don't need to hear it.'

Pollard stared. Even Catherine Bishop raised her eyebrows. Knight waved his warrant card under Pollard's nose.

'DI Knight. I'm here to ask you some questions about the death of your brother. I'm surprised to find you at work, I'd have thought Craig being killed would be a good enough reason for any employer to give you a few days off?' Pollard threw his cigarette butt on the floor, took off his hard hat and passed his hand over his face.

'Need the job, don't I? Anyway, better to be here than at home with Mum and Dad crying their eyes out or screaming at each other about whose fault it is.' Bishop glanced at Knight, but rather than ask Pollard what he meant he said: 'What was Craig like?'

'What was he like? What do you mean?'

'As a person, a friend, a brother.'

Pollard shuffled his feet.

'He was all right.'

'All right?' Knight echoed.

Pollard stared at him.

'He's my brother and he's dead, what do you expect me to say? Have you got a brother?'

Bishop shifted uncomfortably. Knight said,

'I have, but since I'm not a suspect in his murder I don't see what he has to do with anything.'

'A suspect? What do you mean?'

'Why else do you think we're here, Mike? Unless you start answering my questions, we'll be finishing this conversation back at the station and I don't think being dragged off site in handcuffs will do much for your chances of keeping your job, do you?'

Pollard's fists clenched.

'You're a f . . .'

'Come on Mike, you'll have to do better than that. What was Craig like?'

All at once, the fight seemed to go out of Mike Pollard. His shoulders drooped, and the hard hat in his hand seemed about to fall to the floor.

'I hated him.' It was almost a whisper.

'I thought you might say that.' Knight said softly.

Pollard led them to a draughty Portakabin and they sat in mismatched garden chairs as he made three mugs of tea. He handed over the drinks and then sat, taking a bunch of keys out of his pocket and throwing them on the rickety plastic table, dropping his hard hat to the dusty floor, any pretence of bravado gone. Knight and Bishop waited as Pollard seemed to gather his thoughts.

'I used to want to be like Craig, you know? When we were younger, I think everyone around here wanted to be like Craig. Maybe that was part of the problem, he started believing he was as good as people said he was. Even when he started getting into trouble with the police, it just made people respect him more. Some people, I mean, I suppose a lot of people just thought he was even more of a tosser than they already did.' Pollard took a sip of tea and shook his head. 'I never thought I'd end up glad of a job labouring on a building site or making tea for coppers, if I'm honest. The way Craig used to talk, we'd be running our own business by now, sitting in luxury offices, getting paid a fortune while other people did the work. I used to believe every word he said. And then he left school, started earning his own money . . . '

Another mouthful of tea and a pause so long that Knight said:

'What work did he do?'

'A mate of our dad took him on as a favour, he was a plumber. Mum and Dad were hoping Craig would learn from him, train properly, work for himself eventually and I hoped so too, thought he might have a job for me. But of course it didn't work out like that. It seemed to go well to start with. Craig enjoyed strutting around buying everyone drinks and Dad's mate was pleased with him. It didn't last. Craig started getting up too late for work and things started to go

missing from the houses they were working in. He got sacked and he didn't
work again. He'd got so big headed – he criticised me all the time, my hair, my
clothes, the music I liked, my friends, everything. I wanted to stay on at school
and do A levels, but he went on so much about how he'd gone out and got a job
to bring money into the house that I left, started labouring and I'm still here. I
went out with Kelly first you know, she was in my year at school. I think she
was the one thing in my life that Craig didn't criticise. She took one look at him
and dumped me. He made sure he got her pregnant too, not only pregnant but
twins. She told me they were in love, were planning on living together, getting
married and all that. I couldn't believe the way he really treated her, have you
seen that house? I only saw it through the window but that was enough, it was
practically empty. I had a proper go at him about it, but what could I do?'
There was a silence. Pollard drained the last of his tea and Bishop waited until
he'd finished before speaking.

'Do you know what Craig did with the money he kept from Kelly and the
children?'

'Oh, you can talk then?' Pollard shook his head. 'Sorry. Not really, but he
always had new clothes, not cheap stuff either and he was out every night. I
know he never touched drugs, couldn't stand them, he'd seen too many of his
old mates ruined by them but he did drink a lot. And he was always meeting
girls and buying them drinks, all the schoolgirls sneaking into the pubs, they're
usually up for a good night and so was Craig, if you know what I mean. Kelly
deserves better than him, they all do.'
Bishop said, 'You don't sound as if you approve of how Craig behaved.'
Pollard sighed.

'I like a drink and a laugh myself but those girls, they get on your nerves,
they're just kids. Not that they're underage for what Craig wanted them for,
they were easy pickings for him, but I just think it's pathetic and when you've

got a girlfriend and two kids at home living the way like they do ... well, it's just wrong, isn't it?'

Bishop and Knight didn't disagree.

'How did you know?' asked Bishop as Knight drove them back to the station.

'Know what?

'About Mike Pollard not being his brother's biggest fan?'

'A few things in his statement and what he said when he heard Craig was dead. "He's been knifed at last then" and "he had it coming", that sort of thing.'

'Do you think he did it? Sounds like Mike's resented his brother for years. Craig bullied him, stole his girlfriend and then to rub his nose in it even more, got her pregnant. Maybe they met on Sunday night or they spoke on the phone, Craig said something clever that tipped Mike over the edge and he went after Craig with a baseball bat.'

'Can you see him doing it?'

'Not as he was today, he soon dropped the big man act. But after a few drinks, in the middle of an argument, a couple of punches thrown . . . who knows? What do you think, boss?'

'I don't think we should rule him out, but why would he send you the photos? That's premeditated, a person who knew Pollard would go that way home and was waiting for him.'

Bishop nodded.

'I know we're looking at it like that, but it could just be to throw us off the scent, make it look like a premeditated killing when in fact it wasn't? Mike Pollard could have punched his brother, grabbed something in the alley and battered him with it, then realised what he'd done and panicked . . . '

Even as she spoke, Bishop knew it hadn't happened like that. It made no sense. Nothing about this case did yet. She changed the subject, starting to feel a little more comfortable with DI Wallpaper now she'd spent a night in his house and knew he had a brother and a sister, that he was human after all. She wasn't quite brave enough to talk about anything other than the case outside the cosiness of his home though.

'I can't believe Pollard stopped swearing like that.'

'I think Mike's a lad who's used to do doing as he's told. I'm wondering if Mr and Mrs Pollard realised too late they'd let Craig get away with too much and came down on Mike like a ton of bricks so he didn't go the same way. Plus, I don't suppose the blokes he works with say please and thank you too often, just order him around.'

'From what Mike said, I think you could be right. If his mum and dad are arguing about whose fault Craig's death is, could be they're each saying the other was too easy on him.'

'Maybe so.'

'Interesting that Kelly Whitcham was Mike's girlfriend first, too. He could be hoping she'll run back to him now Craig's out of the picture, that could be another motive. Or they're in it together. Kelly could be the brains, Mike the muscle.'

Knight swung the car back into the station car park.

'Neither of them have a real alibi. I think it's time we had another talk with Miss Whitcham. You can take one of the DCs, take Dave Lancaster, he's young and I think she might respond better if there's a man there with you.'

'How do you mean? Don't you want to speak to her yourself?'

Knight shook his head and explained about the late night text message.

'She probably won't want to tell you much but I think she'll talk to Dave, or take Chris Rogers. They're both on the CCTV tapes, I bet either one would be glad of a break.'

They went into the station, Knight heading straight for his office and Bishop turning into the Ladies before going off to give Lancaster or Rogers a reprieve from watching CCTV footage. She had a lot more respect for DI Knight after their meeting with Mike Pollard. How many other DIs or DCIs would have picked up on his contempt for his brother? She'd like to think all of them, but she wasn't so sure.

She was making her way down the corridor when she spotted DI Knight heading towards her, smiling.

'I think we'll both go to see Kelly Whitcham after all. I've just found an interesting message on my desk'.

Whitcham had acquired a pair of jeans from somewhere but still wore the hooded sweatshirt Knight had seen her in the day before. She was sitting in the living room of her mother's house, feet drawn up onto the settee underneath her. Her hair needed washing, her face was pale and her expression showed plainly she was not particularly pleased to see Knight again. She didn't so much as glance at Bishop as Knight introduced her.

'Why didn't you reply to my text?' she asked, glaring at Knight. Whitcham's mother tutted then left the room to make the tea she'd offered as she showed them in. She'd displayed no interest or concern at their appearance at her front door. Knight and Bishop sat in armchairs either side of an unlit gas fire, the top of which was covered with framed photographs, school pictures mainly. Several were of Kelly Whitcham herself, the gap toothed smile and pigtails a sharp contrast to the scowling adult version that sat opposite them. Whitcham's daughter and son smiled out from a blurry shot that looked as though it had been printed at home rather than developed professionally.

'How are the children?' asked Knight. He could hear them playing upstairs. Whitcham snorted.

'As if you care.'

Bishop opened her notebook.

'Kelly, one of your neighbours from the house you shared with Craig says Craig's brother Mike was a regular visitor to the house, that she saw him at the front door almost every night. Can you explain what he was doing there and why you told DI Knight he only visited "a few times"?'

'Why should I?'

'Because this isn't a social call, Miss Whitcham. We're here to ask you questions about the murder of your boyfriend. If you haven't realised how serious this is, maybe you should start thinking about it now. If you don't start being a bit more cooperative we'll see if you're more in the mood to answer questions down at the station.'

Whitcham stared at her, then turned on Knight.

'Are you going to let her talk to me like that? Is she allowed to? You're her boss, aren't you?'

Bishop leaned back in her chair and crossed her legs at the ankles, looking a lot more relaxed than Whitcham did.

'You seem to be under the misapprehension that DI Knight is a friend of yours, Miss Whitcham.'

'I'm not under any "misapprehension". He was nice to me yesterday and I don't see that anything's changed to make him not even speak to me today. I've done nothing wrong, it was my boyfriend that was killed. I'm one of the victims and you're talking to me like I'm a criminal. I could have you done for this!'

Mrs Whitcham came back into the room with a tray of tea and biscuits.

'Stop shouting, Kelly, you'll upset the children.' she said placidly, handing out the mugs of tea. Knight and Bishop thanked her.

'They're only accusing me of killing Craig.' Whitcham spat.

'I'm sure they're just doing their job. How will they find out who killed him if they don't ask questions?'

'There's no point asking me since I didn't do it, they'd be better off asking whoever did.'

Mrs Whitcham gave another tut and went back out of the room, closing the door firmly behind her. Knight leant forward.

'Kelly, we'll get this over with a lot quicker if you just answer the questions.' Whitcham glared at him over the top of her mug.

'I didn't kill him. There were times I might have felt like it, but I didn't actually do it. Mike came to the door to check me and the kids were all right, that's all. It was daft really, all I could do was talk to him through the letterbox. There's no way he came every night though, whatever the lying, nosy bastards in that street have told you.'

Bishop pretended to look through the notes in her pad.

'You said that on the night Craig was killed you were at home with your children as usual. You didn't see anyone, you didn't speak to anyone.'

'Yes, same as every other night. Have I got to go through all that again now? Didn't they write it down the first time?' Whitcham sipped her tea, pulled a face and slammed the mug onto the coffee table in front of her.

'So you've got no real alibi?' asked Bishop.

'Alibi? What do you mean, alibi? I was at home with my children. I was locked in, the doors and the windows as well. I couldn't have got out if I'd wanted to, which part of that don't you understand?'

Bishop leant forward and looked Kelly Whitcham in the eye.

'What I don't understand, Kelly, is why you would live like you were doing with Craig Pollard when you could have got out of that house fairly easily. You're not stupid, you've got qualifications, you had a good job. Why did you stay?'

Whitcham looked away.

'What do you mean?'

'You could have smashed a window and attracted attention to yourself or even climbed out. Apparently one of your upstairs windows needs mending, so they can't be that hard to break. You could have asked Mike Pollard for help.'

Whitcham sneered.

'Oh yeah, right. What could Mike have done? Craig would have killed him.'
There was a pause, Whitcham biting her fingernails as she realised what she had said. Bishop broke the silence.

'So why, when you could have escaped the house, did you stay? You've already said you weren't scared of Craig, that he wasn't violent. Why didn't you just say "Look Craig, I've had enough, I'm leaving, going back to my mum and taking the kids". Why couldn't you do that?'
Whitcham shook her head helplessly.

'You don't understand . . . '

'Understand what?'

'What he was like, what Craig was like. He just . . . he had a way of making you believe everything he said. Charming, I suppose.'

'Charming enough to make you believe that living in an almost empty house was normal? That your children having no clothes or toys was normal? I know he was good looking but come on, Kelly.' Bishop scoffed.

'How would you know he's good looking? I'm more your type, aren't I?'
Bishop kept her face blank.

'Not as clever as you thought you were, are you?' taunted Whitcham. 'I always know. How could you tell if Craig was good looking or not?'

'I'm gay, Kelly, not blind. I can see when a man's attractive.'
Whitcham's eyebrows rose theatrically.

'Maybe that's why you wanted to come to question me eh, Sergeant? Maybe you fancy locking me in a cell for the night and paying me a visit?'
This time, Bishop didn't bother to hide what she thought as she stared at Whitcham, taking in her unwashed hair, grubby clothes and sour breath.
Knight asked softly, 'What did Craig know about you, Kelly?'
Whitcham froze, the mocking expression disappearing from her face.

'What . . . what do you mean?'

'Well,' Knight said in a friendly tone, 'as DS Bishop has pointed out, you could have got out of that house and situation any time you wanted, especially with your children being there too, so why would you stay? If Craig hadn't threatened you physically, what had he frightened you with?'

'I don't know what you mean.' Whitcham whispered.

'I think you do, Kelly.'

She closed her eyes.

'All right. I'd done a few things when I first met Craig, just things to help him out. He said if I left he'd tell people, tell you lot.'

'He said he'd tell the police? So these "things" were illegal?'

'I suppose so. Nothing major, just keeping a lookout, selling a few things. But Craig said it was enough, I'd go to prison and the kids would go into care and I'd never see them again. I thought at least in the house we were all together and we were safe, even if it wasn't luxury.'

Knight glanced at Bishop, who said, 'You realise how this looks, Kelly? You've no real alibi, you've got a motive and even if you didn't kill Craig, which let's face it you could have, you might have got someone else to do it for you.'

'Really? Like who? It's hardly something you'd ask a mate to do as a favour.'

'A person you had a relationship with who's never really got over you, who had his own reasons for wanting Craig out of the way. We'll leave you to think about it.' Knight said, standing up and placing his mug on the coffee table.

As they drove back the station, Knight's phone rang. He handed it to Bishop, keeping his eyes on the road. Her conversation was brief.

'Forensics. Apparently, there were no fingerprints at all on either the picture from Pollard's pocket or the ones I received at home, just mine on the picture of me and loads on the envelope – Post Office staff and so on.'

'None at all on the one from Pollard's pocket?'

'No.'

'Which suggests it was put there deliberately by a person who was very careful to leave no trace of themselves, rather than Pollard having taken and printed it himself.'

'I suppose it does.' said Bishop with a shiver.

8

Steve Kent felt terrible. The crossing from Zeebrugge to Hull had been a
nightmare, the ferry feeling to Kent as if it must surely capsize any moment.
He'd spent the night curled on his bunk, staring through the porthole into the
blackness of the night sky and wishing himself elsewhere, anywhere would do.
Staggering out of his cabin early that morning in search of coffee he was greeted
by smiling stewards who assured him that the crossing had been a little choppy,
sure, but nothing out of the ordinary. Kent couldn't agree. It was the fourth time
he'd made the journey and it had been the worst so far by quite a way. He
enjoyed his job but much preferred driving around the UK to having to make
these sea crossings. It wasn't too often though and it paid well, it was just a little
rough on the stomach, or on his stomach at least. He wondered whether one of
the freshly baked croissants he could smell would help then decided against it
and sat back in his chair, eyes closed. They were due into Hull in half an hour or
so, maybe a quick nap would make him feel better. As he shifted in the seat his
mobile began to ring and he swore under his breath. He checked the display and
frowned. Talk about a blast from the past.

'Dave?'

'Steve?'

'All right mate, what's up? Not heard from you for in years.'

'Thank God for that, I thought you might have changed your number. Have
you seen the news?'

'News? What news? I'm on a ferry mate, have to drive over to Belgium and
France every now and again. I've not seen any TV or newspapers.'

'Craig Pollard's dead.'

Kent's eyebrows raised under the brim of his baseball cap.

'Dead? What do you mean?'

'I mean dead, murdered. They're not saying how, but somebody's killed him.'

'You're joking. Doesn't surprise me though, he was a mouthy little shit when we knew him and I doubt he's changed much over the years.'

'Exactly, that's what I mean. What if we get the police knocking on our doors?'

'Why would we?'

'You know why. We knew him years ago and . . . well, you were there, you know what happened.'

'Yeah, years ago, twelve years ago. Why would they come for us now? No one knows about it.' Kent took off his hat and ran his hand over his shaved head. The voice on the other end of the line was anxious, panicked.

'Pollard knew about it.'

'Of course he fucking knew, it was his fault!' Kent smiled apologetically at a passing middle aged woman who was frowning disapprovingly at him. 'I can't talk here; let me call you back later.'

He stuffed the phone into his pocket and stood up to make his way back to the cabin for his bag. Craig Pollard dead, and not accidentally. He couldn't say he was sorry, despite growing up near Craig. They'd been mates, good mates, but one Sunday afternoon all that had changed and they'd gone their separate ways – himself, Craig, Nick and Dave. They'd all sworn to keep the secret and Steve Kent himself had never told another soul what had happened. It couldn't come out now. The life he had, the life he'd worked for would be over. Would they still be in trouble? He didn't know but surely they would be. Hopefully with Pollard dead the whole thing would be put to rest for ever. He hadn't spoken to Craig Pollard since that day, had exchanged a few phone calls with Nick and Dave but even that hadn't lasted. He'd wanted to turn his back on that time in his life, to forget the whole thing. He'd never been able to, of course, but he'd lived with it. And now? He hoisted his rucksack onto his shoulder. He'd have to wait and see.

Staring out of the window, Dave Bowles pursed his lips and chewed his thumbnail, then got up and paced the room. It was all very well Steve saying that it was years ago, no one knew, it was fine. This was the day Bowles had been dreading for twelve years. He'd known that it would all be brought up again. There *was* another person who knew apart from him, Steve, Nick and Craig. The others may have forgotten that, but Bowles hadn't. He didn't know what to do. He had to find out more, but how? He couldn't just saunter into the police station for a chat and they weren't giving much away in the press. He sat down again, took a deep breath and forced himself to calm down and think rationally. Craig Pollard had been just the sort of loud-mouthed idiot who would get himself into a fight he would come off worst in, Bowles knew that as well as Steve Kent did. If that was what had happened, then they were safe, Bowles himself was safe. If that was true though, why were the police being so cagey? Surely they would have the culprit in custody by now, bar room brawls usually being quite public. If Pollard had been killed in a punch up or a knife fight, would it even have made the news? Bowles didn't know. He'd have to watch, wait and keep his fingers crossed, much as he'd been doing for the past twelve years.

Knight sat in his office, frowning down at the reports on his desk. Well into the second day of the investigation and they seemed no closer to understanding why Craig Pollard had died or who had killed him. Although Pollard had been known to the police, he'd never served any time in prison so there were no old cellmates to talk to and none of his friends could help, or so they were saying. His mobile phone records hadn't arrived but Knight still didn't expect to gain much from them. Pollard's mobile phone hadn't been found with his body, of course, so they couldn't look there for help either.

Knight read through his notes, made earlier in the day after talking to Kelly Whitcham and Mike Pollard. He couldn't seriously see either, or both of them killing Pollard, but at the moment they had no one else in the picture. It didn't sit right though. The Catherine of Aragon/Catherine Bishop message just didn't fit with that; they were missing something and he had no idea what. Kelly Whitcham might have the brains to dream up the messages, but why would she bother? The calling card left with Pollard's body and again with the photo sent to DS Bishop's house had no parallels with any investigation he'd been involved in before. If Bishop herself had no idea what the pictures were about, Knight wondered what chance the rest of them had. He needed to talk to the DS again, to ask her to think about every possibility, every link, every case she'd ever worked on and every arrest she'd made. Bishop was a local girl, having grown up in a neighbouring county. Although Knight didn't necessarily consider this ideal for a CID officer, it did have its advantages. People might confide things to someone they perceived as a local more willingly than they would an "outsider". It seemed an old fashioned attitude, but it was one Knight knew from experience still existed. Bishop may have the key to the puzzle without even realising it. Knight didn't doubt she'd thought long and hard about her own involvement, but it must be there, something she'd missed. The whole situation was strange, an incident that looked like a simple fight gone wrong made much more complicated by the presence of a couple of sheets of paper.

Knight thought again about the photograph of DS Bishop lying reading in her pyjamas, the shot taken through her own window. The person who presumably killed Craig Pollard must have been less than ten metres from Catherine Bishop at that moment. How was that affecting her? It must be on her mind. Would it impair her ability to do her job? Should she be reassigned, away from the investigation? From what he'd seen of Catherine since his arrival in Northolme, Knight thought she would be all the more determined to stay on the case. He needed to talk to her and he got to his feet. Before he reached the open door however, there was a knock and the head of one of the DCs, Anna Varcoe, appeared around it.

'Sir, something's just turned up we thought you should hear about.' Varcoe came into the room, a sheet of paper in her hand. 'We've had a phone call into the main switchboard, a bloke wanting details of Craig Pollard's death. Said he'd known Craig years ago and wanted to send a sympathy card to his parents, but that he wanted more details of how he'd died and the circumstances so he didn't say anything insensitive. Sally-Anne on the desk tried to keep him talking while someone else got through to one of us, she thought it could just be a journalist fishing but that it could also be important. Anyway, he panicked and backed off, said it didn't matter and put the phone down.'
Knight sat back down and gestured for Varcoe to do the same.

'Interesting. As you say, could be a journalist but then again . . . Was the call recorded?'

'Yes and I've requested a copy of it, shouldn't take long. It's also being traced. In the meantime, Sally-Anne wrote down everything he said while she had it in her head.'
She passed the sheet of paper over the desk to Knight. The neat handwriting said: "Hello, I . . . I'm wondering if you could give me some information about Craig Pollard. I know he's dead and I want to send a card to his Mum and Dad, I knew him years ago you see and I thought I should but . . . well, I don't want to say anything to upset them, upset them more than they already are, I mean. Can you tell me how he died? And why?"

"I'm sorry, that's not information I have access to. Could I take your name, please?"

"There's no need, I'm not involved. As I say, I've not seen Craig for years. I just need a few more details, I don't want to put my foot in it."

"Yes, sir, but that's not information I have. If you give me your name and some more details I can ask one of the investigating team to call you back? Your name please sir, and you say you knew Mr Pollard years ago? Would that be at school or through work maybe?"

"No, it doesn't matter, I . . . I just thought you might tell me why, or how . . ."

"They would call you back as soon as possible, sir, I can assure you. If you could please give me your name, address and contact number?"

"No I can't, I'm sorry. I don't know anything. Look, I've got to go."

Knight shook his head in amazement.

'How did she remember all that?'

Varcoe smiled, tucking her hair behind her ears.

'Shorthand. She wrote it down as they spoke.'

'Brilliant. I didn't know people still did shorthand.'

'Sally-Anne does. She's a legend, worked here forever.'

'Lucky the call came into her then.' Knight examined the transcript again. 'Interesting that he wants to know why Pollard was killed, he says that twice. Although he asks how he died twice as well, but it just seems an odd thing to ask with his cover story. As you say, he could still be a journalist but I doubt it.'

Varcoe nodded.

'I know what you mean, sir. Journalists are usually more confident, not as hesitant.'

'So what are the other possibilities? He could have killed Pollard and be trying to find out how much we know, but then he might as well just turn up here and confess. He could be someone who knows or has seen something but he's too frightened to come forward.'

'Or he's been warned off.' Varcoe added.

'True. Or there was some truth in what he said, he knew Pollard years ago and wants to know more to go around telling the rest of the town, or he just wants to know in that way people do when they stop to stare at an accident or a fire or something. We need to know where the call was made from, Anna. I know you're onto that.'

'I am, although we won't know until tomorrow at the earliest now.'

'As long as it's been actioned. Trouble is, Craig Pollard knew a lot of people and it's going to be next to impossible to narrow down who might have made that call. Who knows how many years ago he knew Pollard, if he ever did.'

Anna Varcoe nodded her understanding. Knight had been impressed with the little he'd seen of the DC so far. She was bright, quick thinking and made a decent cup of tea, which was more than he could say for DC Rogers.

'The location's crucial then, sir. As soon as I hear something back on it, I'll let you know.'

As Varcoe got to her feet and left Knight's office, he caught himself staring after her, the smile still on his face. He shook his head, amused. Maybe he was ready to move on after Caitlin, but gazing soppily at young DCs wasn't really the way to do it. He stood again. Time to talk to DS Bishop.

'You've done what?' Steve Kent bellowed.

Dave Bowles cringed, holding his mobile phone away from his ear. He'd expected Steve to go mental when he told him about the phone call to Northolme police station, but standing here listening to it actually happen was another matter entirely. Thank God they weren't face to face.

'You stupid, stupid bastard! If they weren't looking for you already, you can be fucking sure they are now! What were you thinking?'

'I don't know, I panicked, I just . . . I thought they might tell me.'

'Of course they weren't going to tell you, they're the police, not some sort of public information service! Jesus, Dave. Tell me you didn't use your mobile?'

'No, 'course not. Phone box.'

'Where?'

Bowles frowned.

'What do you mean, where?'

'Where was the phone box, Dave? Christ!'

'Oh, middle of nowhere. No one saw me, I'm sure of it.' Bowles lied. He hadn't thought and had used the nearest one he could find.

'They better not have done. I knew you were stupid Dave, but this takes the fucking biscuit. If they come for you, and they might do now, don't mention me do you hear? And do me a favour, take the sim card out of your phone then cut it up and throw the bits in the river. Get yourself a new pay as you go phone and sim, I don't want any links between us.'

'I thought you said we didn't have anything to worry about. We've done nothing wrong, that's what you said.'

'We haven't this time but I don't fancy explaining what happened before, do you? Especially now Pollard's dead.'

'There's still Nick to think about. And that lad.'

'Nick isn't stupid, he'll keep his head down. And the lad . . . we don't know he saw anything. If he did why didn't he come forward at the time, or since? He's had twelve years to think about it.'

'Maybe he didn't see anything then. Maybe he doesn't know. They said it was an accident after all.'

'It was an accident, that's the point, and I'm not going to be dragged into something that I didn't do. Get that phone and sim card sorted. Don't ring me again, not from your new number either. Remember what I said, Dave. I wasn't there if they come for you.'

Steve Kent shoved his phone back in his pocket. He should have known Dave would do something stupid, though at least he hadn't gone to the police station in person and made a tearful confession. Kent paced around the living room of his flat. He couldn't deny he was worried too, of course he was, but panicking would get them nowhere. He was still sure Pollard's death was the result of a fight, an argument, something Pollard had got himself into as a result of his big mouth and cocky attitude. Until Kent heard differently, he was going to keep believing it. The worst thing he could do now was panic; he knew he mustn't let Dave's hysteria infect him too. Nick was an unknown. Kent had no idea where he was but presumed the news of Pollard's death would reach him eventually. He may have moved away or even emigrated. Kent had considered that himself, anything to make a new start, to become an anonymous face. In the end he had moved, albeit within the same county. Far enough though, away from the town, the moor, the memories and the old friends.

Catherine Bishop's desk in the main CID room was in the corner and she sat with her back to the wall. She could see the whole room, all the comings and goings. It was quieter now but there were still people around. Looking at the notes and the day's reports from the DCs and the rest of the team, it seemed to her they were no closer to finding Craig Pollard's killer than they had been the previous day. Trying to find any of the girls Pollard may have met in the pubs around the town had proved as fruitless as their attempts to talk to his friends. Perhaps Pollard wasn't as popular as his brother claimed. The post mortem had given them nothing new to go on and so far all the forensics had confirmed was that Craig Pollard's blood had been found with his body and no one else's. Bishop ran a hand through her hair. She'd had a headache since mid afternoon. She'd been trying not to think about the picture left with the body or the message posted to her, and especially not the photo taken of her, through her own living room window for Christ's sake. Why? If the idea was to frighten or intimidate her, the killer was in for a surprise. Initially it had been a shock, the photograph in particular, but in the end Pollard had been attacked and killed, not Bishop. She considered Knight's suggestion again, that the killer may have been posing a challenge to her or to the force but she couldn't understand that either. The evening meeting with Kendrick and Knight was in twenty minutes time and it was looking like she wouldn't have much to report. It was frustrating and somewhat worrying to have so little information coming in so early. She bent over the reports again, elbows on the desktop, forehead propped on her fingertips. Nothing. There was nothing there, nothing stood out. Leaning back in the chair now, she puffed out her cheeks in frustration. DI Knight was making his way across the room, eyes mainly on the worn carpet tiles though occasionally he would smile at someone, respond to a greeting. He was a strange one. He reached her desk and stopped, gesturing to the pile of papers in front of her and the emails open on her ancient beige monitor.

'Anything?' he asked, taking a chair from a nearby desk and dragging it over to sit by Bishop.

'No, afraid not.'

There didn't seem much else to say. Bishop waited; he'd come to her after all. Knight chewed on the top of his thumb, staring across the room at nothing in particular.

'I know I've asked you this before and no doubt you've been through it over and over in your head, but are you absolutely sure there's nothing you can think of that will help us? It might not even be related to the job, it could be someone you've met outside of work - a friend, an ex, a partner? Something in your past? I know,' he said, as she sighed. 'I know, but we're missing something. We've nothing to go on, nothing to move things forward, nothing to tell Pollard's family and nothing for DCI Kendrick or the Superintendent. Won't be long until she wants some answers.'

Bishop leaned back in her chair.

'I know sir and believe me I've been thinking about it all day, it's been in the back of my mind all the time but I can't think of anything and to be honest it's driving me mad. Some detective I must be, I'm the clue and I've no idea what's meant by it. I just can't think of anything or anyone. I've never arrested Pollard, never questioned him, never had anything to do with him except hearing other people moaning about him for being a mouthy bastard who seems to get away with everything. There are no end of coppers in this town who would have loved to have seen him sent down for a while, teach him a lesson, but we've never been able to catch him doing anything serious enough to make it happen.'

Knight glanced at her.

'What are you thinking he might have been up to?'

She shrugged.

'Drug dealing? All those flash clothes must have come from somewhere and he seemed to know everyone and be in town every night, he had plenty of opportunity.'

'But no one has suggested he was dealing have they? We've never found any drugs on him at all and his brother said Craig had never touched them, that he'd seen too many mates ruined by them. Nothing in the post mortem either.'

'It's just a suggestion. Then there's the fancy Pollard seemed to have for teenage girls. I thought we might get something from that, pissed off dad or older brother but nothing's turned up so far.'

Knight nodded.

'I thought we might find something there too. We still could, we're going back to the colleges tomorrow and the heads of the secondary schools are talking to their students, but would you come forward, especially if you were underage?'

'Maybe not, but we might get a friend that points us in the right direction. Pollard's dead after all, someone might want to do the right thing and help us out. Even if the bloke was what most of us would call a complete arsehole, did he really deserve to have his head smashed in and to be left lying in his own blood in a stinking alley?'

Knight stood.

'Someone obviously thought so. By the way, you're welcome to use my spare room again tonight. I'm not sure how you're feeling about things . . .'

Bishop followed him across the room.

'Thanks sir. If you're sure, that'd be great. It's just that photo, it's hard to get the thought out of my mind that he was there looking at me. It's one thing dealing with someone when they're standing in front of you, however big and ugly they are, but when someone sneaks around it's different.'

They were in the corridor now, heading for the meeting room and DCI Kendrick.

'From what forensics are saying we're looking for the invisible man anyway.' Knight said. 'No trace at the scene and no evidence, at least not yet.'

Bishop grimaced.

'I know. Things are really going our way.'

9

I need to move on to the second and at the moment I'm finding it difficult. It's not that he deserves anything less, it's just . . . I can't explain it, even to myself. It's reluctance. Craig was different. I was ready, even eager to get that done, but this time I'm more wary. One death could be explained away, even with the calling card I left for them, a prank or a joke. Another death seems to make it much more serious; a lunatic on the loose maybe? There's also more of a chance of alerting the others or of one of them coming forward with the whole story. I could stop now. Pollard was the one I wanted most after all, the ringleader, the rotten apple in the barrel. The others are just weak, not evil as he was. They were still there though, they stood by and let it happen, thinking more of themselves than of Tommy, too afraid of Pollard to stand up to him. So was I though, I need to remember that while I'm passing judgement.

10

Bishop shovelled the last of her chicken bhuna into her mouth and let out a long, satisfied breath. Knight, tearing off a final piece of naan bread, glanced up at her and smiled.

'Perfect,' said Bishop. 'Just what you need on a freezing cold, rainy night.' She took a sip of beer. 'Especially when your case is going to shit.'
Knight picked up his plate then leant across the table and took Bishop's. He rinsed them, dumped them in the sink and sat back down.

'I know I keep banging on about it, but we're missing something. Whoever killed Pollard will be sitting somewhere laughing at us.'

'It feels like we've got nowhere to go. DCI Kendrick didn't exactly mince his words, did he?' Bishop sighed. 'And he's right. A murder around here, whoever did it's usually still next to the body when it's found, knife in his hand, blood on his fists, but this? Have you ever heard of a case like it, sir, when you were in the Met? You must have seen all sorts of goings on.'

'Please call me Jonathan. We had someone phone the station and accuse a DC of murder once, a bloke had been knifed in a fight over a woman. Wasn't the DC at all, it was his cousin, though it caused a few headaches for a while. But I don't think you're being accused of anything here . . . '

'Mainly because I didn't do it!' Bishop interrupted. Knight held up a placatory hand.

'I *know*. It could be a plea for help, for understanding, just two fingers up at you and coppers in general . . . it'd help if they'd been a bit more specific though, instead of pissing around with reproduced oil paintings.'

Bishop raised an eyebrow. She couldn't remember having heard Knight swear before.

'What about the photo, what do you think he meant by that? If it were of someone else and more recent, someone close to Pollard like his brother or Kelly Whitcham, it would make more sense. They could be gloating about killing him then, rubbing their noses in the fact that they're watching them suffer or even accusing them, but why me? It doesn't feel like a threat, but then again it's shaken me up, I don't mind admitting it.'

Knight got to his feet again, crossed to the sink and began running hot water into the washing up bowl.

'I'm not surprised. If it had been a "knight" chess piece in the pictures, I'd feel the same.'

'Oh yes, I'd not thought of that - Bishop and Knight.'

She smiled at him hesitantly. Knight's mobile began to ring and he took it out of his pocket, frowning at the display.

'I'll take over, sir . . . Jonathan.' Bishop said. 'Where do you keep your washing up liquid?'

In the living room, Knight took a deep breath and touched the phone's screen to answer the call.

'Hello? Caitlin?'

'Jonathan? I thought you were never going to answer, I was going to leave you a voicemail.'

'I've only just got home, I was eating.'

'Working late? There's a surprise.'

'It's a murder investigation, Caitlin. As you know, we can't always persuade people to kill each other during office hours.'

'As charming as ever, Jonathan, and as defensive. It's nice to hear people are just as brutal in the sticks as they are down here in civilisation.'

'Did you ring me just to have a go, or . . . ?'

'Oh, no, there's a point. I'm pregnant.'

Knight's eyes widened and his sudden dry mouth was nothing to do with the curry he'd just eaten.

'So why are you telling me?' he managed to say. 'Hadn't you better phone Ben or Dom or whatever his name was?'

'His name was and still is Jed, as you well know. And I don't need to phone him, he's here now. We're living together.'

Knight sat down heavily.

'How wonderful for you. So, again, why are you telling me instead of floating ecstatically around Mothercare together?'

'You're so funny, Jonathan, you really are. I'm four months pregnant, so if you can manage to work that out on your fingers that means, God help us all, that the baby could be yours.'

Knight shook his head, exasperated.

'You're unbelievable. It won't be my baby, we were barely speaking at that point, never mind anything else. It's Jed's baby and you know it, this is just you winding me up for your own amusement. You're probably sitting there with a gang of your friends with me on speaker phone for a laugh.'

There was a pause. Caitlin spoke again, quieter now.

'I'm pleased you think so highly of me, Jonathan. The truth is this baby could be yours or, as you so kindly point out, it could be Jed's. I don't know and I won't until after the birth. I just wanted you to know it was a possibility but obviously just calling you out of the blue was the wrong way to go about it. I'm sorry, I'll go. Take care Jonathan.'

Knight stared at his phone. Caitlin had never apologised to him before, never acknowledged that perhaps she'd made a mistake or was in the wrong. He wasn't sure how long he'd been sitting there when Catherine Bishop quietly came into the room with the tea.

'All right?' she said, holding a mug out to him, then when there was no response: 'Jonathan?'

He started.

'Sorry. Thank you.'

Bishop crossed the room and sat down holding her own mug close, wondering how quickly she could finish her tea and politely get out of Knight's way. Then, to her amazement, he began to talk.

'That was my ex on the phone. Ex girlfriend. She's pregnant.'

'Oh.' She had no idea what else to say.

'Yeah.'

'How long since you split up?'

'Just before I moved back up here. That was one of the reasons I transferred. She'd been seeing someone else for a while and eventually I found out.'

'You hadn't suspected?'

'No. Some detective I am. You know how it is, working long hours, knackered when you do eventually get in. Some weeks we barely saw each other and she didn't like that. She needs lots of attention, she's hard work to be honest. Not sure now what I ever saw in her except at first - she's gorgeous but there's nothing underneath that if you know what I mean. She's like some amazing painting that you admire in a gallery but you know you couldn't live with at home. Too much for me, too loud, too confident and I think I bored her to death. I'm sure she's much happier with Jed. Is that even a real name?'

'I don't know.' said Bishop softly. 'So she's having your baby?'

Knight smiled ruefully.

'Helpfully, she isn't sure. All she can say for sure is she's having someone's baby.'

'So until the birth . . . '

'Depends if the baby comes out wearing a striped shirt and braces or a police uniform. Jed works in the City doing something mere mortals can't hope to understand.'

'You've met him then?'

'Once, at some posh do Caitlin dragged me to. Her friends seemed to think I was something the cat had sicked up. They used to call me "Caitlin's policeman friend".'

'Charming.'

'It's just how they were, I don't think they meant anything personal. I didn't fit in with their view of the world. They want the police to be sorting things out on the streets out of their sight, not at their fancy parties.'

'Caitlin goes to a lot of these types of things then?'

'It was part of her job, though to be honest I couldn't even tell you what she actually did. Lots of dinners and drinks parties and mincing around London as far as I could tell.'

'How long were you together?'

'Only six months. Long enough for both of us.'

'And you moved here when you split up?'

'Moved back here. This is where I grew up, not far away. I'd had enough of London and I wanted a complete change.'

'It'll be quieter, if nothing else. I did wonder why someone would leave the Met to come up here.'

'Like I say, I was ready for a change. I'd been down there long enough.'

'Not as challenging though?'

'I don't know. I've not had a case like this before.'

11

A few seconds passed before Steve Kent realised what had woken him. He'd had a few drinks last night, more than a few, and needed some sleep. When he heard the phone still ringing, however, he stretched over the side of his mattress and onto the floor to retrieve the phone from his jeans pocket. Only one person ever phoned that number and it wasn't someone you wanted to have a missed call from.

'Got a job for you tomorrow. Be at the lock up at ten pm.'

The call was terminated with Kent having had no chance to speak even if he'd wanted to. He knew he was to be at the lock up two hours before the time given so if anyone was listening he'd have been and gone before they showed up. As always there was no choice, no chance to refuse or protest. He sometimes wondered if he'd done the right thing getting involved; after all he'd tried to keep out of trouble. Then again, he had his legitimate day job and if he did a few deliveries here and there, cash in hand, no questions asked or answered then who would know or care? He'd never asked what was in the brown parcels he was asked to deliver or collect, though he could have a guess. It was something he usually tried not to think about. There had been a larger parcel once, quite heavy and rectangular, as deep as a shoebox but about three times as long. He definitely didn't want to think about what had been inside that one.

The deliveries he *really* didn't want to think about were the three people he'd had to collect in Southall one day and bring up to Lincoln. Two young women and an even younger man, only about eighteen. Their blank eyes and pale faces would stay with him, as would the pathetic looks of gratitude and attempts at thanks they'd given him when he'd brought them bottles of water and egg sandwiches back from the services where he'd stopped for a pee. He couldn't let them out of the back of the van of course, he'd been given strict instructions about that. They didn't seem to be able to speak much English but he did hear them exchange a few words in a language he'd didn't recognise. When he'd arrived at the address in Lincoln and opened the doors they'd been huddled together as if comforting each other. It didn't sit well with him. Delivering parcels was one thing, people were another. He wanted no part of it but had no idea how to get himself out of the situation. He could tip the police off, give them the addresses he knew, but he'd probably be signing his own death warrant or at the very least setting himself up for the beating of his life. He didn't know for certain, but if his suspicions were right and the man in charge was who he thought it was, the death warrant was a certainty. The bloke who phoned him wasn't the boss, just one of his minions but even he sounded threatening enough. They wouldn't think twice about killing him if the rumours were to be believed, and Steve Kent did believe them. That the boss was now dealing in people came as no surprise. Kent had only seen him in the flesh once but he'd somehow ended up being one of his men and was starting to feel out of his depth. The delivery jobs had been occasional at first, once every couple of months, but now it seemed the phone was ringing every week, even a few times a week. Perhaps the boss and his cronies had decided Kent could be trusted, maybe he'd passed his probationary period and was now accepted as a fully fledged member of the gang. Not exactly something he'd rush to put on his CV.

Nick Brady had been made redundant three times in as many years and was starting to feel a little sorry for himself. Take this last job for example. All right, it wasn't as if he was saving lives or doing some good in the world but he turned up and picked the right things, packed them in the right boxes and kept his nose clean. No sneaking out for a fag break every half hour like some of the lads, no coming in late and going home early. All he expected in return was his wages in the bank when they were supposed to be, and they'd been late two months running. Now, no great surprise, he'd been laid off – permanently. Bloody brilliant. He should be okay for the rent this month but he'd have to find something else quickly or he'd be out on his ear, back to his Mum's. He didn't want that. He'd have to go down to the job centre in the morning, see what they had. If past experience was anything to go by, it wouldn't be much.

Nick opened the door to his flat and picked up the post on the way in, just a gas bill and his credit card statement. He left them unopened on the table and went through to the bathroom for a shower, wanting to wash his former workplace off him for good. As he pulled his T shirt over his head, his mobile rang in his jeans pocket. He wrestled it out and checked the display.

'All right Mum, what's up? I'm just getting in the shower, got a bit of bad news, actually - I've been made redundant again.'

'Oh no, Nick, you don't have much luck with jobs do you? Your Auntie Kay's coming round later, I'll see if Uncle Martin's heard of anything going at the steelworks.'

Nick shook his head silently. He'd have to be desperate to work with Martin Newsome. The bloke was a nightmare, full of big mouthed bravado about his latest drinking exploits and nights out with the lads, conveniently forgetting he was a married man of fifty three.

'Anyway,' his mum went on, 'I'm ringing about something I've seen in the paper. That lad you knew at school, always in trouble, you were mates for a bit. Wasn't his name Craig Pollard?'

Nick's eyes narrowed.

'Yeah, Pollard. Why?'

'He's dead, been murdered apparently.'

'Murdered? Come off it, Mum.'

'It's true.'

'What, because it's in the local rag? More likely he got drunk and said something clever to the wrong person and they knifed him. It wouldn't surprise me.'

'I'm just telling you what it said in the paper. They've interviewed his mum and she's saying the police don't care, that they haven't done anything.'

'They must have done.'

'Well, they've not arrested anyone, that's what she means.'

Nick felt a familiar dread in his stomach. It couldn't be, it couldn't have anything to do with it.

'Which paper, Mum? I'll nip out and get one.'

'Why don't you just come round and read ours? I've got a cake in the oven.'

Knight lay back on his pillows, willing himself to relax. Caitlin's news had hit him like a body blow. He still didn't believe she was carrying his baby, but if the chance was there – and he supposed Caitlin should know – it was a possibility he was going to have to get used to. He couldn't understand why she'd chosen to tell him now. The baby wasn't due for another five months, why hadn't she waited until nearer the time? She may have thought it was his right to know now, maybe Jed had persuaded her to tell him, perhaps one of her less nauseating friends had? He knew he'd need to speak to her again, but not now, not tonight. A baby . . . He'd thought about what it might be like to be a father, of course he had but never seriously, just with a sort of passing curiosity when a colleague or friend's child was born. The biggest surprise was that Caitlin had allowed herself to become pregnant at all. He couldn't imagine her pushing a pram around the designer shops she favoured or carrying the baby onto the Tube. Knight shifted as his hand unconsciously crept up to his right shoulder blade. He knew how fragile life could be, his job had taught him that early on and it continued to reinforce the lesson most days. In some ways he hoped the baby would be Jed's child, mostly for its own sake. Another part of him though felt a slight hope, a stirring of emotion at the thought of being a father.

He was there, she knew it, but she couldn't see him. It was dark, unnaturally so, the blackness so thick and complete it seemed to engulf her. Catherine Bishop reached out a trembling hand, attempting to make sense of the place, trying to find her bearings. The fetid air felt heavy and hot. A scurrying sound, the scratching of tiny claws. The sound of another person breathing but no one in sight. Bishop froze, span around. Nothing. No one, but he was there. A cruel, mocking chuckle.

'Are you lost, Catherine? Feeling helpless?'

Two hands in the middle of her back, a hard shove. She fell to the floor, clattering without dignity. He laughed as she cried out. Flashes of light, hundreds of them, blinding and dazzling, unwelcome and threatening. Catching at her most vulnerable, her most exposed. Forcing her to gaze at herself, her flaws, her weaknesses, everything she tried to keep hidden during the day. This was night though, the blackest of nights.

The lights died away and he was gone. Catherine awoke with a cry.

12

DCI Keith Kendrick didn't often lose his temper, impatient irritation being his usual state of mind, but when he did the whole station knew about it. Bishop stumbled towards her desk, coffee in hand to ward off the morning. She squinted at Chris Rogers who was making strange gestures with his hands, pointing towards Bishop and miming wringing someone's neck.

'What's up with you?' said Bishop, plonking herself heavily in her chair. 'Twitch getting worse?'

'You'll have a lot more than a twitch when the DCI gets his hands on you.'

'He should be so lucky. What are you on about?'

'Apparently, Craig Pollard's mum's been shouting her mouth off in the local paper: her poor little boy dead, police not bothered, useless, piss up in a brewery, arse with both hands, etcetera, etcetera.'

Bishop groaned.

'Oh God . . . '

'Kendrick's looking for you and DI Knight. He came storming through about five minutes ago and said to tell you to get to his office before your backside hit your chair.'

Bishop got up resignedly.

'That's just bloody great.'

She approached the DCI's office, hearing what sounded like Kendrick muttering as she tapped lightly on the door. Kendrick barked 'Come in!'

'DS Bishop, good of you to join us,' Kendrick snapped, nodding at the spare chair in the corner. Knight already sat in the seat opposite Kendrick, eyes fixed on a spot just above the DCI's head. Bishop lowered herself carefully into the chair after removing what looked like a complete change of clothes from the seat. She held the suit and shirt on her lap, not really sure where else to put them.

'So,' said Kendrick, throwing a copy of the previous night's local newspaper across the desk towards Knight, 'How do you two propose I explain this to the Superintendent?'

Knight shuffled his chair to one side so Bishop could lean over to read the article too. The gist was, as DC Rogers had said, that Craig Pollard's mother was claiming the police had done absolutely nothing to find the person responsible for her son's death, that they weren't even trying, had barely spoken to herself or her husband and had offered them no idea when they might expect to bury their son. A photograph of a tearful Mrs Pollard clutching a gilt framed picture of Craig dominated the front page along with the headline "MOTHER'S ANGER AT POLICE FAILURE".

'We're doing our best.' muttered Bishop.

Kendrick leaned forward.

'I beg your pardon?'

Bishop made herself meet his eyes.

'We're doing the best we can, sir.'

'Are we, Sergeant? Then why is Craig Pollard's killer not sitting in one of our delightfully welcoming interview rooms? Why did Craig Pollard's killer not spend last night staring down into a bowl of prison soup, hoping the showers would be safe? Why aren't we all digging out our black ties to go to Craig Pollard's funeral and telling his parents how sorry we are, but that at least we've caught the bastard?'

Bishop kept quiet. There was no reasoning with Kendrick in this mood, it was best just to let him burn himself out. She hoped Knight would realise this too, but then one of them would have to speak.

'Cat got your tongue, Sergeant?'

Bishop stared at the floor, fiddling with one of the buttons on the suit jacket she held. Kendrick glared.

'Leave that button alone, that suit cost a bloody fortune!' He stood abruptly, snatched the suit from Bishop and stuffed it under his desk along with the shirt and tie. 'We'll look even better if I have to go to a press conference about this fiasco with no buttons on my suit. Now,' he took the newspaper back, 'Anyone got anything to say? I know this isn't the run-of-the-mill drunken assault that got out of hand, but we must have something I can take back to the Super? DI Knight?'

Knight chewed his thumbnail.

'No more than last night, sir. The main issue is the messages relating to DS Bishop, but we have no idea what they mean. Until we do . . . '

'Until we do, we just hope the killer happens to wander into reception and give himself up?'Kendrick was getting worked up again. 'Brilliant. Mrs Pollard will love that. I can just see the headline now,' he spread his arms wide, 'Police admit they have no bloody idea. All suggestions gratefully received!'

'We do have some points to follow up.' Knight said calmly.

'Really? Well, that's a turn up,' said Kendrick. 'Let's follow them then, shall we? I want you both back here at two with something new to tell me.'

As they were obviously dismissed, Knight led the way out into the corridor. Bishop offered him a weak smile.

'Well, that was fun.' she said.

Knight grinned.

'Let's get a cup of tea.'

Bishop treated herself to a chocolate muffin as well as tea and Knight choose a piece of flapjack.

'Best make sure the DCI doesn't come in and see us,' she said. 'Not after he's just ordered us to find Craig Pollard's killer before lunchtime.'

'We won't be hanging around,' said Knight. 'Anna Varcoe's got a location for that anonymous phone call, a phone box in town. She's off getting the CCTV footage now. We need to know who made that call, so she's telling them we need it prioritising.'

'Agreed, sir. He must know something. What are we going to do about Mrs Pollard?'

'Not much we can do now really. She's got a point, I suppose. She doesn't know about the messages, so in her eyes we just need to pick up whichever drunken gobshite Craig had a run in with. You and I know it's not that simple. We've no forensics, no witnesses, nothing from the post mortem that can help, no obvious motive or suspects. We've already talked about Kelly Whitcham and Mike Pollard, but I don't honestly think either of them are our killer. So, back to the messages and the phone call. They're all we have.'

Bishop nodded.

'Makes sense.'

'We need a list of Pollard's school friends from his parents, if they'll even talk to us now. Can you speak to the family liaison officer again please? I'll work with DC Varcoe and try to get an image we can use from the CCTV stuff. Maybe Pollard's parents will recognise whoever made that call if we get really lucky. We could check with Kelly Whitcham and Mike Pollard too. Someone must know who he is.' Knight ran his fingers through his hair, his hand straying to his shoulder blade. Bishop frowned, then pretended not to notice.

'Assuming he really did know Craig Pollard years ago, of course.' The last of the chocolate muffin disappeared into Bishop's mouth.

'Assuming we get an image. Assuming the CCTV camera was working. Assuming he wasn't wearing a mask or a balaclava or a fucking motorbike helmet!'

Bishop stared at him, eyebrows raised. She stood up. 'I'll speak to PC Stathos, sir.' she said and walked quickly away. Knight, feeling slightly guilty, closed his eyes and pushed his chair back. It seemed they were going to need some luck.

Kendrick's two o'clock deadline was still a few hours away when Bishop arrived back at the station. She crossed the CID room to her desk, smiling at some of the uniforms that were scurrying around. Taking out her notepad, she flipped through the list of names she'd scrawled during her visit to Craig Pollard's parents. This would be one in the eye for Knight after the way he'd snapped at her earlier. She wouldn't show him he'd annoyed her, but he'd probably realised. Irene and Pete Pollard had provided a short list of names and a quick phone call to Mike Pollard had added a couple more. The information wouldn't necessarily be much use on its own, but depending what Varcoe and Knight got from the CCTV tapes, both her list and any image produced could be used together to narrow down any suspects. After the frustration of the last couple of days, it had been good to get back to actually making progress. She didn't often feel as if she was wasting her time, but a little of that had crept in. Her personal involvement in the case was beginning to come to the front of her mind more often and that was something Bishop didn't want. She knew herself well enough to realise the only way to keep any worry, concern or fear about why Craig Pollard's killer had identified her at the scene at bay was to keep the case moving forward, to make sure they found the answers as soon as possible.

Knight leant forward, squinting at the image on the screen. Anna Varcoe scrubbed at her eyes with her knuckles, the beginnings of a headache making its presence felt.

'And this is as clear as it gets?' said Knight. It was more of a statement than a question. Varcoe nodded.

'We've worked with worse. Someone might recognise him.'

'And no motorbike helmet . . . '

Varcoe glanced at him, bemused.

'No, sir. Not as far as I can make out.'

Knight got to his feet.

'Okay. If you talk to DS Bishop, she was trying to get a list of Pollard's school friends together. If she's got something, we might have our mystery man in an interview room this afternoon.'

Varcoe left him gazing at something only he could see on the wall. She shook her head as she made her way to the CID room. *Inspector Wallpaper strikes again,* she thought, though he had said more to her today than ever. Even he couldn't ignore the unsolved Pollard case breathing down their necks, especially with Kendrick on the warpath.

Catherine Bishop was sitting at her desk in the corner, frowning into the mug she held. Varcoe approached, waited.

'All right, Anna?' said Bishop, peering further into the cup.

'Something wrong with your drink, Sarge?'

'I've dropped half a Rich Tea in it, I was hoping I could salvage something. I think it's a gonner though. What's that?'

Varcoe held up the printout.

'Our mystery caller. Craig Pollard's "old schoolfriend".' To Bishop's relief, Varcoe refrained from illustrating the quote with her fingers.

'Hmm, that was quick. Let's have a look.' said Bishop. Varcoe handed over the sheet. The image was a little blurred, grainy, the man's face turned slightly away from centre. 'Not exactly a looker, is he?' Bishop tipped her head to the side, turning the paper in her hands then glancing up at Varcoe, who grinned.

'Don't know, Sarge. Hard to tell from that, I'd have thought.'

'I've been running the names we got from Mr and Mrs Pollard through the PNC, but nothing so far on any of this lot. Thought we might get lucky, but I should have known better. Fancy a trip out to the Pollard house with me?' Varcoe shuffled her feet.

'What's the mood like in there?'

'The mood? Mrs Pollard's liable to snap at you like a shark that's just come off hunger strike as soon as she knows you're a copper - I was there this morning. Alexa Stathos is still there, making loads of tea and trying to stay out of the way.'

'What about the story in the paper? Didn't Alexa know about it?'

'You would think. Seems Mrs Pollard was sneaky, and I suppose Alexa can't be there all the time. Helen Bridges wrote the story, of course, and we know her of old, don't we?'
Varcoe nodded, sighing.

'Oh yes, she'll want to get the nationals involved if she can then. Remember the story she did about the Chief Constable getting out of paying a parking fine? Talk about a load of trumped up rubbish.'

'He did get out of it though, didn't he?' Bishop whispered theatrically. Varcoe smiled in spite of herself.

13

By one o'clock, Bishop and Varcoe were feeling a lot less cheery. Craig
Pollard's parents hadn't been able to identify the man on Varcoe's printout and
they'd been more or less ordered off the premises after a few minutes. PC Alexa
Stathos smiled apologetically as she showed them to the door, then told Bishop
and Varcoe in a furious whisper that she didn't know what she was still doing in
the Pollard's house because they obviously resented her presence and could they
talk to someone about it please? Bishop promised to see what she could do.
Back in the car, Varcoe turned to Bishop.

'So what now, Sarge?'

Bishop sighed.

'I think we should go to the pub.' Varcoe waited. 'No? Okay, maybe we
should go back to the station. I've got a meeting with His Highness DCI
Kendrick at two and I don't know what'll happen if I'm late, he'll probably
have my head cut off and stuck up on the outside of the station as a warning to
others. We do have time to go via the building site Craig Pollard's brother
works on though. Looks like he's our final chance until we go to Pollard's old
school.'

'There's always Kelly Whitcham.'

'True. Let's see what Mike says first though, I don't think Kelly was around
when Craig was at school. If we don't have any joy, as I say, we'll go to the
school, the pubs and maybe – don't let Kendrick hear – the local press.'

'You know where this building site is then?'

Bishop started the engine.

'Let's hope I can remember.'

The drive took about ten minutes. Bishop chatted away about all sorts of things, Anna Varcoe adding comments when she could get a word in. Varcoe couldn't remember working like this with the DS before and she was enjoying the experience. She'd once been told Bishop could be prickly and difficult to get on with but she'd never found this herself and wasn't one to judge on hearsay. All sorts of gossip travelled around the station, rumours, scandals and plain lies, but Varcoe tried to keep herself away from it as much as she could. She also didn't want to be the talk of the station and had always kept her working life and personal life as separate as she could. It had worked pretty well so far.

Bishop bumped the car up onto a grass verge and brought it to a halt. They climbed out and made their way over to the nearest builder who nodded his head towards a muddy path through the site. Following it was a tricky business as it was potholed and wet, but they made it through unscathed to where Mike Pollard was unloading sheets of insulation from the back of a trailer. Bishop sauntered over.

'Afternoon, Mike. How's it going?'

Pollard turned.

'How's what going? I've spoken to you once today already, can't you leave me alone? Have you found out who killed my brother yet?'

In response, Bishop stuck the printout under Pollard's nose. He stared at it.

'Who's this?'

'We were hoping you could tell us.'

Pollard took the sheet and held it up to the light.

'Looks like one of Craig's old mates Nick . . . no, Steve something.'

'Steve who? This is really important, Mike.'

'I don't know, I just knew him as Steve. Used to be a pal of Craig's years ago. I'm sure that was his name.'

Bishop took the paper back.

'And this was when Craig was at school? Was he a school friend or did Craig know him from somewhere else?'

Pollard shook his head.

'I don't know, honestly. I think it was after school, maybe when Craig was working but I'm not sure. They didn't want me hanging around with them.'

'And there's nothing else you can tell us about him?'

'I don't think so. They were quite matey for a while but I think they had some kind of an argument. Maybe not though, Craig had so many friends back then, different ones every week it seemed like.'

'All right, thanks Mike.'

Pollard turned away, back to the insulation. Bishop and Varcoe left him to it and made their way gingerly back to the car. Bishop dropped into the driver's seat and sighed heavily.

'Shit.' she said.

'It's a start.' Varcoe said.

'I know, but the DCI wants a finish. There must be a million Steves in town and that's assuming Pollard remembered the right name and that this mysterious Steve even lived here. He could be from anywhere.'

'We'll have to go to the school, then.'

'Not now though, I need to get back to the station. You go on there, take someone with you. Here you go.' Bishop held out the now slightly creased printout. Varcoe reached out and took it from her quickly as Bishop threw the car into gear and sped off.

Knight paced the conference room as Bishop shot through the door. It was a couple of minutes after two o'clock, but there was no sign as yet of the DCI. Catherine Bishop ran her hands through her hair as she sat down. Knight stood beside her.

'How did you and DC Varcoe get on?' he asked.

'We got a name from Mike Pollard, but only a first name. Pollard's parents didn't recognise him. Mike says the bloke's called Steve, but obviously that's about as helpful as him being called John Smith. Anna's on her way over to the school Pollard used to go to now to see if anyone there knows our man, but I think it's a bit of a long shot to be honest. Mike Pollard thinks Craig might have been friends with our mystery caller after school. Anyway, will there be any teachers left now who even remember Craig Pollard, much less all his mates?' Knight settled in the seat next to Bishop.

'Maybe, maybe not, but we have to try it. This case is a bloody nightmare. Every report we write might as well just say "We don't have a clue."'

They both turned to look at the door as Kendrick's unmistakeable voice was heard in the distance, followed by him guffawing. Bishop and Knight stared at each other and Bishop made the gesture with her index finger screwed into her temple to indicate "He's mad". It wasn't something she'd done since school, but it made her and Knight smile. They heard footsteps outside the door.

'Brace yourself.' Knight murmured.

'Fee fi fo fum.' whispered Bishop.

There was something about Keith Kendrick that meant everyone sat up straight when he entered a room and Bishop and Knight were no exception. Bishop felt the urge to chant 'Good afternoon DCI Kendrick', as if she was at primary school.

Kendrick yanked a chair from under the conference table and settled his considerable bulk in it.

'In case you're wondering,' he said 'the probably only momentary lifting of my bad mood is due to DI Hawkins bringing in two members of the gang we think are responsible for all the four by four thefts we've had recently. The other two men involved are being collected from their respective nasty little day jobs as we speak. So. Let's keep this elation of mine going. What have you two got for me?'

Knight handed him a new copy of the image of the mystery caller.

'His name's Steve.' Bishop added helpfully. Kendrick stared at the paper, his huge hands turning the page around to look at it from every angle as if that would make it clearer, just as Bishop had done.

'Have we found him? Had a little chat about why it's extremely rude to refuse to leave your name and number when you call your friendly local police station for a cosy chat about a murder victim?'

Bishop shifted in her chair. Knight said,

'Not exactly. We only know his first name so far. DC Varcoe is off at Pollard's old school now, trying to find out if anyone there can help.'

Kendrick was drawing himself up, no doubt in preparation for another rant, so Bishop interjected quickly:

'And we're compiling the details of every Steve in the area who's around Craig Bishop's age to see if any of their surnames ring any bells with Craig Pollard's brother or parents. It was Mike Pollard that gave us the name Steve in the first place.'

Kendrick settled back down.

'And he's sure about the name?'

'He seemed sure, sir. He did say another name at first, Nick I think it was, but then changed his mind.'

'Steve, Nick . . . why couldn't Pollard pal around with people called Archibald or Horatio? It'd make our job a bit easier. Should we be looking at anyone called Nick or Nicholas too?'

Bishop glanced at Knight.

'We could do, sir. I'm not sure how long it would take . . .' she said.

Kendrick stood up.

'It'll take as long as it needs to, Sergeant, but I don't want to miss something and have to start again later. Have Pollard's parent's seen this?'

'Yes, but they don't recognise him.'

'Show them again, dangle the names Steve and Nick in front of them, see if it gives them a nudge in the right direction. I want this charmer interviewed as soon as we can. Right now, it seems he's the only lead we have. Or am I wrong? Do you have any other little titbits for me?'

They shook their heads.

'Didn't think so. Keep me informed.'

Kendrick strode out and Bishop and Knight breathed sighs of relief.

'Could have been worse.' commented Bishop.

'Much worse.' Knight agreed.

Bishop's mobile rang and she dragged it from her jacket pocket.

'Anna?'

Anna Varcoe's voice was crackly, but audible enough.

'Hello, Sarge. Not having much luck I'm afraid, the only teacher who would have been here when Pollard was is part time now and not at school until tomorrow. We've got a home address and mobile number, but there's no sign of her at home and the mobile's not ringing. We had a word with her neighbour and apparently she does a lot of walking so she's probably up in the Peak District somewhere with no signal. I'll keep trying. Do you want us back at the station?'

Bishop asked Varcoe to take the printout back to the Pollards to see if the names they had been given jogged their memories. Ending the call, she saw her phone was showing she'd received a text message and opened it:

Bored of marking essays. Fancy a drink tonight? L

Eyebrows raised, Bishop sent back: May b a late one.

The reply was almost instant: Wouldn't expect anything else. Come round when you're ready.

Totally confused but thinking it was worth a try, Bishop typed: Food?

Again, a quick response: If you bring a takeaway.

Smiling, Bishop sent: No prob. See u l8er

No grammar and text talk. Louise would hate it. Knight was waiting for her.

'Sorry, sir. Just a friend. I'll probably see her later, depending on what time we finish.'

'You're welcome to stay as long as this goes on you know.' Knight said, holding the door open for her. He had heard Bishop crying out during the night, muttering and mumbling in her sleep and was becoming concerned about how the case was affecting her, bright and breezy as she seemed.

'Thank you. I just don't want to be in your way or outstay my welcome.'

'Not at all,' said Knight, 'it's good to have some company.'

He was surprised to hear himself say it, and even more surprised to find he meant it.

14

Catherine Bishop drove across town to Louise's new address after collecting a Chinese takeaway, feeling strangely nervous. DI Knight had given her his spare key, told her to enjoy herself, to be careful and to let him know if she was going to be out all night. She'd frowned a little at that, as if he thought he was her dad or something, until she'd seen the grin on his face. *Careful,* she'd thought *you'll be liking him next.* He certainly seemed to be coming out of his shell a little, although she'd noticed some of the other officers still glanced at each other and smiled when he was around. He was just so awkward somehow, especially when compared with DCI Kendrick and the other DI. Still, as a boss she had no real complaints, at least so far and that was all she needed to worry about. She was almost there and the butterflies in her stomach increased. She was suddenly conscious of the mud on her boots and the fact she'd come straight from the station with no time for a shower or even a quick wash. She gave herself a mental shake. *It's Louise, she's seen you looking like this a million times, looking much worse than this too. It's not like you need to impress her.* She had to admit that a tiny part of her wanted Louise to suddenly realise what she'd been missing, although after a thirteen hour day she was unlikely to be looking or smelling her best.

Bishop saw a spot by the kerb where she could leave the car. It was at the wrong end of Louise's street, but it would have to do. She clambered out, heaved the bag of food over the gearstick and awkwardly locked the door. There were footsteps behind her and she tensed, feeling vulnerable with her hands full. She remembered Knight's warning to be careful as well as the message left with Craig Pollard's body and fought the temptation to spin around to see who was there. The distance to Louise's door seemed miles. She should have parked beneath a streetlight. *Come on, Catherine, you're a police officer,* she said to herself sternly. Squaring her shoulders, she turned around, eyes scanning the street. Nothing. There was no one there. Bishop sighed and began to walk down the street, watching and listening, feeling incredibly alert although she was tired. Louise's house was in sight when there was another sound, running feet some way behind her. Bishop gasped, walking faster, images from her dream of the night before racing through her mind. She was level with Louise's front gate, the footsteps growing closer and closer. Bishop, almost running herself now, had to stop to fumble with the bolt on the gate. Eventually she yanked it open and hurtled through, onto the gravel path. A figure rushed by on the pavement behind her and a flash of light lit the dark sky for a second, then was gone. Bishop knocked as loudly as she dared on Louise's front door, trying to control her breathing. She was fine, the figure was just a kid, there was no danger. The fact that the light had looked just like those in her dreams was a coincidence, it hadn't been a camera, there was no one out there now. *You're okay*, Bishop told herself. There was movement in the house and the door opened. Louise appeared, glass of wine in one hand, paperback novel in the other. She'd had her hair cut shorter than Catherine remembered. It suited her, drawing attention to the structure of her face.

'Come in, Catherine. How are you? Long day?'
Bishop followed her into a short hallway, forcing herself to stay calm.

'You could say that. I'm fine, thanks. I like your hair. How are you?'
She held out the bag of food and Louise took it, leading the way into the kitchen where the table was set.

'No candles?' Bishop joked, some of her bravado returning now she was on the right side of a locked door, though her heart still pounded.

Louise smiled tiredly.

'Not tonight. How are you really? You look exhausted. Are you working on the Craig Pollard murder? I couldn't believe it when I read about it, it just doesn't seem like the sort of thing that would happen around here.'

She poured Bishop a glass of water which she took gratefully and started to serve the food. 'Beef and black bean?'

'Yours, of course. Mine's the chicken fried rice.'

Louise glanced at her.

'That's a new one.'

'I'm not really hungry.'

Louise didn't comment and they ate in silence for a while, Bishop picking at her food. Eventually she said, 'This was a surprise.'

'What do you mean?'

'You inviting me here.'

Louise took a sip of wine.

'I invited you here because you said you'd be working late and I thought it made more sense than me sitting in a pub somewhere waiting for you. I just thought it'd be nice to catch up, that's all.'

'Nice? I thought English teachers didn't use that word.'

'Yes, nice. Although I'm starting to wonder why I bothered.'

Bishop covered her face with her hands.

'I'm sorry.' she said, her voice muffled. Louise stood, walked around the table and put an arm around her shoulders.

'Come on,' she said. 'Come and talk to me.'

In the living room, a log fire blazed. The lights were dimmed, the colours neutral and calming. Bishop felt herself instantly relax as Louise led her by the hand to the settee.

'I'm sorry.' Bishop repeated.

'Been doing your big brave copper act? What's going on, Catherine?'

'You know I can't tell you.'

'Just tell me what you can.'

Bishop relayed the briefest details of the messages that had been left and the photo she'd received, the panic and worry they'd caused her, then the incident just now in the street. Louise listened, staring into the fire. When Bishop was quiet, she said, 'And I don't suppose you've talked to anyone about this? No one knows how worried you've been? What if that person outside just now was the person you're trying to catch? He could have done anything to you. You could be in real danger, Catherine.'

'It was just a kid outside, don't worry. I've spoken to DI Knight. I just need to carry on and when we've caught him, it'll be over.'

'I bet you didn't tell him how you've really been feeling. You need to talk to people.'

'He's my boss, not my therapist. He needs to know I can do my job or else I'll be off the case, shunted across to DI Hawkins and her bloody car thefts. This is what I've worked for, I can't let some psycho with a screw loose scare me into giving it up.'

Louise held up her hands.

'All right, all right, I get it. No need to shout.'

There was silence for a while, until Bishop started to get to her feet.

'I need to go and get some sleep, Louise. I'm sorry I've been such a pain in the arse.'

Louise reached out, gently holding her arm.

'I wanted to talk to you.'

Slowly, Bishop sat back down. Louise took a deep breath.

'When you sent that text the other night, it got me thinking. I do miss you, I have done since I moved out. I just wanted to see you again, to talk and . . . I don't know. We've kept in touch on and off, but I've not actually seen you for ages. We were happy, weren't we? If hadn't been for your job . . .'

'My job is still here though, all the problems you had with it will still be problems.'

'I know. I know they will, and I understand you love your work and you need to do it. I just miss you , I miss how we were at the beginning.'

'We can't go back there though.'

'Maybe we could.'

'What do you mean?'

'I can be more understanding, I promise. We could keep our separate houses, just see each other more often? When you can?'

Bishop stared.

'Where has this come from? When you left, you told me I was married to my job, that I'd chosen the job over you, over our life together, over our future and now all of a sudden you can compromise? Why has it taken you six months to work it out?'

Louise had tears in her eyes.

'I miss you. I just . . . miss you.'

'You miss me, or you miss someone coming home to you, eating with you, sharing a bed with you? There's a difference. I didn't know if I missed you for yourself or if I missed the company at first.'

'Well, that's honest. And what did you decide?'

'I missed you. But you left, you walked out.'

'After you agreed it was for the best.'

'What choice did I have? None. You gave me two options, us or the job and to me that's not something a person who loved me would force me to decide. In the reply to my last text, you said exactly the same, that I'd miss my job more than I missed you. Why have you changed your mind?'

'I haven't, I just see that I could have been more understanding, that's all.'

'But why now? Are you saying you want us to get back together? It's all come out of the blue.'

'I'm just saying it would be good to see more of you, maybe see how things go.'

'Good of you to throw me a few crumbs! Do I have any say in this? You're also presuming I'm still single, which is a bit of a cheek really.'

'Are you?'

'Yes,' Catherine admitted, 'but that's not the point.'

'You know my friends Amy and Beth?' Bishop groaned. 'I know you don't like them, but I was talking to them and they're building a house, thinking about starting a family when it's finished. It just got me thinking about us, how we happy we used to be. I just thought, what if I've thrown away my chance for a future like that?'

'You didn't throw it away, we agreed it wasn't going to work. I'll admit, I wanted you to stay, I've missed you, but we're the same people in the same situation.'

Louise got up and took a tissue from a box on the bookcase, then sat back down.

'I don't want to argue with you, we've done that before.'

'We'll always come back to things we've said before because the old issues are still there.'

Louise looked at Catherine, holding her gaze.

'Is it just the issues that are still there?'

'What do you mean?'

Leaning forward, Louise took her hand.

'Catherine, all I'm asking is if we can try, just take it slowly. I know how I was, I know I said things, that I wasn't very understanding or supportive. You said you missed me.'

Bishop glanced away.

'I know. But what if we try and everything's the same? My job takes up more time than ever. Would you really want to cope with that again?'

'Other people do. I know it seems sudden but it's not really, I've been thinking about it for a while. I just don't want to look back in a few years and wish I'd at least talked to you about it.'

'And you knew I'd come running?' The face of the woman that she had seen in the briefing room flashed into Bishop's mind and she blinked, thrown for a second.

Louise moved away.

'This has obviously been a mistake.'

'I'm trying to make sure you realise that nothing's changed. Just because we're both still single, it doesn't mean it would work if we got back together.'

Frowning, Louise stood again, went into the kitchen and brought the wine bottle through. There was a tiny amount left and she poured it into her glass then drank it down, still standing.

'You're right. Maybe you should go now then.' Her voice was cold and Catherine got to her feet feeling torn.

Louise followed her to the front door and Bishop turned, wondering what she was supposed to do.

'Bye then.' she said helplessly.

'Thanks for the food.' Louise replied. They stared at each other, eyes sending wordless messages. Slowly, they moved closer until they stood face to face, bodies almost touching.

'Stay tonight?' whispered Louise.

Knight woke sweating, panicking, knowing he'd probably screamed in his sleep. The dream was back, more vivid and terrible than ever: the blindfold, the smell of petrol and hatred, the snarled threats and promises. The punches in his gut, the kicks in his ribs and between his legs, the sound and feel of his shirt being torn from his body. Then the weight, someone kneeling on the small of his back, his arms being held, his legs pinned down, no idea how many there were or what they would do to him now, if he would even survive. The first touch on his back, his shoulder blade, on the flesh there. A cold, piercing sensation that instantly turned into red hot agony. The terrible realisation that it was a knife, that they were cutting him, that his blood was running over the front of his shoulder and down his back. They were laughing and taunting him, promising he would never forget this night, saying that he would forever have a reminder of it just in case he thought of doing something so stupid again. Lying there when they'd dumped him at the side of the road, cold and shivering, losing blood, knowing that he'd brought this on himself.

15

For the second time, Knight's sleep was interrupted, this time by his mobile phone. He groaned and turned over. It felt as if he'd only slept for minutes, but a glance at the glowing figures of his bedside clock told him it was about four hours since his dream had woken him, six fourteen am now. He fumbled for the phone which was still chirping away somewhere near the clock. Finally grabbing it, he raised it to his ear.

Thirty seconds later he was out of bed and scrabbling for clothes then rushing across the landing. He pounded on the door of the spare bedroom to wake DS Bishop but there was no reply. He stared at the door then remembered and stumbled back to the bedroom, picking up his phone from where he'd dropped it on the bed. Sure enough, there was a text from her. He must have already been asleep when she'd sent it: Staying here, c u at station tomorrow. CB He smiled in spite of the news he'd just received. *Good for you* he thought. Unfortunately, he was going have to disturb her.

Catherine Bishop stretched out a hand and found Louise's warm back. It was true then. She'd woken a few minutes before, taking a few seconds to remember where she was, why the wall she was looking at was pale yellow and not white. Louise's house, Louise's bedroom. Louise's bed. She stretched then buried her face in the pillow, never having imagined that accepting Louise's invitation to meet would lead to this. Were they back together then? Was that what she wanted? Louise. So familiar, so safe, shared history and memories, friends in common, the knowledge of each other's past and hopes for the future. Everything she thought she'd lost was seemingly back within her grasp and she had to decide whether she wanted to take it or to run. Perhaps staying last night hadn't been the best way to begin making that decision. She realised her mobile was ringing. Where the hell was it? It had been in her jacket pocket and she seemed to remember her clothes were on the floor at the side of the bed. She leant over to look, and sure enough could see the screen of the phone, clearly lit through the fabric of her shirt which was lying on top of it. She heaved herself on to the floor and grabbed it. DI Knight. Not good at this time in the morning.

'Hello? Jonathan?'

'Morning, Catherine. I'm afraid we've got another body with our friend's calling card. Where are you, can I pick you up?'

Bishop gave Louise's address, her head spinning. This changed everything.

'Okay, we won't lose much time if I call in for you. I think I can be there in about twenty minutes.'

He hung up. Bishop slowly got to her feet as Louise's face appeared over the side of the bed, bleary eyed.

'Let me guess,' she said. 'You've got to go?'

'Another body. I'll need some clean clothes, Louise, I'm sorry.'

Louise clambered out of bed, pulling on pyjama shorts and a vest.

'Have a quick shower, I'll sort you something out.' she said.

Bishop kissed her softly on the way out of the bedroom door, trying to ignore the churning of her stomach.

The atmosphere in Knight's car was noticeably tense. Although they'd both attended more crime scenes than they wanted to remember, this somehow felt different, more personal. They hadn't been given much detail, only that the body of an adult male had been discovered and that the same message that had been found with Craig Pollard's corpse had also been recognised at the scene. Bishop was quiet, her mind running through the possibilities of what this meant.

Until they arrived they couldn't begin to answer any of her questions, but that didn't stop her mind racing. She was wearing some of Louise's clothes, a black pinstripe trouser suit and a light grey shirt. It was strangely comforting to carry Louise's smell with her, a tiny piece of the old familiarity in a world that suddenly felt very strange. Louise had provided a new toothbrush, been very understanding and had even waved her off at the door. Perhaps she really was determined to turn over a new leaf. Bishop closed her eyes then opened them again, knowing she needed to concentrate, to focus on making sense of whatever was waiting for them. She glanced at the sat nav Knight was religiously following. It reckoned they would arrive at their destination in around four minutes. She gazed out of the window, not that there was anything to see but darkness. She could imagine the flat countryside and bare fields, the grass a washed out, paler version of its summer self. Three minutes. She couldn't mention the running figure from last night now, it would have to be later.

Knight coughed and cleared his throat. She wanted him to say something, anything, but he just kept driving, his fingers gripping the steering wheel tightly, his lips pressed tightly together. Two minutes. The sat nav's computerised voice suddenly boomed out making them both jump, instructing Knight to turn left at the next junction. Knight braked and slowed right down. It was a tiny break in the hedge, barely noticeable in this light. Out of the darkness loomed a figure in a high visibility coat. A uniformed constable stood rubbing his hands together by a line of cones and a 'POLICE ROAD CLOSED' sign. Knight stopped the car next to him and wound down the window, digging for his warrant card in his jacket pocket. The constable leaned in.

'Sorry, sir, this road's closed, as you can see. I'm going to have to ask you to turn around.'

'DI Knight and DS Bishop – here you go.' The constable took the warrant card from him and scrutinised it.

'Okay, thank you, sir. I'll move a few cones for you. Just up the road, they're sorting some lighting out.'

Knight nodded his thanks and wound the window back up.

'Freezing out there.' he muttered.

Bishop leant back in the seat, staring through the windscreen. Knight pulled onto the grass verge behind a battered burgundy Volvo estate.

'Doctor Webber's here then.' Bishop said tonelessly, pressing the seatbelt release button. Knight turned off the engine and they climbed out into the cold, damp morning.

'Doctor Webber?' Knight asked.

'You'll see.'

They made their way further down the lane, past scene of crime vans and hurrying people. Sure enough, the area was suddenly bathed in a yellow glow as several large spotlights sparked into life. Mick Caffery bustled up to them.

'Morning. You'll need to get suited up before you go any further. The body's over there where the blue van is.'

He pointed. There was an obvious concentration of activity in that area, white suited figures scurrying around, all sorts of equipment being ferried that way.

'Any early thoughts?' asked Knight.

Caffery sighed.

'Take the Pollard scene, add a van and a more scenic location and there you go.'

'Similarities then.'

'Practically the same, except this poor sod's lying on his front next to a van. It's registered to a local courier company. Back of his head's smashed in all right though. The doctor's having a look at him now. Photographs and filming just about finished I think.'

'And the same message as last time?'

'Oh yes, exactly the same. Under his foot, the top trapped so it didn't blow away.'

Bishop swallowed, nausea rising from her stomach. *Deep breaths,* she told herself firmly. A sudden urge to run came over her, the impulse to get as far away from this place and from this case as possible. She fought it, clenching her hands into fists. *Come on, Catherine, get a grip.* Knight turned and Bishop wondered for a second if she had spoken out loud.

'There are some suits in the car boot.' Knight told her. Bishop followed him back down the lane, still struggling with unfamiliar and unwelcome feelings. They pulled on the scene of crime suits silently, each lost in their own thoughts, then made their way back to where they'd left Caffery. He was talking to another white suited figure who turned as Knight and Bishop approached. It was all Knight could do not to gasp. Bishop had to hide a grin in spite of it all.

'Good morning, Doctor Webber.'

Jo Webber smiled back, her perfect features made even more attractive by the shadows cast on them.

'Hello, Catherine. I asked you last time we met to call me Jo.'

'Jo, then. This is DI Knight - Jonathan.'

Webber turned to Knight.

'Pleased to meet you. You'll want to know about our victim?'

'Please.' squeaked Knight. Bishop bit her lip but Jo Webber didn't seem to have noticed.

'Well, cause of death looks like being the trauma to the back of his head. Time of death – I'm not going to speculate now, but some time last night. He's not been out here that long – obvious really, as he would have been found before now, not that you need me to tell you that. I'll do the post mortem later this morning, I'll say eleven thirty.'

'Eleven thirty.' echoed Knight.

'That's right, Inspector. I presume you'll be attending?'

'I . . . yes, I'll be there.'

Webber smiled again and swept away. Knight rounded on Bishop.

'You could have told me she looks like a bloody supermodel!'

Grinning openly now, Bishop said 'I thought I'd let you have the pleasure of discovering that yourself. Rather her than Doc Beckett then?'

Knight didn't bother to reply and they hurried after Caffery, who was already striding his way towards the blue van. Knight didn't like laughing and joking at a crime scene. He knew why people did it; to try to protect themselves against the horrors they saw every working day, but he could never approve of it. Doctor Webber's appearance had stunned him, it was true, but she was forgotten now as he stared at the body in front of them. The wreckage of the man's head was stomach-turning and he felt Bishop tense beside him. The blue van's driver door was open, the victim lying on the road face down as Caffery had said. From his position, it seemed he had either just climbed out of the driver's seat or was doing so when he was attacked. They couldn't be sure of course, but it looked that way to Knight. They were lucky a passing vehicle hadn't run him over as he lay there. He said as much to Caffery, who agreed and explained that the man who had discovered the body had been travelling in the opposite direction.

'It's a quiet road and chances are it happened very late or in the early hours.' Caffery pointed out.

'Okay.' Knight pondered. 'So the victim's driving along, minding his own business, then suddenly decides to stop, presuming of course he was driving.' Caffery beckoned to them and they followed him to the back of the vehicle. SOCOs had been working on the road and there were several numbered yellow plastic markers. Caffery explained they identified skid marks made by the van.

'Don't quote me on this yet,' he said, 'but it looks to me as if he was travelling at speed and slammed his brakes on. We'll keep looking.'

Frowning, Bishop said, 'So maybe there was an obstruction in the road or a vehicle coming towards him?'

'Could be either of those, or both. Something that forced him to stop, at any rate. If it was a vehicle, and it didn't brake sharply, we probably won't have tracks. We've not found any yet anyway, though it's obviously early days.' They moved back around to the side of the vehicle where the body lay. Caffery left them and went to speak to a member of his team. Bishop glanced at the A4 paper under the victim's shoe then quickly averted her gaze to his face, or what little was visible. Knight stared down at him too.

'Seems strange that he was out here in the middle of nowhere. Even if he's a courier or delivery driver, you'd think he'd stick to the main roads wouldn't you, for quicker journeys? And why was he out so late?'

'It does seem odd, now you mention it. Although if he was using a sat nav, they can take you to some strange places if you're not careful.' Bishop glanced at Knight. 'Another body, sir, the same message.' She felt nausea rise into her throat again and wished she had some water to hand. Swallowing, she rubbed her hand across her mouth.

'Yes. We need to find out who he is as soon as we can.'

'Hopefully they'll be able to move him soon.'
They both span around as a loud metallic banging suddenly started, apparently coming from inside the blue van.

'What the . . .' exclaimed Knight, as Bishop gasped 'Shit!'
They ran around to the back of the van, almost colliding with Caffery and two of his SOCOs. Caffery stared, hands on hips. A padlock was threaded through a latch that had been drilled into the van doors.

'Someone locked in there . . . '

'Shall we open it?' asked one of the constables.
Everyone looked at each other. The noise grew louder and faint shouting could be heard too.

'Sounds like they're terrified.' Bishop observed. Knight stepped back.

'We'll have to open it.' he said. 'They could have been in there for hours.'
Caffery nodded.

'It's been dusted for prints, I think we've got everything we can from it out here. Pass me a suit, we'll need the clothes from whoever's in there. They could be the one who killed him for all we know.'

A uniformed constable stepped forward with a hammer and gave the padlock a few hefty blows. Protective suit in hand, Caffery stepped forward, reached for the handle and pulled. The doors flew open so suddenly that the young woman who was pounding on them from the inside almost fell on top of Caffery. He spoke softly, indicating she needed to change into the suit he handed to her. She looked bemused but obediently disappeared back inside. Caffery held the door closed until she emerged again, wearing the same outfit as the rest of them. Reaching into the van, Caffery brought out her clothes in evidence bags. She gazed at the surrounding group and seemed to single out Bishop.

'Please . . . water?' she said, her English heavily accented. She swayed on her feet and Bishop moved forward quickly, taking her arm.

'All right, you're okay.'

The uniformed constable was beckoned back over and he led the woman gently to a nearby squad car. She sat in the back, gratefully sipping from a bottle of orange juice. Knight ran a hand over his hair.

'That might explain why he was taking the scenic route.' he commented dryly.

'As good a reason as any,' agreed Bishop. 'As if things weren't complicated enough.'

They gave the woman in the squad car sideways glances.

'We need to interview her.'

'Yep. Sooner the better.'

They walked over to the squad car and the constable closed the back door as they approached.

'How is she?' Bishop offered a smile in the woman's direction.

'She doesn't speak much English, Sarge, so it's hard to say. She's not as pale as she was though.'

'So we're going to struggle to interview her?'

'I think you'd need an interpreter, sir.'

Knight took out his mobile. 'I'll get someone set up at the station to help us.'

16

In the video interview suite, Bishop and Varcoe sat opposite the woman and the interpreter, a man from the local university who seemed to speak every European language you could mention. They now knew her name was Milica Zukic. She was thin, her light brown hair lank, in need of a wash and a cut. She wore a navy sweatshirt and jogging bottoms that the desk sergeant had produced from somewhere. Doctor Whelan was plump, bespectacled, mid forties and very keen to help. Knight sat in the next room, in front of a monitor. He wanted Catherine and Anna to conduct the interview, but he also wanted to see what Milica Zukic had to say first hand. He had a briefing scheduled after the interview with the DCI and also the Super, who wanted to attend. Knight hadn't seen much of Superintendent Jane Stringer so far but he had known that she would be involved sooner or later, especially after this latest development. He focused on the monitor in front of him. Bishop smiled reassuringly at the young woman on the other side of the table. 'Please could you ask Milica to tell us where she's from, a little about her background and how she came to be in the UK?' she said to Whelan. He nodded eagerly.

Bishop closed the door of the interview room softly behind her, leaving Varcoe with Dr Whelan and Milica Zukic. Knight met her in the corridor.

'I feel like I need a shower.' she said, shaking her head. Knight nodded.

'I know what you mean. How about we put her in one of the cells for now? She could have killed him, of course, but I didn't see any blood on her or in the van and even if she changed her clothes afterwards we'll find them. She could have been in the passenger seat, lunged across and attacked him as he drove, forced him to stop then nipped out and smashed his head in when he got out, but I really don't see it. For a start, he looked quite a big bloke and she must be what? Eight stone?'

'About that I should think. Anyway, she couldn't have padlocked herself into the back of the van. Plus, we need to consider the link to the Craig Pollard murder and how could she have even met him, never mind killed him?'

'True. Since she was on the move, there must be a grubby shithole somewhere expecting her and as soon as the news breaks about the latest murder, which no doubt it will soon, they'll realise she must have been found. At least in a cell she'll be safe and can get some sleep. Can you get onto Intelligence, find out if any of the names she's mentioned ring any bells? We'd better ask about her papers too, see if she is actually allowed to be in the country. When we've got a name and address confirmed for our victim, we'll get a photo over to Pollard's parents and brother again,. Maybe they'll recognise him.'

Bishop hesitated then said,

'Sir – Jonathan - do you think I'll be taken off the case?'

'Why?'

'Two victims, both found with messages that refer to me. I thought I might be, I'm just thinking about how it might look to the public or to a jury?'

'Do you want to be taken off it?'

'No, not at all. If anything, this second murder makes me all the more determined to find out what the hell's going on.'

Knight grinned.

'Just what I expected you to say. I can promise you, Sergeant, I'll do what I can to make sure you stay where you are.'

Bishop let out a breath, grateful for Knight's understanding but also for the fact that he hadn't seemed to notice her discomfort at the crime scene earlier.

'Thank you.'

'I need to get to the Super's office now, but let's catch up later.'

Knight strode away and Bishop headed over to the custody sergeant to arrange to check their guest in.

17

Knight paused outside the Superintendent's door, hearing Kendrick's rumbling tones inside the office. He knocked and Kendrick himself yanked the door open. The room was light and airy, the walls painted an uninspiring magnolia, the carpet tiles a slightly newer looking version of the stained and tired looking ones that covered the floor of the CID office. A few plants dotted the room and there were the usual chipped bookcases and battered filing cabinets. A low coffee table and a couple of armchairs stood in one corner. Stringer had attempted some personal touches such as a brightly coloured rug on the floor and a few cheerful, modern prints on the walls. The Superintendent herself was a tall, slender woman with immaculately styled straight blonde hair and perfect, understated make up. She could easily play the role of the headteacher of an exclusive public school, or a lady of the manor.

Jane Stringer stood as Knight entered the room, offering a pinched smile. She wore a tailored black skirt with a matching jacket and a pristine white blouse. Her appearance and whole demeanour conveyed a clear message to Knight – "I am in charge here. Get me results".

'Jonathan. Do sit down.' She gestured at the chair next to the one in which Kendrick had resettled himself. Stringer smoothed nonexistent creases from her skirt, straightened a silver photograph frame that she judged to be slightly askew on her desktop and sat.

'Thank you, Ma'am.' Knight sat up as straight as he could. Like Kendrick, Jane Stringer had that effect.

'Now.' Stringer clasped long, elegant fingers in front of her, 'How have we got on with our unexpected witness?'

'I'm not sure she witnessed much at all Ma'am, I'm afraid.' Knight said. 'The basic facts: she's twenty two and from Serbia. Her uncle Dimitar is well known and important there. It was he who suggested perhaps his niece would care to try her luck earning some money in the UK. He told her she could make a fortune.'

Stringer shook her head and Kendrick gave a snort.

'I wonder how she was going to do that?' he remarked.

'Well, she said her journey to Britain alerted her to the fact that the future might not be as bright as her uncle had painted it. She mostly stowed in the back of vans or the cabs of lorries and she still isn't sure how she had actually arrived in the country. One of the trucks she had been on must have crossed the sea by ferry. She's sure she didn't fly in, but . . . '

'Surely she would have known.' Stringer commented. Knight nodded agreement, then resumed his story.

'The last lorry, the one she must have crossed the sea in, took her to some sort of garage with a small apartment attached. A young man had met her, gave her food and said she could have a shower. After a few hours rest on the bed, during which time she dozed but didn't sleep, she heard raised voices arguing. She heard her uncle's name several times but didn't understand enough English to follow the rest. After a while, she heard footsteps on the stairs. A second man came in; he looked like a wolf, she said. "Vuk" is a Serbian word for wolf and in her mind, that was what she called him. She heard other people call him Ron afterwards.'

Stringer opened a desk drawer, removing a smart looking notepad and an elegant fountain pen. She wrote few lines then glanced at Knight.

'Go on, please.'

'He told her he told her this was usually when he would "try out" the new arrivals himself before sending them on, but as she was the "precious" niece of Dimitar Raskovic, he would control himself.'

'Very good of him.' Kendrick put in scornfully.

Knight sat back, organising his thoughts. The Super wouldn't want all the details, not everything Zukic had told them, but he felt it was essential that as much of her story was heard as possible. They had all heard very similar versions before of course, but Zukic had given them names, she was observant and intelligent and Knight felt they had a good chance of catching up with the traffickers using her information. He began to talk again, almost watching the events unfold in his mind as he spoke, much like Zukic must have, though his were imagined images not painful memories as hers were.

'This "Vuk" grabbed her and bundled her into the back of a van. She thought they drove for over an hour, closer to two, when eventually they stopped. He came to the back doors of the van, stuck his head in and told her that she needed to get out and walk with him into a house without drawing attention to herself. If she did anything stupid, he warned, even her uncle wouldn't be able to save her.'

'Did she notice anything at all that could help us?' Stringer wanted to know.

'It was a terraced street from her description, a row of very similar houses. She could hear traffic noise and sirens, the sound of children playing nearby.'

'Town then, not out in the countryside somewhere.' Kendrick observed.

'Inside the house was a woman. Huge, Milica said.'

'Obese?' asked Stringer.

'Yes, apparently so. They hustled Milica down the hallway, which she described as dark with a dirty red carpet, and into the kitchen. The whole house stank of perfume and cigarette smoke, she said, but the kitchen was the worst. It was filthy, she could describe it all in detail. The Vuk had gone and she lost it a bit, demanded to know where she was and what was going on. This woman slapped her face and yelled at her then a huge bloke came in, picked Milica up and carried her upstairs and into a bedroom. They locked the door and left her there to calm down. Eventually, the woman came back and asked Milica if she was going to behave herself. She said she would. The woman introduced herself as Ivona and said Milica was going to live in the house, work there doing the cleaning and also go out to factories or wherever she was needed.'

'So she just cleaned? It wasn't a brothel?' Stringer asked, pen poised.

'Oh yes, it was a brothel,' Knight said, grim faced. 'She talked about cleaning the bedrooms around the sleeping girls, said some were even younger than her seventeen year old sister at home in Serbia. There were rooms with hearts on the doors that she was only allowed into when she was told to clean them. The 'heavy' work went on in there, Ivona told her, but she was excused as she was Dimitar Raskovic's niece – there were other girls for that, Ivona said. Milica was just the cleaner.'

'Bad enough.' Kendrick said, stretching his legs and cracking his knuckles. Stringer frowned distaste at him.

'And what about our victim, Jonathan? How did she come to be in the back of his van?'

'She couldn't tell us a lot. Yesterday, Ivona came in in a hurry and told Milica to pack up her stuff quickly, that they were moving out. The Vuk came and took Milica to some kind of building, smelt like a garage, she said. He locked her in, told her to wait quietly and that she'd be collected. Our victim arrived some time later and helped Milica into the back of his van. They'd been driving along at what seemed to be a normal speed when they stopped very suddenly – she'd been dozing, she thought, but she slid along the floor of the van and hit the partition. She could hear the driver shouting, then he slammed the door and she heard nothing from him after that. She couldn't say how long she had sat there, hours she thought, but they didn't move off again. She couldn't see anything, being in the back and she couldn't get out. She must have been freezing.'

Stringer gave a curt nod.

'So she was able to give us some names, although who knows how much help they'll be. Who's following up on this, DS Bishop?'

'Yes, she's liaising with Intelligence to see what she can find out.' Knight said firmly. Kendrick glanced at him.

'It would be very positive if we could close down a gang of people traffickers as well as catch whoever killed Pollard and this new victim, Inspector.' Stringer said pointedly.

'Yes, Ma'am, it would,' Knight agreed. 'I'm sorry, but I'll have to leave now if I'm to make it to the PM on time.' he said, half getting to his feet.

'Fine.' said Stringer, already turning back to her computer. 'Keep me informed, Jonathan.'

'Yes, Ma'am.' Knight said, fighting the urge to salute her.

18

Knight had attended several post mortems in his career, but this would be his first since his transfer to Lincolnshire. He'd struggled to find a parking place and was dangerously close to being late. In his experience, being late for a post mortem was usually seen as incredibly rude by the person performing the procedure. From his brief meeting with Jo Webber earlier that morning, he doubted she would see it any differently. A minute before eleven thirty, according to his watch. Knight hurried through the door and glanced around. The room was as expected, spotless white tiles, temperature cool if not cold, white clothed figures moving purposefully. Disinfectant and formaldehyde hung in the air, bleach too. Other smells would follow, Knight knew. As with crime scenes, it wasn't always so much what you saw at a post mortem, it was the smells and the sounds. You could, in theory, avert your eyes from the horror but the smell couldn't be avoided. It was everywhere, seeming to creep inside your nose and your body, out through your own pores to mingle again with the stench of the room or the scene. Sounds were the same. The noise a saw made as it cut through human bone was not one Knight thought he would ever forget if he walked out of the room now, left the force and never attended another post mortem. You would always remember certain details, and Knight supposed that was the way it should be.

A technician bustled forward bearing a scene of crimes suit for Knight. He thanked the figure, unable to determine who he was speaking to because of the hood and mask that they already wore. He stepped into the suit, pulled it up over his clothes and was struggling with the zip when another figure approached. This one had yet to don her mask and hood, and Knight once again felt his stomach lurch at the sight of Dr Jo Webber.

'Inspector Knight, you're here. Good, we're ready to start.'
She indicated the stainless steel table that stood in the middle of the room, brightly lit by overhead spotlights. The body lay waiting. He'd taken a quick phone call from DS Bishop just as he'd arrived at the mortuary and now knew their victim's name was Steven Kent, aged twenty seven. Steve was the name Mike Pollard had mentioned, but the victim wasn't the man from their CCTV footage. Back to square one with that. Officers were on their way to Kent's home to begin their search, and though Bishop had said they were struggling to find a next of kin, they would need to be identified and informed quickly. Kent's parents had apparently died together in a car accident a few years earlier. Kent hadn't been married, but there was probably a girlfriend or partner. Officers would be en route to his workplace too as his colleagues would surely know about his family and domestic situation.

With hood, face mask and gloves now in place, Knight followed Webber over to the table, and Steven Kent's body. He gazed down at the dead man, naked under the glare of the spotlights. Knight stepped back, as far from the table as possible. Webber glanced at him then began to speak, relaying the details she'd just been given about Kent's identity to the others in the room and for the benefit of the recording equipment. She also described Kent physically: his eye colour, hair colour, ethnicity and so on. Webber also noted a scar on Kent's abdomen which seemed to indicate he'd had an appendectomy. At this point, Knight's feeling of dread became more apparent. He knew Webber would soon make the Y-incision and the internal examination would be underway. He bit down on the inside of his lips behind his mask. Knight had never pretended autopsies didn't affect him and distrusted any officer who claimed to be immune from the affect they had. Seeing a fellow human being cut and opened up like meat in a butcher's shop just seemed wrong, especially with a victim of murder such as this man. It was often the final indignity of a body that had been attacked and broken, a life cut short because of anger, calculation or senselessness. There were other reasons, of course. It was a procedure that needed to be completed however, to help Knight and his colleagues catch the person that had killed Steve Kent and possibly Craig Pollard. Knight steeled himself as Dr Webber crossed the floor to the body again.

Knight stepped out into the corridor, glad it was over. He stood for a few seconds, breathing in the fresher air. The door behind him opened and Dr Webber appeared.

'If you'd like a quick chat Inspector, you could go up to my office - upstairs and second on the left.'

'Thank you.'

She looked at him.

'Are you okay?'

'Fine thanks, just . . . '

'Catching your breath?'

'Something like that.'

Her smile was understanding.

'I'll see you in my office.'

She disappeared again and Knight trudged off in the direction she'd indicated. The stairs were scuffed tiles and his footsteps echoed around him. He reached a small square landing, the walls painted a sickly green. A battered wooden door held a name plate bearing Webber's name, black lettering on a silver background. Knight paused outside, not sure whether to go in. It seemed a little presumptuous so he stood outside, feeling like a naughty schoolboy waiting for the headteacher. He soon heard footsteps and the doctor appeared, now wearing black trousers and a tailored red shirt, suit jacket in one hand, paperwork in the other. No wedding ring Knight noticed, though that meant nothing considering the procedure she'd just performed. She smiled as she saw him standing there.

'You should have gone in.' she said, pushing through the door and holding it open for him.

'I didn't like to. Anyway, the door might have been locked.'

'It might,' she agreed, 'but it wasn't. My secretary's next door, so I don't bother too much when she's there, I just lock my papers away and take my laptop with me.'

The room was fairly small, pale blue walls in here, navy carpet tiles. There were several filing cabinets, a scuffed wooden desk and a couple of threadbare chairs. Dr Webber seated herself behind her desk. Knight couldn't help noticing her own chair was a well padded leather number, looking much newer and more comfortable than the one he gingerly sat in. She noticed his expression and laughed.

'I bought this one myself. Not that I spend that much time in here, but I like to take care of my back, it soon complains if I don't, it likes some luxury. Now,' she glanced at the notes she'd brought with her, 'Steven Kent.'
Knight nodded, and she leaned back in her chair.

'Obviously I'll be providing a full report as soon as I can, but a few things you'll want to know now. We found no other injuries except those on the back of the skull; no more inflicted by his attacker and no defence wounds. He received three blows to the back of his head with a blunt instrument. A wooden club or bat is my best guess, though there are no splinters or anything to substantiate that. I don't think you should expect much help from the traces we removed from his body, I'm afraid. No alcohol in his system. What else? Blood group A+. Time of death: between eleven last night and three this morning. Of course, it was a cold night, he was lying outside . . . it's difficult to be exact. He died where he fell, the body wasn't moved. All in all, a very healthy young man, except . . . '

'Except his head has been bashed in.'

'Exactly.'

There was silence for a few seconds. Knight glanced at a framed photograph on the wall just above Jo Webber's head.

'Is that your dog?' he asked, just for something to say. Webber followed his gaze.

'Yes, Jess. She's only nine months old, still a puppy really but she's got so big. Anyway,' she stood up, 'I'm sorry but I have a meeting in ten minutes and I need to get across to the other building. I'll get my full report over to you as soon as I can, later today I should think.'

Knight also got to his feet.

'Thank you, Doctor.' he said. 'She's a lovely dog, by the way. We always had boxers when I was growing up. I'd love one, but it wouldn't be fair in my job.'

'Call me Jo. That's what I thought, but my neighbour has her during the day, they keep each other company.'

Knight paused outside the door.

'Thanks again, Jo. No doubt we'll speak again soon.'

She smiled.

'No doubt.'

19

Bishop sat at her desk with her phone wedged under her chin, arms stretched high above her head, hands clasped together as if in prayer. She'd been on hold for what seemed like forever and she'd had about enough. DC Sullivan hovered in front of her desk with mug of tea.

'Just put it down anywhere, it's fine. Thanks, Simon. Honestly, this is a bloody joke, he's only in Lincoln. I could have walked there faster, fifteen minutes I've been waiting for this arse . . . .Hello? DI Foster?' She pulled a face at Sullivan who was laughing as he went back to his own desk. 'That's right, sir, a woman called Ivona. A terraced house, several women apparently being brought in from Serbia, possibly other countries, then forced to work as prostitutes . . . Just anything you have. We think they may have been tipped off that they'd been rumbled. The woman we have here was shipped out of the house all of a sudden, which suggests something was up. She's linked to a couple of . . . sorry, just hang on, that's my boss.'

Her mobile had started to ring. Knight. She answered the call. 'Hello, sir?'

'I'm on my way back to the station, can we get together when I get in? Are you there now?'

'Yes, sorry, just hold on,' She picked up the receiver of her desk phone again. 'Sorry, DI Foster, I'm going to have to go, but if you could let me know about anything you have . . . Oh, of course. I'll go and have a word with her.' She quickly gabbled her phone number and email address, then snatched up her mobile again, 'Sorry sir, yes, I'm at the station.'

'About fifteen minutes then?'

'Fine, see you in the conference room.'

An incident room was being set up, the whiteboards headed with a photograph of Craig Pollard and a space where Steve Kent's face would appear when they had the picture. Autopsy photos, a timeline of Pollard's last day, everything they had so far, which in truth didn't amount to a great deal, had been summarised by the incident room manager, DS Robin Cuthbert. He was known throughout the station as 'Monk' on account of his bald pate surrounded by thick black hair, serene expression and rotund figure. He was standing next to the whiteboards, pen in hand, frowning in concentration as he studied some paperwork propped on the desk beside him. Bishop marched in through the door unnoticed by Cuthbert, strode up to him and clapped her hand down onto his shoulder. Cuthbert jumped towards the ceiling with a squeal.

'Afternoon, Brother Cuthbert, how's it going?'

Cuthbert held a hand to his chest.

'Bloody hell, Catherine, you'll kill me one of these days.'

'Rubbish, you're as strong as an ox. Just to let you know, DI Knight's on his way back from the Kent PM so no doubt he'll be in here some time soon. I'm meeting with him first, but he'll want to see where we are with this lot too.'

'Inspector Wallpaper? I can hardly wait.'

'Now now, Monk, let's give him a chance, shall we? He's actually starting to grow on me.'

Cuthbert snorted.

'Like a boil you mean? A big, juicy boil, growing on your . . .'

Cuthbert stopped as the door flung open again and DCI Kendrick crossed the room in four strides.

'DS Cuthbert, where are we up to?' he boomed.

Cuthbert wrung his hands.

'Well, as I was telling DS Bishop here . . . ' Both men turned around, but Bishop had vanished.

Scurrying down the corridor, Bishop couldn't help smiling to herself. It helped to keep your eyes and ears ever alert for Kendrick, who had a nasty habit of appearing without warning. It wasn't as if he was easy to miss; Cuthbert had only himself to blame. No doubt she'd be seeing him soon enough, he'd probably want to be in the meeting with Knight when he heard about it. She turned into the conference room and switched on the lights. One of the bulbs was obviously faulty and kept flashing on and off.

'Great.' muttered Bishop to herself. She collected three cups of water, prepared in case DCI Kendrick did decide to join them. The room smelt stale, even worse than usual, provoking more mumbling from Bishop. Her mobile beeped as it received a text message and she smiled as she read: Enjoyed last night. Same again tonight? Doesn't matter what time. L x

Louise certainly seemed to want to try again and she felt a small stab of guilt. She definitely needed to do some thinking about whether she wanted to jump straight back into a relationship, albeit a more casual one. Now was definitely not the time to do it though. She set her notebook on the table and took a sip of water. She hadn't drunk the tea Sullivan had made for her and it would be cold by now, even if she had time to nip back to her desk before Knight arrived. Right on cue, the door opened and he wandered in looking as if he had all the time in the world, absent-mindedly brushing rain from his hair.

'Pouring down out there,' he said, pulling out a chair and settling in it. 'How's it going?'

Bishop opened her notepad.

'Steve Kent's flat is still being searched, but it's turned up an interesting find already. A mobile phone with no numbers stored in the memory and that has only ever received calls from one number.'

'Instructions about his dodgy deliveries?'

'Could well be. We're trying to track down the number but I suspect it'll be difficult, if not impossible. It seems Kent was single. According to his neighbour he had a girl living with him for a short while but she moved out over a year ago. The neighbour never knew her name and neither did the blokes he worked with. Kent kept very much to himself. We did find out from them that he has a sister living in Leeds so we've been onto West Yorkshire and they're going to track her down and break the news. It's almost certain he would have had another mobile phone, a personal one, but there's no sign of it so far. It's looking like whoever killed Kent took the phone as we're presuming happened with Pollard. We haven't found it in the area around the crime scene, or anything else. The van's gone off to forensics but we're not expecting much. Seems like the invisible killer's struck again.'

'A person who knows about forensics, about the traces that can be left. Most people have a vague idea about that sort of thing these days though. The victim was attacked when he was vulnerable, as Pollard was. It seems Kent had his back to his killer, climbing out of the van.'

'I suppose that makes it easier for our murderer - hit them when they don't even know you're there. Kent was quite a big bloke, as was Pollard.'

'Around six foot, yes. Doctor Webber mentioned that Kent had only been hit three times, according to what she found during the post mortem, whereas Pollard . . . '

'He'd been hit loads of times.'

Knight nodded grimly.

'Maybe Pollard had pissed our friend off more than Kent had.'

A deep sigh from Bishop.

'Or he's getting better with practice and knew just where to hit this time.'
There was a pause, then Knight sat up straight.

'We need to establish what links Craig Pollard with Steve Kent. I'd like to think we'd have stumbled across that fact without our helpful murderer leaving us another calling card. Has a photo of Kent gone to Pollard's parents and his brother?'

'Yep, the one that's on his driving licence. It's a few years old but I wanted them to see him as soon as possible. Hopefully we'll come across a more up to date one in his flat somewhere.'

'Have you got a copy?'
Bishop rummaged through her papers and handed one over. Knight considered it.

'He doesn't seem to have changed much to be honest, not that he was looking his best when I saw him.'

'What else could Jo Webber tell you after the PM?'
Knight explained what the pathologist had said, then added,

'We keep coming back to the question of why Kent stopped the van. Milica Zukic said they stopped very suddenly, then she heard him shouting. There could have been a vehicle blocking the road, pretending to have broken down?'

'If that's what happened though, why didn't he wait until Kent was bending over the engine and then smack him one? Although I suppose he'd have ended up with bits of brain and skull all over the engine, and if he is forensically aware . . .' Bishop's voice trailed away.

'He wouldn't want to take the chance when he's been so careful, plus there would be no guarantee Kent would stop, especially when he had his passenger locked in the back of the van - not that our murderer would have known that. We still need a name for our anonymous caller, especially if Mike Pollard recognises Steven Kent as the Steve that was Craig's mate. Maybe he was right when he said Nick? We're waiting on the analysis of Milica Zukic's clothes, but

I don't think we'll find any blood or anything to suggest she killed Steve Kent, even if it would have meant she could escape. Where would she go? She doesn't speak enough English to be able to blend in and she knew Ivona, this man she calls the "Vuk" and friends would come looking for her.'

'It seems a bit strange she hasn't picked up more English though, if she's been here a few years?'

'She said she wasn't allowed to talk to anyone though, didn't she, although she must have said a few words to people she worked with at some point. They might have been Serbian too, I suppose, taken in by the same people who brought Zukic here. Did you speak to Intelligence?'
Bishop nodded, screwing up her face.

'Just now. I spoke to a DI, Foster's his name. He's going to call me back. I wasn't able to give him much to go on, just the names Ivona and Ron. There's a member of his team working over here on another assignment, he said to go and speak to her but I've not had a chance yet. We could try to narrow down the area Zukic might have been held in, but . . . '

'But it would be mainly guesswork given how little she can tell us. They've been clever, threatening her, keeping her separate from the other girls, transporting her in vans so she couldn't see road signs or landmarks.'

'Bastards.' said Bishop, with feeling. Knight nodded agreement.

'If they've moved Zukic, surely they will be moving the other girls too? Did Foster mention any raids that might be a reason for the sudden panic? Maybe Ron and Ivona were tipped off.'

'I asked him and he's going to do some digging.'

'Do we have any locals whose card you'd mark for this sort of thing?'

'People trafficking? Most wouldn't be seen dead getting involved, code of honour and all that. Anything organised around here usually has one man behind it though, and I do mean well behind it, he usually keeps his head down these days. Dougie Hughes.'

Knight blinked a few times.

'Hughes?'

'Yeah, you know the type – local boy, dragged up on the worst of the back streets, place so rough even the dog shit wears knuckledusters. He has bigger ideas, starts by grafting on building sites, saves enough to buy a van, drug dealing all the while, sets up a legit firm of builders. Still dealing, takes on a few blokes, branches out into plumbing, buys some warehouse space, takes on a few more blokes, doesn't deal himself now he has minions to do it for him. Throws himself into the legitimate stuff, sets up a taxi firm, a club, a betting shop. Hairdressing salon for his Mrs to work in, beauty parlour, money flooding in, builds the big shopping centre in town . . . The man's a walking stereotype. I wouldn't be surprised if he's got his sticky fingers in this somewhere, he probably owns the courier firm Kent worked for if we can dig deep enough. He might have a bit less cash floating around these days, economic situation and all that, maybe he's moved into dealing people as well.'

Knight said softly, only just audibly, 'Sounds like a Hughes I know.'

'Sorry, boss?'

'It's okay, carry on, just thinking out loud.'

'He has property that could be used; the warehouse space Zukic mentioned, the club, the betting shop - they could all be used to find punters for the poor buggers that are brought into the country, or for cheap labour to work in with not many questions asked.'

Knight was chewing his thumbnail again.

'Plenty of opportunity, yes. Can you see him doing it?'

'Oh, yeah. He's the type, but he knows how to keep his nose clean. We've not been able to send him down for anything yet, he's bloody clever. Of course the more money he's got, the better the people are that surround him, protect him and advise him. They'll know all the tricks and loopholes.'

'It's all supposition though. Do we have anyone closer to him?'

'You mean an informant?'

Almost imperceptibly, Knight nodded. Bishop shook her head regretfully.

'No, sir, not that I know of.'

'We could get Milica Zukic to have a look at him, she might have seen him at some point? I know it's unlikely, but it'll only take a few minutes. Otherwise . . . .'

'I'll sort that and get some mugshots of a few of the well known local pervs and kerb crawlers as well, see if Milica can recognise any of them. It might give us a handle on the location of the house she was held in at any rate.'

'Fine. We should have the full post mortem report later and we're waiting on Mr and Mrs Pollard and Mike to see if they know what could link Craig Pollard to Steve Kent, if anything. DC Varcoe's going to try that teacher at Pollard's old school again today, see if she can give us any more names and she may as well show her the picture of Kent too. Hopefully West Yorkshire will get some info from Kent's sister?'

'You never know. I gave them Pollard's name, she might remember him.'

'We're bound to have some journalists sniffing round before the day's much older, so there'll probably be a press conference. We'll keep the messages out of it, or try to of course. I don't think Milica Zukic's name should be mentioned either if we can help it.'

'We're definitely not considering her as a suspect?'

'Obviously we can't rule her out completely, but as we've said I don't think so. There's no way she could have killed Pollard either, if her story is true.'

'Do you think it might be to our advantage if we let the press know there was a possible witness in the back of the van that Kent was driving though? Not mention a name as you say, but . . .' asked Bishop.

'Try to rattle our man, you mean?'

'Just a thought.'

'It's a good idea. No doubt DCI Kendrick will want a chat soon anyway. I should think he'll want to handle the press conference, probably the Super too.' Bishop rolled her eyes a little at the mention of Jane Stringer and Knight pretended he hadn't noticed.

'A double murder . . . we don't have many of those around here, the press will be panting for some information. Might even make the national news. Good job the DCI has his suit handy.'

'With all the buttons attached.'

20

Keith Kendrick was still making his presence felt in the incident room as Knight opened the door. Kendrick spotted him immediately and beckoned to him. Knight managed a reluctant half smile and joined Kendrick and Cuthbert in the middle of the room.

'DI Knight, just the man. How are we doing?'

Knight told him.

'Superintendent Stringer and I will be holding a press conference at four this afternoon. The Super will want to talk to again you before then though. I'm presuming we expect to have some results from speaking to the Pollards and the rest?'

'Yes, I would hope so. What about Milica Zukic?'

Kendrick raised his eyebrows.

'What about her? I see the need to keep her safe . . . it would be a feather in our cap to shut down a gang of people traffickers, pimps and forced prostitutes as well as solve the Pollard and Kent murders. Wouldn't be a bad way to introduce yourself to Lincolnshire, Jonathan.' Knight made a neutral sound that Kendrick chose to interpret as acquiescence. 'We've had hundreds of journalists wanting to know what's going on, but they'll have to wait. Let's hope we have something concrete for them by four so we don't have to go with a begging bowl asking them to help us out.'

Knight, who had raised his eyebrows at Kendrick's "hundreds" of journalists, made the neutral noise again and tried to move away without appearing to do so. Kendrick noticed.

'I'll set up a meeting with the Super at three o'clock, her office again. I'll see you there.'

To the relief of Knight, Cuthbert and everyone else in the room, Kendrick marched out, slamming the door behind him.

'Thank God for that.' said Cuthbert. 'Now, what was I doing before I was interrupted?'

Knight finally had the opportunity to wander around the room absorbing everything. He'd seen little of DS Cuthbert before but Bishop had said he was a conscientious officer and the usual choice for the key role of running an incident room. Knight paused to read the notes on the whiteboards, Cuthbert watching his progress without appearing to do so. Knight, seemingly satisfied, went out of the room. Cuthbert, astounded, turned to one of the uniformed officers.

'Did you see that? He comes in, struts around then saunters off and doesn't even bother to speak to me. I've worked my arse off this morning to get this lot set up, and he just . . . '

The PC tuned him out and concentrated on the screen in front of her. This had the makings of a long day.

Bishop peered around the open door. The room beyond was small but filled with so much clutter and boxes of files that at first she couldn't see whether anyone was in there or not.

'Hello?' she called.

There was a rustling sound and a figure emerged from behind a bookcase. It was the woman from the briefing room.

'Hello, are you looking for me?'

Bishop cleared her throat.

'Claire Weyton? I spoke to DI Foster earlier, he said you might be able to help me. I'm Catherine Bishop, I think we met in the briefing room? I stood on you . . .'

'Good to meet you again.' Claire Weyton grinned. She was a little taller than Bishop, not that it took much, with glossy dark hair and high cheekbones, her eyes that vivid blue. Bishop couldn't quite believe she hadn't noticed her around the station, but then if she had been working in this dungeon for the past few months it was no real surprise. No one came down here unless they absolutely had to; it was like the land that time forgot. Claire Weyton held out a hand and Bishop shook it. Claire's grip was firm, her hand warm. Bishop blinked a little.

'How can I help?' Claire asked.

Pulling herself together, Bishop said:

'I need any information you can find about a raid that may have been planned on a property that was being used as a brothel where trafficked women were being held.'

'And this place is in Northolme? Nothing springs to mind, but I can check for you.'

Bishop waved a hand helplessly.

'The problem is, we don't know exactly where. It probably isn't in Northolme, we think it could be somewhere else in the county. I have a few names that might help narrow the search down a little?'

'Right. Well, I have my laptop set up over there, there's just room for a desk believe it or not. Shall we have a look?'

'Yes please, if you have time to do it now.'

They made their way through the mess, squeezing around the bookcase.

'There's only one chair, I'm afraid.' Claire said, turning to look at Bishop.

'Oh, it's fine, you need to sit to use the computer.' Bishop replied hastily.

'Thank you. Let me just close all of this down.' Claire said, her hands moving fluidly over the keyboard as she settled in the grubby looking desk chair. 'Okay. You said you had some names?'

'Yes, but if I'm honest what I have is a little bit thin. I only have the name of one of the women who was working there, plus two of the people that were holding them: Milica Zukic, Ivona and Ron.'
Claire Weyton paused, gazing up at Bishop.

'And that's all?' she asked gently. Bishop nodded.

'That's all.' she confirmed miserably. 'Sorry.'

'Well, I like a challenge. I'll write the names down then have a hunt around, see what I can come up with?'

'Sounds good to me. Anything you can find that might help would be a bonus.' Bishop stepped back, bumping into the bookcase behind her.

'I'll see you later then, DS Bishop.'

'You will – and call me Catherine.'
Claire Weyton smiled, already turning back to her computer. Bishop hesitated for a second, then made her way carefully out of the room.

Bishop peered through the hatch in the door of the cell she'd led Milica Zukic to earlier, feeling a little uncomfortable about doing so. Zukic hadn't been arrested and there was no real suspicion that she done anything wrong other than believe the words of a relative she should have been able to trust. Zukic lay on the blue plastic-covered mattress on her side, face to the wall, head pillowed on her arm. The custody sergeant opened the cell door and Bishop entered, closely followed by the interpreter, Doctor Whelan, who had volunteered to spend the rest of the day working on his laptop in the station canteen in case his services were required again. From the jam on his jacket, it also looked to Bishop as if he'd found the time to sample a couple of doughnuts whilst he was there; she'd fallen foul of their explosions herself more than once. Zukic sat up, startled, then turned and smiled warily at them. She looked exhausted, thin and very young. Bishop held up the sheaf of photocopies she carried and said to Whelan:

'Please can you tell Milica I need her to look at these photographs and tell me if she recognises anyone? I might have more photos later for her to look at too.' Whelan nodded eagerly and approached Zukic, smiling and waving his hands as he spoke. Zukic listened, head tilted to the left and then replied. Whelan turned back to Bishop.

'She said that's fine, she just wants to help. She wants to know what will happen to her.'

Bishop tried to add reassurance to the smile she offered Zukic.

'I honestly don't know yet, I'm afraid.'

Whelan spoke again to Zukic, who smiled thinly back at Bishop and stood up.

'Do you want her to look at the pictures here, or . . . ?'

'I think we need a little more room.' said Bishop, glancing around the tiny cell. They always gave her the creeps. She led Whelan and Zukic back through to the main station and then to a small room that was usually a place for visiting solicitors to wait. Zukic dropped into a chair and looked expectantly at Bishop, who took the seat opposite. She held up the first mugshot:that of a balding man who glared fiercely at the camera. Zukic shook her head. This went on for some time. Bishop had only four photos left when the one she held up to Zukic caused the young woman to stare, face paling. She leant towards Bishop, holding out her hand to take the paper. Bishop gave it to her and she gazed at it, visibly distressed. When Milica Zukic eventually spoke, her voice low and panicked. Bishop didn't need Whelan to translate the word "Vuk". Elated, she checked her notes. The man was Ronald Woffenden, aged fifty one. He lived about twenty miles from Northolme. This seemed far too good to be true. She asked Whelan to check that Zukic was sure, that this was definitely the man she called the

Vuk, the same man she had met on her first full day in Britain and who had transported her to the house she had been forced to stay in. Zukic was emphatic, vehement almost – this was the man. Bishop leapt out of her chair and stuck her head out into the corridor, grabbing the nearest person and asking him to track down DI Knight. She quickly showed her remaining photos to Zukic but the result was only more apologetic headshakes. Bishop didn't mind; she had her golden egg. Knight appeared, expression confused.

'What's going on?'

'Milica has just confirmed that this,' she waved the picture in Knight's face, 'is the man she told us about, the Vuk.'

Knight grabbed the photo and studied it.

'She's sure?'

'Positive sir, she's certain.'

They both span around as footsteps hurried down the corridor towards them. It was Claire Weyton, a sheet of paper in her hand, her expression eager.

'Sergeant Bishop? I'm sorry to interrupt, but I think I've found something. The man you mentioned? There's a Ron Woffenden who we suspect of being involved in that kind of activity – we've not been able to really get anything on him as yet, but . . . ' She glanced from Bishop to Knight and paused as realisation dawned. 'Oh. You already know, don't you?'

'Only just.' Bishop reassured her. 'Milica Zukic recognised him from a mugshot. I was going to come straight down to let you know.'

'Do you want me to keep looking?' Weyton asked them.

'Yes please, for now.' Knight said. 'Catherine will let you know if we get any useful information from Woffenden – it might take a while to find him.'

'Okay – I'll grab a cup of coffee and get back to it.'

'Thank you.' Knight called after her. He turned back to Bishop and said: 'Let's bring him in.'

21

DC Varcoe approached Bishop, who was pacing the incident room floor, waiting for the message to say that Ronald Woffenden had arrived in the interview room. Bishop didn't see her and almost knocked her over as she turned at speed.

'Sorry, Anna, bit distracted. What have you got?' In her excitement, she'd forgotten where Varcoe had been.

'Steve Kent didn't go to school with Craig Pollard. I spoke to the school, checked the records and it was pretty clear that wasn't our link, so I went to the Pollard's house again. The reception was a bit less frosty this time and I was even offered a cup of tea. I persuaded Mrs Pollard to get a few old photos out, Craig in the football team, Craig in the pub pool team before he was old enough to drink, all that sort of thing but no luck. However,' she looked pleased with herself, 'Mr Pollard gave me the name of the bloke who used to run the youth club Craig went to for a while – before he got chucked out, anyway. I found him. He's retired now and guess what? He remembers Craig Pollard and Steve Kent being mates. Seems they met at the club, Kent lived out of town. He gave me a few more names too, so I'm going to run them through the computer now and see what falls out.'

'Good work, Anna. Let me know how it goes please. Sounds like you've got the Pollards wrapped around your little finger now then?'

Varcoe smiled over her shoulder as she made for the door.

'Not sure about that but they've definitely calmed down a bit.'

Bishop heard a mobile ringing and in the hubbub of the incident room it was a few seconds before she realised it was hers. She managed to get it to her ear before the voicemail cut in.

'Catherine Bishop.'

'It's DS Etheridge here from West Yorkshire?' Male, gruff voice, didn't really want to be making the call.

'Oh, right, hello.'

'You wanted us to find the sister of a victim for you and break the news?'

'Yes, that's right.'

'Well, we've done that and she wants to talk to you.'

'What do you mean?'

'She says she's got some information she wants to share with whoever's investigating her brother's death and that's not us, so she won't talk.'

'But . . . '

'I know, but that's the way it is.' Etheridge interrupted. 'Do you want her details?'

'Go on then.' Bishop stepped quickly to a nearby desk, fumbling for a pen and scrap of paper. She scribbled down the information and Etheridge was gone.

'What a charming man.' Bishop said in a posh voice to herself. Receiving the call had reminded her that she hadn't replied to Louise's text message and that she had better do it now while her phone was still in her hand and she had a spare few seconds. She typed: Case moving, could be very late, will keep u posted C x She took a deep breath and put the phone away.

I wonder if she ever smiles properly? Knight thought, nodding firmly at whatever Superintendent Stringer had just said about the fast approaching press conference.

'So this Mr Woffenden is on his way in?' asked Kendrick.

'Should arrive any minute.'

'Can I just be sure I understand why we want to speak to him?' Stringer took a sip of water from a crystal tumbler that sat by her elbow. 'Our witness saw Woffenden in the house she was kept prisoner in and we therefore think there may be a motive for him to kill Steven Kent, since it seems he was involved?'

'At this stage, we just want to find out what he knows. We want to know about the brothel he was allegedly involved with, not to mention the people trafficking, prostitution . . . ' Knight shrugged.

'According to Intelligence, he's been a person of interest for quite some time.'

'That's right.'

The phone by Stringer's perfectly manicured hand rang, and she lifted the receiver to her ear.

'Thank you.' she said, and replaced the receiver looking at Knight. 'Mr Woffenden is downstairs.'

Knight met Bishop in the dimly lit corridor of the interview suite, though Bishop had always thought "suite" quite a flattering term for the straggle of grim little rooms.

'He's in Two.' she told Knight. 'Milica Zukic had a look at him through the two way mirror and she's sure it's him. He's not too happy to be here.'

Knight opened the door.

'Finally. Are you going to tell me what the fuck's going on or do I have to guess?'

Woffenden stared aggressively at them as they took their seats. Bishop started the recording, stating her name and rank and the date and time. Knight confirmed his own identity, with Woffenden shuffling in his seat impatiently before mumbling his name.

'So what's this about?'

Knight sat back in his chair, calm and relaxed.

'Mr Woffenden, do you know a man called Steven Kent?'

Woffenden glared.

'Kent? No. Is that it? You could have phoned and asked me that.'

'What about a woman called Ivona?'

'Called what? What are you on about?'

'Ivona. A woman. Do you know of any women called Ivona?'

'No I bloody don't. What is this?'

'It's known as an interview, Mr Woffenden. Looking at your record, I can see you've sat through several in the past. I'm surprised you don't recognise the experience.'

Woffenden sat back, mirroring Knight.

'Well,' he said, 'aren't you clever?' He smiled to himself.

'I'll ask you again. Do you know Steven Kent, or a woman called Ivona?'

'And I'll tell you again, no I don't.'

'Didn't you want legal representation, Mr Woffenden?'

'You what? Why should I? I know I've done nothing wrong.'

Bishop stared at Woffenden, a horrible realisation dawning. She opened the file she held on her lap, discreetly examining the mugshot of Woffenden. *Oh, shit* she thought.

'Mr Woffenden,' she said. 'Do you have any tattoos?'

'Tattoos? No, no way. Not a fan of needles. My twin brother's got a few, a huge one his chest,' Bishop winced, 'but not me. I was ill a lot as a young lad, had no end of blood taken and it put me right off. You going to tell me what that has to do with anything?'

Knight looked like he wanted to ask the same question. Bishop sighed, told the tape recorder the interview had been suspended and then led a bewildered Knight out of the room. In the corridor, she stabbed at the mugshot with her finger.

'Look, you can see the top of a tattoo here. We've got the wrong man, we need his brother.'

Knight groaned as realisation dawned.

'How the hell have we managed that?'

Bishop rolled her eyes and shook her head.

'It's my fault, I should have checked.'

'How were you supposed to know he had a twin brother? What are the odds? We can't blame Milica, she wasn't to know either, or Claire Weyton come to that.'

'I doubt the DCI and the Super will see it like that.'

'Looks like the Mr Woffenden we have through there has done his brother a big favour then.'

'Seems so.'

They went back in and resumed the interview for the tape.

'So where's your brother?' Knight said.

Woffenden grinned hugely.

'You mean Ron? No idea, mate, I've not seen him for weeks. I've been minding his flat for him and when your brave boys in blue came looking for Mr Woffenden, I naturally did what any good citizen would and came quietly.'

22

Ron Woffenden rubbed his eyes. It had been a long drive, not wholly unexpected, but still sooner than they'd thought. At least he could lay low here for a while. It was the usual sort of place, a terraced house in a run down street, an area where no one made eye contact or spoke to each other. Perfect. Don had done him a big favour but he'd have to stay away from his brother now, be out of contact for a while. He still wasn't sure how they'd got onto him so quickly; maybe the tip off about the raid had been accurate after all. No one had believed it, but they'd moved on anyway. There were always more houses to go to and it didn't take long for the punters to realise you were there. Lucky that Don knew next to nothing about his brother's work really.

If Kendrick had been annoyed the previous day, it was nothing compared to the ranting he treated Knight and Bishop to when he heard about Woffenden. He stormed around his office smashing his fist into his palm, reminding Knight of John Cleese playing Basil Fawlty.

'What were we playing at? How the bloody hell are the Superintendent and I supposed to explain this one at the press conference, which if I could remind you, is in less than an hour? Do you want to see us chewed up and spat out in the morning papers? We shouldn't have gone haring after Woffenden to bring him in, we should have been cautious and watched him – the right one. The whole lot of them will have disappeared for good, Ron, his mates and all the poor cows that slave for them. How the hell are we going to get to them now?' Bishop bit her lip and Knight kept his eyes on the desktop. Their silence infuriated Kendrick.

'Do either of you give a toss about this?'

'We still have Milica Zukic.' Knight said.

'And what bloody use is she now, the poor lass? She led us straight to Woffenden and what happened?'

'The killer of Steven Kent, who may or not be linked to Ron Woffenden, doesn't know that the passenger in the back of Kent's van didn't actually see the murder. We could use that to our advantage in the press conference and not mention Woffenden at all. There's no reason anyone should know about it.' Knight spoke calmly.

Kendrick sat behind his desk, his fury finally exhausted.

'Go on.'

'We know Pollard and Kent were mates when they were younger, but we don't know of any link between Pollard and Zukic, Pollard and Woffenden, Pollard and Ivona or Pollard and the house Zukic was held in. That could be because there isn't a link. Kent may have done some delivering for the people Woffenden and Ivona are involved with and no more.'

'So at the press conference . . . '

'At the press conference, we say we have a person helping us with enquiries who was a passenger in the vehicle Kent was travelling in shortly before his death. It was DS Bishop's suggestion.'

'Put the wind up the killer?'

'Something like that. We wanted Woffenden brought in because he was a link to Kent, but he's also part of this trafficking gang and the sooner we speak to him the better. That's not to say finding Woffenden will bring us any closer to whoever killed Pollard and Kent. I think we're agreed that the same person killed them both?'

'The message seems to confirm that.' Bishop pointed out reluctantly.

'Or someone wants us to think it's the same person.' Kendrick added..

'The two messages were identical though.'

'The fact is, we just don't know. I'll speak to the Super about all this and see how she wants to play it. You two better get out of here before she comes for a quiet word with you as well.'

Kendrick turned pointedly to his computer screen.

Back in the CID room, Bishop threw herself into her chair.

'Was there any need for that? It's not like we brought in the wrong bloke on purpose.'

Knight found himself a seat.

'He's right though. Woffenden will have gone to ground along with the rest of the gang.'

'What are we going to do with the other Mr Woffenden?'

Shaking his head, Knight sighed.

'Kick his arse out of here I suppose. We won't get away with charging him for anything. He actually said 'Donald' for the recording, just quietly.'

'Smug bastard, I'm sure he enjoyed stringing us along.'

'No doubt. We need to find somewhere safe for Milica Zukic too, especially if she's mentioned in the press conference.'

With a grin, Bishop said 'Don't tell me you're thinking of inviting her to stay with you as well?'

'No more spare rooms, Sergeant, unless you're not coming back again tonight?'

Bishop blushed, the first time Knight had seen her even remotely embarrassed.

'Not sure, have to see how it goes. I need to tell you about the call I had from West Yorkshire . . . '

23

Anna Varcoe reached for her coffee and took a sip, then scowled, had a quick check around and spat the cold liquid back into the cup.

'I saw that.' said Bishop from the other side of the room. She got up from her chair and came to stand beside Varcoe. 'Any luck?'

'It's a bloody nightmare, Sarge. This investigation is like unravelling wool – just when you think you're getting somewhere, you find more knots.'

'Tell me about it.' Bishop said with feeling. 'Fancy a trip to Leeds?'

Varcoe looked up.

'Leeds? Why?'

'A little bird there has told us she has some information. Come on, get your bag.'

Varcoe got to her feet and picked up her jacket.

'A little bird? Who do you mean?'

'Steven Kent's sister. Last one to the car park can drive.'

Knight stood at the back of the press conference watching Stringer's face growing redder by the second. He was pleased he wasn't sitting at the highly polished wooden desk at the front of the room where DCI Kendrick was attempting to reassure the assembled journalists, and in particular local reporter Helen Bridges, that bringing the murderer of Craig Pollard to justice had always been a priority and that it hadn't taken a second murder to force them to take Pollard's death seriously.

'So you do admit there's a link between the two cases?' Bridges asked, pen poised.

'We can't comment.' Kendrick folded his arms then remembered it made him seem defensive and uncrossed them.

'Come on, Chief Inspector, two men with their heads beaten in, their bodies found a couple of days apart? Did Pollard and Kent know each other? Should young men in the area be worried? Can you confirm you're investigating both deaths simultaneously?'

Kendrick cast a panicked look at Stringer, who cleared her throat.

'No comment.'

Bridges gave a scornful laugh.

'Are you actually going to tell us anything Superintendent, or should we just all leave now? Your statement gave us nothing.'

Kendrick leant forward.

'We can tell you that we have a possible witness to the Steven Kent murder and that the person is helping us with our enquiries.'

'Man, woman, what did they see?' Bridges was out of her chair again.

'No further comments about the witness.' Stringer said firmly. Bridges looked outraged.

'You can't just say you have a witness and leave it at that.'

'We can, Ms Bridges, and we have.'

Bridges continued to splutter and a young man stood up.

'Superintendent Stringer, would it be fair to say that at this point in time you have no idea who killed Craig Pollard or Steven Kent?'

Stringer took a deep breath.

'It would be fair to say our investigations are ongoing in both cases. That's all everyone, thank you.'

She stood quickly and began making her way towards the end of the table and escape. The media liaison officer looked shell shocked. Knight thought it would be a good idea to make himself scarce and headed back to his office.

Jodie Kent's house was warm and bright, as was Kent herself, or would have been had it not been for the news of her brother's death. She welcomed them in, apologised for the mess though there was none and offered tea or coffee. She was pale, grief plainly visible on her face, but she managed a smile as she handed them their drinks. They went through to the living room where a toddler was playing with a brightly coloured toy kitchen. Varcoe smiled down at him and was rewarded with a grin.

'He's gorgeous.' she told Kent.

'Thank you. He's almost walking, we've got to watch him every minute.'

'Firstly, Ms Kent, please allow me to say how sorry we are for your loss.' said Bishop formally. She hated these occasions, always uncomfortably aware how trite every condolence could sound when you had never met the victim.
Kent bowed her head.

'Please,' she said, 'call me Jodie.'

'Thank you, Jodie. DS Etheridge from your local station called to say you had some information you wanted to share with the officers investigating your brother's death. Is that correct?'
Kent nodded.

'I didn't want to tell Etheridge. The woman that came with him to tell us about Steve was nice, but he was a . . . pig.' she said, glancing at her son.

'I see. I'm really sorry about that.' Bishop said quickly.

'Oh, don't you apologise for him, you don't even work with him do you? You're from Lincolnshire. I grew up in Northolme. I came here to university, then met Mark and never moved back.'

'Were you close to Steve?' asked Bishop gently.

'I'd say so. He's . . . he was a few years younger, we used to fight when we were little, like you do, but as we grew older we got on fine. He used to call in if he was out this way with a delivery, he stayed over occasionally . . . My partner's a paramedic and works long hours like yourselves, so I was glad of the company if Mark was working. After Mum and Dad were killed, Steve and I were each other's only family. He loved Sam,' the child looked up and smiled, recognising his name, 'and he and Mark always got on well. We all used to watch football and have a few beers.'

'Your brother worked as a courier?'

Kent nodded, shifting anxiously in her chair. *Here we go,* thought Bishop.

'Yes, that's what I wanted to talk about.'

'Steve's job?'

'He called here the one night, it was about seven o'clock. I asked him if he wanted tea, wanted to stay and he did. We'd eaten and we were sitting in here watching the TV when Steve's mobile rang. He got a strange look on his face, like he felt guilty or was worried. He took the phone out of his pocket and I could see it wasn't his usual mobile. He had a fancy one - all singing, all dancing - but this one was really plain and simple. He listened to whoever was ringing but he didn't say a word, not hello or goodbye or anything. He put the phone away and sort of slumped down in the chair. I could tell he didn't want to talk about it, but it seemed really odd to me. I asked if it was work and he mumbled something. I couldn't tell what he was saying and then he changed the subject. I thought it was weird and I mentioned it to Mark when he came home, but we didn't worry too much, it was just strange. Then the other night, Steve was staying again and I could tell he was worried. He was quiet and snappy, not himself at all.'

She paused and took a mouthful of her tea, then pulled a crumpled tissue from her pocket and wiped her eyes.

'You're doing really well, Jodie.' Varcoe said quietly.

'Mark was here, he said he'd take Steve down to the pub and talk to him, see if he could help. They came back later than usual and Steve was in a state. Mark said every time he went to the bar he'd had a double whiskey, according to the barmaid. He could hardly stand up, so Mark brought a duvet and pillow down and we just left him to sleep on the settee in here rather than try to get him up to the spare room. Mark told me Steve had said he could be in trouble, his mate Dave had done something daft that could drop them all in it. He'd mentioned some deliveries too, stuff he didn't want to be involved with. Mark wasn't sure what he meant and Steve said he'd been doing a few cash in hand jobs outside of work, good money. It had been fine to start with, a few parcels, but he was worried he was getting in over his head. He wouldn't say any more than that.'

Kent's son reached out a pleading hand to his mother and she excused herself, saying she needed to fetch the child a drink. Bishop looked at Varcoe, who nodded. Both thought Kent had something new to tell them, hopefully something significant. Kent was back, bending to give the child a plastic lidded beaker. She sat back down, hugging a cushion close.

'Anyway, when we were sure Steve was asleep, I think he probably passed out to be honest, I took his keys from his jacket pocket and Mark went to have a look in the van.' Her eyes sought out Bishop's willing her to understand. 'He didn't want to, neither of us did, but we were worried and we thought if we knew what was going on, maybe we could help. Mark came back in and he was shaking his head. He said I'd better go and have a look, so I went out to the van and opened the back doors. There were sandwich cartons in there, some empty bottles of water, blankets . . . I didn't understand, it looked like people had been in there, travelling in there, but why would they be? Why wouldn't they sit in the front? I went back in and asked Mark what he thought. The only idea we could come up with was that Steve had taken a person, or some people, in the van who didn't want to be seen. Why would that be? It had to be something dodgy, didn't it?'

Bishop and Varcoe kept quiet, and Kent continued her story.

'It could just have been some labourers or farm workers I suppose, but . . . anyway, we didn't know what to think and we couldn't ask Steve. We did write these down though.' She took a sheet of folded notepaper from her pocket and handed it to Bishop. 'They're postcodes from Steve's sat nav.'

Varcoe glanced at Bishop who shook her head slightly. No sat nav had been found in Kent's vehicle.

'I'm not sure if they'll be any use to you. We were going to drive to them when Mark had his next few days off and see if we could find out what Steve was up to, but it's too late now.' Jodie Kent fought to keep her composure. 'I don't think he would have done anything illegal, I'm sure it was just a favour for a mate, cash in hand, that sort of thing. He wouldn't have been involved in anything really dodgy.'

24

Back in the car, statements from Jodie Kent and her partner who had been asleep upstairs taken, Bishop unfolded the paper again. There were ten postcodes written neatly in blue biro. Six were Lincolnshire area codes, the rest further afield.

'How much do you bet that one of these is Milica Zukic's brothel?'

'I should think it's almost definite. Question is, which one?'

'Only one way to find out. I'll give DI Knight a call. Do you fancy some more driving?'

Starting the engine, Varcoe pulled a face.

'Not much choice, Sarge, we're about sixty miles from home.'

'Don't be facetious, Anna, it doesn't suit you.' Bishop grinned, rummaging in her bag for her phone. 'Hello, sir, how was the press conference?' She couldn't help but smile as Knight filled her in on the grilling Stringer and Kendrick had endured, then told him about the postcodes given to them by Jodie Kent and the new name she had given them – Dave. Another popular one for Kendrick to moan about. 'What do you want us to do? We're just leaving Leeds, we could have a look at the Lincoln address on the way back to the station or shall we leave it for tonight?'

Knight pondered for a few seconds before agreeing it was a good idea to see what they could find out that evening.

'Drop Claire in Intel an email too,' Knight said tinnily. 'See what she can dig up tomorrow.'

'Put your foot down, Anna.' said Bishop settling back into her seat. She should have driven, she reflected, it would have kept her mind busier. She glanced in the wing mirror, studying the car behind them. *Paranoid*, she thought. She welcomed the chance to contact Claire again though, feeling like a schoolgirl with a crush on a pop star as she thought about it.

'Shouldn't Milica Zukic visit this place with us?' Varcoe asked.

'She probably will eventually. Let's see it ourselves first. We don't know if one of these places was where she was held and even it was, chances are it'll be empty now. As DI Knight keeps saying, the person who killed Pollard and Kent may have no involvement with the gang that kept Milica prisoner.'

'We know Pollard spent just about every penny he had, Sarge – what if he was a punter at this place?'

Bishop frowned, thinking.

'Milica Zukic did say some of the girls seemed younger than her sister, who was only seventeen, and we know from Mike Pollard that Craig was keen on girls who were just legal – who's to say his tastes didn't run to even younger?'

Varcoe grimaced, hands tightening on the steering wheel.

'He wouldn't be the first, Sarge.'

'Let me speak to the DI again.'

Knight was wandering around the incident room, looking lost. DS Cuthbert watched him, then muttered to PC Lawrence:

'Do you think he even knows where he is?'

The constable smiled warily.

'He must have done something right to be a DI.' she pointed out.

Cuthbert snorted.

'Maybe they were desperate, or having a two for one offer or something.'

Knight glanced in their direction then moved away. PC Lawrence looked worried.

'You don't think he heard, do you?'

'Do you care?'

'Of course I care, I don't want to be a constable all my life.'

'I don't think cosying up to DI Knight will do your chances of promotion any good, if I'm honest. He's not set the world on fire since he's been here, has he?'

'He must have seen all sorts in the Met though.'

'Seen it, yes, but solved it? We don't know about that, do we? We know nothing about him, proper mystery man.'

'I'm not getting involved in slagging him off, anyway.' The PC turned away and Cuthbert moved off, scowling. Knight was now standing facing the wall, mumbling into his mobile phone. Cuthbert rolled his eyes and went back to the whiteboards.

'I've got a couple of people running the same checks on the name Dave that we ran on Steve and Nick, so we'll see if that gets us anywhere. Pollard's parents and brother are being contacted too to see if they remember anyone called Dave. He could be our mystery caller, but he could be our killer too, we need to remember that.' Knight said.

'Yes, sir. What do you think of DC Varcoe's suggestion that Pollard could have been a paying customer as well as perving around town?' Bishop's voice echoed in Knight's ear.

'I can't hear you very well. We can show his photo to Milica Zukic, unless you did that earlier?'

Bishop admitted she hadn't thought of it.

'I'm not sure if our interpreter is still here; probably not, but even without him I'm sure Miss Zukic will understand what we want her to do if I show her the photo. Did you get an up to date shot of Steven Kent from his sister?'

'We did.'

'Okay, good. I'll see you back here.'

Knight disappeared into the corridor.

'Off to save the world.' muttered Cuthbert.

25

Milica Zukic stared up at the ceiling of the cell she'd now been lying in for about seven hours, save looking at the photographs with Bishop and Doctor Whelan. Whelan was pleasant and reassuring. He'd told her that the police meant her no harm and that the only reason she was in a cell was for her own protection. Could she believe that? Did she have any reason to trust the police? No, but then she had no real reason to distrust them either. She shivered, shuffling on the bunk. The sweatshirt she'd been provided with wasn't very thick and she needed to shower and wash her hair. She thought about her parents in Serbia worrying about her and hoped her uncle had told them she was safe. She'd been stupid to believe him; she should have known what he said was too good to be true, but he was family and if you couldn't trust your family . . . She worried too that her sister had suffered the same fate, that even now she was locked in a house somewhere in Britain, barely surviving a living hell. Compared to the other girls in that house and many others like it, Milica knew she had been lucky. She shivered again, wrapping her arms around her body.

The door opened and Milica shrank back into the corner where her bunk met the wall. The man entered the cell was smiling, his eyes kind. She recognised him as the inspector who had spoken to her earlier. He held a tray of food which he offered to her: sandwiches, a banana, cake and a bottle of orange juice. She smiled gratefully and took the tray. He had a sheaf of papers under his arm and he studied them while she ate. Milica felt she could trust this man. She couldn't have said why but she was sure of it, and she felt her body relax. Her meal finished, she placed the plates, banana skin and empty bottle tidily on the tray and looked expectantly at Knight. He stepped forward and offered her a sheet of paper, which she took and studied. It was another of their photographs, a man a little older than herself. She considered. Had she seen him before? No. Never. Shaking her head apologetically, she handed the sheet back to Knight.

'Sorry.' she said, smiling hesitantly. He smiled back, shrugging.

'Thank you for trying.' he said. Milica, understanding "thank you", shook her head, meaning *It was nothing*. She wanted to ask him what would happen now, where she would go and if she was to stay here whether she could wash or at least have a blanket. She didn't have the words though and felt stupid and inadequate. Knight beckoned to her with his hand and she got warily to her feet. He opened the cell door wide and in the corridor stood a young female uniformed police officer who was smiling pleasantly. Zukic looked at Knight questioningly.

'You go with PC Roberts.' said Knight, using a few more hand gestures. Zukic understood the gist of what he was saying.

PC Roberts pointed at herself and said, 'Natalie.'

Milica smiled in understanding, made the same gesture and said, 'Milica.' Smiling broadly now, the two women shook hands. Knight walked quietly away.

Bishop and Varcoe sat squinting through the darkness at a row of dilapidated terrace houses, car engine idling.

'That's number twelve, green door.' Bishop said, slouching lower in her seat as a scrawny man lurched unsteadily down the pavement. She tensed, but he passed them without a glance.

'Weird how it looks just the same as all the other houses, but then I don't suppose they'd want to advertise what was going on inside.' Anna Varcoe said, turning the car's heater up another notch.

'People must have some idea though, surely?'

'You would think so, but then as we know people are good at turning a blind eye to things they don't want to get involved with.'

'True. Come on, let's get out of here. I think we have to say this is a possibility, but we need Milica Zukic to confirm it. It could be perfectly innocent, just a place Kent had to bring an everyday parcel to, but . . . I don't know.'

Varcoe glanced over her shoulder and accelerated away from the kerb.

'No signs of life anyway. No lights on, no queue of punters in the front garden.'

'Do you call that a garden? Looked like the local tip to me. We'll see what we can find out about the place when we're back at the station. It's bloody freezing, and I'm dying for a warm drink.'

As Varcoe concentrated on finding the way through the warren of identical streets, Bishop typed a text: Sorry, will b 2 late talk tomorrow C x

Louise might not be happy, but she couldn't worry about that now.

Sitting at the table in the conference room, Bishop wrapped her hands around a mug of tea, savouring the heat as it defrosted her fingers. Knight looked exhausted and Bishop was sure her appearance wasn't much better. Varcoe had gone to her desk to check up on the house they'd just visited, hoping to discover who owned it, but at this time of night her best chance would probably be to wait until the morning. Anna wanted to have a quick look before she went home though, conscientious as ever. Kendrick arrived, also tired-eyed and in need of a shave.

'Okay, let's make it quick, I think it's time we were all at home.' Keith Kendrick said. 'What do we have?'

He seemed satisfied with the progress they'd made for once and they agreed to meet again first thing to discuss the actions for the day. Varcoe had stuck her head around the door at one point and said she'd not managed to find anything but would get back onto it first thing. As they made their way to the car park, Bishop said hesitantly:

'I hope you won't mind if I stay with you again, sir?'

'You know I don't mind. Let's get out of here, shall we?' Knight hurried towards his car, head down against the cold wind. Bishop followed, hands jammed into her coat pockets. There had been no wind when they'd arrived back at the station forty minutes before. Winter was definitely setting in. *Lucky I'm not the superstitious type,* thought Bishop, rooting through her bag for her car keys. Why did she never think to have them ready in her hand as she left the station?

Neither Knight nor Bishop saw the figure huddled in the bus shelter across the street.

26

Dave Bowles turned off the television, stomach churning, breathless. His throat was choked and he tried to swallow but couldn't. Steve Kent was dead. Steve Kent, who he'd spoken to a few days ago, who had insisted all was well, was dead. Bowles' hands were twisted together, pressing against his pursed lips. He stood up then sat again, forcing his hands to unclench. Not only was Kent dead, he'd been killed in the same way as Craig Pollard had. To Bowles, that could only mean that he had been right all along and that Kent had been wrong. Twelve years after the event, the boy now a man and hunting them all, taking revenge. Bowles unconsciously made a sound somewhere between a moan and a whimper. He could be next. Only himself and Nick were left. He would have to find Nick, he didn't know what else to do. He daren't ring the police again, not now. He had never imagined this. He had thought the police might come for him one day but never this, not the murder of the four of them, one by one. It was barbaric, some form of personal, primitive justice and he wasn't willing to leave himself at risk. He could go to the police of course, tell them all he knew and hope for mercy, for understanding, but he daren't risk that. He would try to find Nick. He knew where Nick's parents used to live, maybe they were still there. It was a start. He hurried to his bedroom, grabbed his rucksack from the wardrobe and blindly threw clean boxer shorts, a couple of T shirts and a few pairs of socks into it. He knew he was panicking, not thinking straight. It was probably a terrible idea, but he couldn't stand the thought of staying here waiting for his own death, seeing the face of the boy at last. He'd never been a fighter and knew a man that could kill Pollard and Kent without being caught would overpower him easily. He'd always been the smallest. Bowles slammed the door behind him and ran down the stairs.

27

I knew of course that Kent's body would be found at first light, if not before, but I didn't realise there was another person in the van. There was no one in the front with Kent though, I'm certain. They must have been in the back. Interesting. No doubt Kent's out of hours livestock deliveries have been noticed now. That will open a real can of worms. I'm confident that even if their witness saw me, the suit will have made it impossible to describe me. Height and build, perhaps, but I have made adjustments for those too. I'm certain I'm safe, for now at least. Anyway, I still have work to do.

28

Louise read the text from Catherine, shook her head resignedly and dropped the phone onto the sofa. *At least she sent a message this time,* Louise thought. She hadn't always remembered.

Bishop stared at the red numbers of the clock in Knight's spare room. She couldn't explain why she hadn't wanted to see Louise - too much too soon perhaps. The person running behind her still played on her mind too and she remembered that she still hadn't mentioned it to Knight. She needed time to think about what she wanted to happen with Louise, and a murder case left room for little else. She was tired, yet her mind wouldn't allow her to rest. The grimy terrace house she'd seen with Anna Varcoe flitted across her mind, images of the suffering of the girls that may have lived there. She didn't like to admit that to her at least, finding the people responsible for the virtual imprisonment of Milica Zukic and the others, however many there were, had become as important as finding who had killed Craig Pollard and Steven Kent, if not more so. If the person who had committed the murders was also part of the gang, so much the better. She hadn't asked if Claire Weyton had discovered anything further about Ron Woffenden or the mysterious Ivona, and Knight hadn't mentioned it in the briefing with Kendrick. The image of Claire's face, those blue eyes, the jolt of electricity as they'd shaken hands . . . No. There was no point dwelling on it. Bishop had her self-imposed rule and she wasn't going to break it now, no matter who she met. She wrestled her mind away.

She wondered how Louise had reacted to her text. Knowing her, she would have sighed and gone about her business. It was only when Bishop had eventually arrived home, usually waking Louise up in the process, that the arguing had started in the past. Bishop wasn't naive enough to believe that their relationship could ever be as exciting as it was when they'd first met – part of that was because they hadn't known each other and there was so much to explore, to discover. If they were to try again, it would be different, more mature perhaps, with no surprises. Maybe it could work. She sighed and turned over, ignoring the voice in her head that told it never would. At least here in Knight's house she felt safe and could relax a little, though it seemed her unconscious couldn't. Hopefully, there would be no repeat of the dream she'd had the previous night. In the dark, still bedroom she felt all at once very alone.

Knight wondered how Caitlin was, and the baby she carried. He should ring her and talk to her. Not now though, not tonight, not there would ever be a good time. His thoughts drifted to Milica Zukic. She was spending the night in a budget hotel with PC Roberts keeping a watchful eye on her. It was the only solution they'd be able to find, for tonight at least. The wary expression on her face had touched him, as had the watchfulness in her eyes. To be betrayed as she had been by a member of her family must hurt. They would need to give her the opportunity to speak to her parents, he should have thought about that earlier. Insensitive. Another action for tomorrow.

29

The wind drove freezing rain against Dave Bowles' face as he trudged down the long driveway. The house was large and imposing, uninviting. Bowles was beginning to regret rushing out in panic, especially after spending a long and uncomfortable night in a bus shelter - not to be recommended at this time of year. Still, he was alive and he intended to stay that way. Bowles ran his hands through his soaking hair and straightened his jacket. This wasn't the sort of place he was used to. Raising his hand to ring the doorbell, a thought struck him. What if Nick had killed Craig and Steve? Had he worried for years as Bowles had, struggled to sleep as the guilt washed through him? Nick could have cracked and seen disposing of Pollard and Kent as a way to ensure his own involvement stayed secret. Bowles thought it was possible. He could be delivering himself straight into Nick's hands, ringing the doorbell of a wanted murderer, a man who had already killed twice. Bowles' hand hovered mid air and he backed slowly away from the white painted door, stepping quickly onto the gravel. It was too late, however. The door opened to reveal a woman in her sixties, hair tightly curled, wearing a high-necked lavender blouse, a grey skirt and sensible flat shoes. She looked disdainfully at Bowles.

'Do you know what time it is? Can I help you?' she said, her tone implying that she very much doubted it.

'I was looking for Nick.'

'Nick? I think you have the wrong house.' She began to close the door and Bowles stepped forward.

'His family used to live here, it was about ten years ago?'

She shook her head imperiously.

'We've only been here three years, I've no idea who was here before.'

The door slammed. Cowed, Bowles walked away. It had been a stupid idea anyway. He reached the end of the drive and glanced around, not sure what to do next. What about Pollard's brother? He was younger, but he might know what was going on. Bowles set off walking again, then stopped. Surely the police would have spoken to Mike Pollard though? If they were looking for Bowles, which he suspected they might be since he'd made that stupid phone call, he couldn't take any risks. His shoulders slumped and he turned resignedly to plod back the way he had come. He'd have to go home. If Nick found him, he wouldn't fight.

30

Anna Varcoe had arrived at her desk early. Even DI Knight and DS Bishop were nowhere to be seen and they were usually around first. She made a mug of coffee and sat down, quickly checking through her emails. Nothing to distract her from digging into the ownership of the house she and Bishop had seen the previous night. They didn't know for sure that the property was anything to do with either the murders or the traffickers, but while she waited for someone to give her further instructions she was going to see what she could find out.

The door opened and she glanced up. DC Simon Sullivan, pale and drawn, stumbled into the room and tottered over to his desk.

'All right, Si?'

Sullivan groaned, head in his hands.

'No sleep whatsoever again, she's either teething or she's got a cold. I'll get more peace here with people giving me orders every two minutes. Where is everyone? I thought Catherine slept here these days?'

The door opened again and Bishop slunk in.

'No, Simon, it just feels like I do.'

Sullivan ducked behind his monitor. Bishop's desk phone started ringing and she shuffled across to pick it up. Varcoe and Sullivan kept their heads down as she had a short and very terse conversation with the caller then slammed down the receiver, scowling.

'That was our helpful DI from Intelligence, calling a day late to confirm that the address we were at last night, Anna, was going to be the site of a raid but that somehow the occupants got wind of it and disappeared. Tell me something I didn't know, you useless sod.'

'Can't he give us any more than that? No names?'

'Not so far. Be fair Anna, it's taken him nearly a day to tell us that much. We don't need him anyway, we've got one of his team in the building, Claire. She's been much more help than him so far.'

'Bloody hopeless.' muttered Varcoe.

'At least we know we were in the right place.'

'It still might not be the house Milica Zukic was held in.'

'True. And it gets us no nearer to whoever killed Pollard and Kent.'
There was a silence while they considered Bishop's statement. All three sighed.

'You know Claire Weyton's gay, Sarge?' Sullivan asked softly.
Bishop glared at him.

'Don't you start.' she snapped. 'Honestly, this place . . . '

'I'll make some drinks.' said Sullivan hurriedly, pushing his chair back and scurrying out of the room.

'There are still the other postcodes to check though.' Varcoe brought them back to the point. Bishop nodded.

'I know, but let's face it, we're getting nowhere fast. No forensic evidence for one thing, how can that be?'

'Everyone's an expert these days, people have ideas about covering their tracks.' Varcoe shrugged.

'Think they can, you mean. But this . . . how can you leave nothing, absolutely nothing behind?'

'I don't know.'

'We're missing something. We have been from the start, way before Kent was killed. The boss said so and he was right.'

On cue Knight arrived, looking as dejected as the rest of them. He knew his job was to motivate the team but this morning it would be a struggle, both for him and for them. The beginning of another day of following leads that came to nothing, talking to people who couldn't help, of wading through piles of paperwork and reports and getting no nearer their goal. The rest of the team straggled in, one by one.

Knight glanced around again, taking in the despondent expressions and slumped shoulders. Sullivan approached, holding out a mug of tea. Knight took it, offering a tired smile.

'Thank you.'

Sullivan nodded back. 'No problem, boss.'

Knight said, 'Can we all go through to the conference room, please?'

He led the way, the rest following him, glancing at each other with raised eyebrows. Kendrick generally headed the morning briefings with Knight commenting occasionally. This morning, however, the DCI was nowhere to be seen. When everyone was seated, Knight took a deep breath and stood in front of them.

'I know that from the beginning this case had been unusual; firstly the way Pollard's death looked like a simple fight gone too far and the messages concerning DS Bishop,' All heads to turned to look at Bishop who stared resolutely at Knight. 'And now the murder of Steven Kent. We know the two have to be linked, but how? We do have a couple of leads - we know now Pollard and Kent did know each other, but why they've both been killed still needs explaining. We've had a panning in the newspaper with regard to the Pollard murder but we're hoping that by telling the press we have a witness from Kent's van that we might see some movement.'

DC Rogers raised his hand.

'How do you mean, boss? We've not made Milica Zukic's identity public, have we? Do you mean knowing there was a witness could draw the person who killed Pollard and Kent out, that it might panic them?'

'Possibly. We don't want to risk naming Miss Zukic, at least not yet. We know there's a tenuous link between Pollard and Kent and we need to find our mystery men, Nick and Dave - either of them could be our killer.'

'Or both.' Sullivan added.

'Or neither.' Anna Varcoe put in.

Knight nodded.

'We still haven't identified our anonymous caller and again, Nick or Dave are in the frame. We need to find them and we're going to do that today. We also know Steve Kent was delivering more than parcels – more work on that today. Obviously, our priority is finding out who killed Pollard and Kent. If we can also round up a gang of people traffickers, so much the better. Today's the day we get a breakthrough; we've got the leads and we've got the right team to follow them. See DS Bishop for your duties and we'll meet again at five.'

Knight strode from the room.

'Bloody hell,' said Sullivan. 'What did he have for breakfast?'

31

Nick Brady sat eating freshly baked Victoria sponge in the warm kitchen of his mum and dad's bungalow. He was still feeling pretty fed up about losing yet another job but the cake and his mum's encouragement were helping. She bustled around the kitchen, chatting about this and that as she washed pots, iced fairy cakes and folded washing. Brady sat quietly, sipping coffee and trying not to think about Craig Pollard. A huge tabby cat sauntered in, looked around and leapt onto Brady's lap. Brady shifted as she kneaded him with her claws. She could be vicious and he didn't want to upset her.

'Wimp.' said his mum, scooping up the cat and shooing her away. They both heard the letterbox clang shut and Brady got up to retrieve the post and the local newspaper which also lay on the doormat. He picked it up, unfolded it and received his second nasty shock of the week. Kent. Steve Kent was dead. Craig Pollard and Steve Kent, both dead in a week. It couldn't be a coincidence.

'Nick?'

He blinked and turned towards her, holding out the newspaper.

'Mum . . . '

She took it from him, fumbling in her apron pocket for her glasses.

'Steven Kent?' She stared at him. 'Don't tell me you knew him too?'

Brady nodded wordlessly and his mum shook her head.

'What's going on? This used to be a nice town and now we have two young lads murdered in a week. What does it say the police are doing?'

She held the article up to the light, peering at it through half closed eyes.

'You need your eyes testing.' Brady said automatically.

'Rubbish, there's nothing wrong with my eyes. It's a good thing you moved out of town, Nick, I'd watch my back if I was you.' She was only half joking. Setting the newspaper on the table, she went across to fill the kettle again. Brady agonised; he wanted so much to confide in her, he always had but he'd never been able to find the right time and it was too late now, there was too much at stake. This meant there was only himself and Dave left. He couldn't remember Dave's surname. Knowles? He'd been a strange lad, credulous and naive and he'd only tagged along a few times. Pollard had only included him so they could take the piss. Brady shook his head silently. What a little cruel little shit he'd been back then. He'd paid for it since though and seemingly, so had Pollard and Kent. What the hell was he going to do?

32

Knight made his way to his office and slumped behind his desk. His team were all experienced police officers and he knew they would have seen his speech for the hope and hot air it really was. There was nothing else he could say. They had to follow every lead, go through every statement, chase up every Nick and Dave in the system in the hope that some luck would come their way, because he knew so far they had nothing. Craig Pollard's mother was right, the journalist Helen Bridges was right, Kendrick was certainly right. Knight had to admit that after the fascination, horror and heartbreak of London he'd expected, hoped, that Lincolnshire would be a place where he could take stock and work out whether he wanted to leave the police force altogether. He would do his job and no more. After the lucky escape he'd had there would be no more playing outside the rules, no more heroics. Knight was ready for the quiet life, but Lincolnshire obviously didn't agree. As Caitlin had said last time they'd spoken, people were the same wherever you went, from the most primitive conditions to the wealthiest homes. The circumstances may be different, the cultures and lifestyles, but in the end the basic urges and instincts were the same the world over, as they had always been. Knight knew he'd been a fool to expect an easier ride. Wishful thinking perhaps, but not the mindset of a man happy in his work. Knight thought again of Caitlin, of the baby she carried, and took out his mobile.

She answered immediately, though he could hardly hear her through the background noise. It sounded as though she was at some kind of celebration, though surely even Caitlin wouldn't be at a party at eight in the morning.

'Jonathan? Hold on, just let me . . .' A door closed, there were footsteps then another door creaked open and silence. 'Jonathan? Are you still there?'

'Yes, I'm here. How are you?'

'Oh, you know.'

'Not really,' said Knight. 'I've never been pregnant before.'

Caitlin made a small sound, not quite a laugh, more of a sniff.

'Me neither. It's very strange, I can tell you.'

'Strange? How do you mean?'

'Well, the thought of a little creature growing inside as you go about your day, listening to what you're doing, changing and developing. Weird, don't you think?'

'I'm not sure I'd say weird, though it probably would take some getting used to. Does it kick? Can you feel it moving around?'

'Careful, Jonathan, you almost sound interested.'

'Of course I'm interested.'

'You didn't sound it last time we spoke.'

'Well, what did you expect? You phone me out of the blue to tell me you're pregnant, that the baby might or might not be mine? It's not the sort of conversation you have every day, is it?'

'I suppose not, and I did say I was sorry. To answer your questions, I haven't felt the baby move or kick yet; that's normal, but it should happen any time. Do you want to see a copy of the scan I had?'

Knight swallowed.

'Yes, if you want me to see it. Can you see if it's a boy or a girl?'

'No, and I don't want to know until the birth anyway.'

'Fair enough.'

'I'll email it over now, I'm at my desk.'

'I thought you were out somewhere.'

'No, just a very noisy meeting. What's your email address?'

Knight gave it, then waited. Caitlin stayed on the line. He could hear her breathing but she didn't speak. The email arrived and Knight hesitated, then opened it.

'Have you got it?' Caitlin asked. There was slight scratching sound and Knight imagined her filing her nails, the receiver held under her chin.

'Yes, I'm looking at it. It's amazing. I didn't know you could email them.'

'One of the IT people saved it onto my computer, I didn't ask how. Can you see the head?'

Knight leant forward, peering at the screen.

'I think so.'

'Looks like an alien, doesn't it?' She laughed softly.

'Has Jed seen this?'

'Of course he has. He came with me, he saw it on the screen.'

'Oh.'

'Don't be like that. Jed's my partner, of course he wanted to be there.'

'But the baby might not be his?'

'No, but even if he's not the biological father, he'll be part of the child's life.'

Knight grimaced.

'I suppose so. And the baby's healthy, growing and . . . all that?'

'Yes, fine so far.'

'Okay, that's good,' Knight glanced up as Bishop peered through the window in his office door, then tapped on the glass. 'I'm going to have to go, but can we keep in touch?'

'Of course we can.'

'I'll speak to you soon then, and Caitlin?'

'Yes?'

'Take care of yourselves, won't you?' He hung up on her surprised laughter. 'Come in.' he called to Bishop. She sat down in the chair on the opposite side of his desk. 'Okay, Catherine?'

Bishop shook her head.

'Not really.'

She held out a sheet of paper. It was creased and had obviously been folded several times. Her hand shook slightly and Knight frowned. It was another print out of a photograph, the front door of a house with a blurred figure approaching it.

'Is this you?'

'Yes, it arrived here in this morning's post. I stayed with my ex the night before last, when I didn't come back to your house. I heard running feet behind me as I walked down her street and I rushed up to the door as he passed. I didn't get a look at him, but he must have been following me. I remember a flash of light, that'll be when he took the picture. Now he knows where Louise lives. I'll have to warn her.'

'I don't think she'll be in danger though, it sounds as if he could have attacked you when he took this but he didn't. All the same, we need to be careful. The fact that he sent this here seems to suggest he knows you're not staying at home too. Are you sure you want to keep working on this? You can always go to a safe house too until we catch him.'

'And play Scrabble with Milica Zukic? I want to find him, sir.' Bishop hoped she sounded surer of that than she felt.

'Right. We'll keep this to ourselves for now, but we need to be vigilant.' Knight didn't like it, but he also didn't want to lose Bishop from his team. The DCI wouldn't like it either, but . . .

'I can be vigilant.' She lifted her chin.

'Good. Milica Zukic should be arriving any minute, I want her to have a look at that house you and DC Varcoe were at so we can find out if it's where she was held. I want to find out as much as we can about Woffenden and Ivona, all of them, plus who's really in charge. Did we find out who owns the house?'

'No, but Anna's still on it. She came in early to get on, she knows it could be crucial.'

'I wish we knew where Woffenden's gone. He hasn't left the country but that's as far as we know. He seems to be the key, he could lead us to the people that run the whole operation. I've started some discreet enquiries about Zukic's uncle too, but I'm not sure how far we'll get with them. We can't be too obvious, especially since they've flown the nest once already.'

'That was only one property though, there must be more.'

'No doubt, but I don't want to cause any panic or put Milica Zukic in any more danger than she is already.' He changed the subject, deliberately trying to keeping his voice casual. 'What do you know about Dougie Hughes?'

Bishop blinked, confused.

'Dougie Hughes? I told you, sir, he more or less runs the area.'

'What about personally?'

'Personally? I'm not sure what you mean?'

Knight shook his head in exasperation.

'Neither am I really. As I said, Hughes is a name I heard in London more than once and I thought there could be a connection.'

'Personal . . . well, Hughes' wife is called Bernice, she runs a hairdressing salon as I told you before. Lots of hair, red nails and lipstick. High heels and tight leopard skin seem to make up most of her wardrobe, just how you'd expect a gangster's wife to dress. She looks like a character in a film or a soap opera. They've got a son, Richie. He's good looking but stupid, spends most of his life wondering which way everyone else went I think.'

Knight nodded.

'Ever heard of Paul or Malcolm Hughes?'

Bishop frowned.

'No, but what. . .'

With a quick glance at his watch, Knight stood up.

'It's probably nothing. If you haven't heard of them, don't worry about it. That's what I wanted you to say.'

Bishop followed him out of the office, puzzled.

'But if they're linked to the case . . . ?'

'They're not, at least I don't think so. If they are, you'll be the first to know.'

Knight strode ahead leaving Bishop to follow, feeling slightly annoyed. How could she work with him if he kept secrets from her? Talk about dangling a carrot, fishing to see what she knew and then shutting up shop. It wasn't fair and she didn't think it very professional either. However, she trusted Knight without quite knowing why. She hurried forward into the small room where Milica Zukic, PC Roberts and Knight were already waiting. Zukic smiled shyly.

'Hello, Miss Zukic.' Bishop said, with a polite smile, not expecting a response and was startled to hear the reply:

'Good morning.'

Knight grinned at her and Roberts beamed proudly.

'I've been giving Milica a quick English lesson.' she explained. 'Just a few phrases that might help her.'

'Good idea.' said Bishop. 'I'm impressed. You don't speak Serbian though Nat?'

Roberts shook her head.

'No, but there's no need to. It's surprising how much you can say with mimes and drawing, pointing and that sort of thing.'

They were interrupted by the arrival of Dr Whelan the interpreter who came bustling in, greeting them all loudly and complaining about the weather, reminding them it wasn't long until Christmas and wasn't the price of petrol scandalous?

Knight politely interrupted him and explained what they were going to do, then stood back whilst Whelan told Milica, who listened intently. Bishop noticed her clothes were new - jeans and a red hooded sweatshirt with a white T shirt underneath, black leather boots. She sidled up to Roberts, who explained that she'd been instructed to take Milica somewhere for some new clothes and been given the money to do so. They'd bought toiletries too, all from the nearest supermarket and Bishop and Roberts agreed Milica's appearance was much improved. Bishop wondered where the money for the clothes had come from; she wouldn't be surprised if Knight had paid for them himself.

Milica had spoken to her parents and also her sister which had calmed her. Roberts also said Milica seemed happier, not as frightened than she had appeared yesterday and she was certainly less pale, smiling at Knight as he opened the door and led them out to the car. Bishop drove them to the address and Milica peered cautiously through the window. She nodded firmly - this was the place. Bishop drummed her fingers on the steering wheel. She didn't understand what Knight had hoped to gain from this. Yes, they now knew this was definitely where Milica had been held, but did that knowledge move the case forward? Not that she could see. Had they really needed Whelan? Knight seemed pleased though, beaming at Zukic and Roberts. They headed back to the station. Bishop parked the car and went back up to the CID offices, still slightly bemused. Varcoe called her over.

'I think I might be getting somewhere, Sarge.'

Bishop hurried over.

'Really? Show me.'

Varcoe pointed to her computer screen. 'The house is owned by a company, Central City Solutions. Another company owns that company, which is again owned by another – you get the picture. Anyway, long story short, the company behind all of them is R & D Maintenance.'

'Sounds like two odd job men.'

'I doubt they've ever done any odd jobs in their lives, just dodgy ones. The R is Richie Hughes, the D his mate Damien Spencer. I bet it's just a sham company, set up to hide whatever else they're involved in and we all know what that's likely to be.'

Bishop's face lit up.

'So Dougie Hughes is involved, I bloody knew it.'

'It was a dead cert really, but you can bet we won't be able to prove it.'

'And Richie Hughes and Spencer will say they'd no idea what the place was being used for, they just let to a company who let it to another one and so on.'

'Same old story, but it's a start.'

'You better tell DI Knight what you've told me. I think he's in his office. Great work, Anna, I know this must have been really tedious.'

Varcoe smiled and went off to find Knight. Bishop glanced at the clock on the wall. If she was quick, she could have a sneaky cup of tea and a doughnut.

The canteen was quiet and Bishop sat at a corner table, sank her teeth into the doughnut and closed her eyes. She restrained herself from moaning out loud, but the temptation was there.

'You look like you're enjoying that.' a voice said.

Bishop opened her eyes, mouth still full. Claire Weyton stood in front of her, mug in hand, grinning mischievously. Bishop attempted to smile back but couldn't and had to make do with a lop-sided leer.

'Do you mind if I sit down?'

The mouthful of doughnut finally disappeared and Bishop was able to speak.

'Of course I don't mind, why should I mind?' *Calm down*, she said to herself. Claire sat down and took a sip of her drink.

'I still haven't found any more details about the people you were asking about. I think DI Foster has been in touch though?'

Bishop snorted.

'Yeah, for what it was worth.'

Claire smiled uncertainly. 'Oh . . .'

'I didn't mean . . . sorry. I just meant that you've been much more helpful.' Bishop backpedalled. Mentally, she kicked herself. *Very smooth*, she thought. There was a short pause.

'You look tired.' Claire observed.

'Thanks.' Bishop grinned.

'No, I'm sorry, I didn't mean . . .' It was Claire's turn to blush as she fidgeted with the handle of her cup.

'It's okay, I must look tired. I definitely feel it.'

'We always feel guilty you know, going home at five thirty when all of you are still hard at work.'

'There's no need to, honestly. We signed up for this job knowing it would mean long hours and weekends. You get used to it.'

'It must cause problems in your personal life though.'

Another snort from Bishop.

'You can say that again.'

'Have you . . . do you have a partner?'

Claire sounded hesitant, almost shy, no longer confident and knowing as she had before.

'To be honest, it's complicated. I did have, we lived together but she moved out around six months ago. Then the other night, she sent me a text. I went round to see her and she was talking about us trying again, getting back together. The thing is, she moved out because of my job. She couldn't handle the hours I had to work, like we've just talked about. She's a teacher, so fairly regular hours, work she can do at home . . . '

Claire nodded in understanding.

'Regular holidays . . . '

'Exactly. She was fine at first but she got more and more fed up with it and in the end she more or less said it was the job or her. I hesitated and she took that to mean I was choosing the job.'

'And were you?'

'I didn't think someone who loved me would ask me to choose. Sorry, I don't know why I'm telling you all this.' Bishop shook her head.

'Because I asked. I just . . . I thought maybe we could have a drink or something, when you're not as busy of course, but if you're getting back together with your ex . . . '

'I don't know if I am, or even if I want to. I'm still in the same job after all, and I don't intend leaving it. The same problems will be there as far as I can see.'

'Maybe you could work through them?'

'We did try. I think Louise just lost patience and so did I, if I'm honest. In the end, I just thought that if we were right for each other, we'd have worked harder to save the relationship.'

'I can understand that.'

'I would like to go out for a drink with you, if you still want to after what I've told you of course.' She sounded hesitant, even to her own ears, though it was the last thing she felt. Claire emptied her mug and pushed back her chair, her eyes never leaving Bishop's.

'I definitely still want to.'

Bishop gazed back, felt her stomach dissolve.

'You know the hours I'm working at the moment though . . . '

'I can wait.' Claire smiled. 'I need to get back but I'll email you my mobile number. Take care, Catherine.'

'You too.' Bishop watched Claire take her cup over to the counter and exchange a few words with Sally who was working on the till, both ending up laughing. *She's bloody gorgeous*, Bishop thought, not quite able to believe what had just happened. She had forgotten all about her doughnut and had a pleasant surprise when she realised most of it was still waiting on her plate. She saw Chris Rogers at the counter loading his tray with a plate of lasagne and chips, a mug of coffee and a chocolate cookie. He spotted Bishop and headed towards her.

'I've just seen Claire Weyton, was she in here with you?'

'She was in here, yes.'

'With you?'

'It's a big room, Chris, with plenty of chairs.'

Rogers speared a few chips and pushed them into his mouth.

'Ha, she was then. Bugger, I owe Simon a tenner now.'

'Mind your own business.' Bishop retorted, unable to fully suppress a grin.

'We just want to see you happy, Sarge, that's all.'

'That doughnut's made me very happy. See you later.'

33

Back in the CID room Knight was standing with Simon Sullivan, studying a piece of paper. Knight beckoned Bishop over.

'We've narrowed down the list of local Nicks and Daves to these. DC Sullivan and DC Rogers are taking half the list, DC Varcoe and DC Lancaster the other half. Hopefully by the end of the day we'll have found our men, or at least have more of an idea who we can disregard.'

'Fingers crossed.' Bishop nodded.

Sullivan moved off and Knight turned to Bishop.

'We need to check out the other postcodes on the list Kent's sister gave us.'

'Do you want me to do it?'

'I've got a meeting with the Super and DCI Kendrick. You know I've told the team we'll meet at five back here, do think you can make it around those postcodes before then?'

'I'll do my best. Will Miss Zukic be with me?'

'It's tricky with her not speaking English and I don't think we can ask Doctor Whelan to stay around, I'm not sure the budget would stretch to it.'

'She could let me know whether she recognises a place or not though?'

'That's true. Okay then. She could always talk to a translator later I suppose, if she can give us more information about a location. It doesn't help that we've no idea what these places will be.'

'I'll just check my emails quickly and I'll be on my way.'

Bishop strode out of the station and onto the street, Milica Zukic at her heels. Glancing over her shoulder to check Milica was still with her, Bishop crashed into a tall, solid figure as she rounded the corner towards the car park.

'I'm so sorry,' Bishop said, steadying herself. She glanced at the person she'd almost knocked over, then looked again as she recognised Mike Pollard. 'Mr Pollard? What are you doing here?'

Mike glared at her, adjusting his jacket and pulling his knitted hat further over his ears.

'You could have broken my ribs, why don't you look where you're going?'

'I asked you what you're doing hanging around outside the police station, Mike?'

Pollard was furious.

'I wasn't "hanging around", as you put it. I'm on my way to a job interview, if you must know.'

Bishop raised an eyebrow.

'At the police station?'

'No, not at the police station. You must be joking, I can do better than that. It's with a solicitor, not that it's any of your business.'

'All right Mike.' Bishop beckoned to Milica Zukic. 'It might be a good idea to surround yourself with people who know the law.'

She marched off leaving Pollard gawping after her, his expression thunderous. Once in the car, she sent Knight a quick text explaining what had happened. It was time they had another look at Craig Pollard's brother and probably his not-so-broken-hearted girlfriend too.

Bishop wanted to sing along to the radio as she drove but didn't want to subject Milica Zukic to her voice. Milica seemed happy enough, though Bishop wasn't convinced she understood where they were going. She seemed pleased just to be out of the station and Bishop could understand that. The first postcode took them to a village, a row of stone cottages, pretty and well maintained. Milica shook her head. She seemed to be looking wistfully at the scene and Bishop wondered if she was thinking of her home and family or was thinking about the life she could have had. She wanted to tell Milica that she was young, that she could still achieve all she'd planned but of course she didn't have the words to do so. The next postcode brought them to another village and another headshake from Milica. Bishop was beginning to feel a little dispirited and hoped this wasn't going to be a waste of time. It was a similar story with the next two places, a housing estate and a warehouse complex. Milica had obviously never been to either before. A half hour drive brought them to the location of the final postcode and this time as soon as Bishop slowed the car down, Milica was sitting forward, alert. She nodded her head firmly several times and said a few words before remembering that Bishop couldn't understand her. Bishop knew what she meant though – they'd arrived at a row of lock up storage units, each about twice as big as the average garage attached to a house would be. She assumed this was where Kent had collected Milica. They'd have to call in Doctor Whelan to be sure, but what else could Milica mean? Bishop parked in front of the first lock up, turned off the engine and looked around. There was no one in sight. She turned to Milica, trying to say through mime that she was going to get out of the car to have a quick look around and that Milica should stay where she was. Milica frowned at first, then smiled and nodded again.

Bishop got out and wandered over to the first set of double doors. She wouldn't have been able to get inside any of the units even if she had wanted to, which without a warrant wasn't advisable. She just wanted to walk around, make sure there was nothing suspicious. For all she knew, there could be frightened girls behind any of these doors. She stepped closer, eyes searching, then heard an engine behind her and turned. A white van had appeared. It parked next to her car, the driver's door flew open and a man leapt out wearing gloves and a baseball cap with a dark scarf covering his face, leaving only his eyes exposed. He ran to the passenger door of Bishop's car, wrenched it open and reached inside, grabbing Milica Zukic's arms and trying to drag her from the car. She screamed then shouted, struggling and kicking. The man realised her seatbelt was still fastened and tried to reach across her to undo it with Milica pushing his hands away. Bishop stared, frozen, then ran back towards the car shouting, 'Stop, police, what the hell do you think you're doing?' The man glanced wildly at Bishop as she bore down on the car, struggling to yell into her Airwave handset for backup. She had no choice, but running towards a man who could be armed when she was alone probably wasn't the best idea. Bishop was almost at the car, still bellowing at him that she was a police officer, Milica still fighting and screeching in Serbian, when he seemed to finally take in what Bishop was saying, abruptly dropped Milica back into her seat, sprinted back towards the van and scrambled in. His vehicle shot forward down the line of lock ups, hurtled around the corner at the end and out of sight. Bishop gabbled a description of the van into her handset as she wrenched open the driver's door of her car and set off in pursuit, Milica still shouting and leaning forward hoping to see which way her would-be abductor had turned.

34

Bishop sat at her desk, head in her hands as Varcoe silently placed a mug of tea at her elbow as she passed on the way to her own workstation. Knight stood beside Bishop, frowning.

'You did nothing wrong, you know. I would have done exactly the same.' he said.

Bishop lifted her head and stared at him.

'He almost had her, if it hadn't been for the seatbelt . . . I should have locked the door or stayed in the car.'

'She's fine, that's all that matters, and on her way to a safe house.'

'I'm going to get my arse kicked for this though, aren't I?'

'For protecting a witness, ensuring her safety?'

'She ensured her own safety, I wouldn't want to be in a fight with her.'

'The DCI is just happy she's still in our hands. It's after five, let's get to the conference room.'

Bishop slowly got to her feet, noticed the tea and picked it up raising it shakily to her lips.

'Thanks, Anna.' she said, as the DC followed her to the door. 'How did your Nick and Dave hunting go?'

'Pretty well, we narrowed our list down to two Nicks, three Daves. Not sure how the others got on. Are you okay?'

'Oh, I'm fine, don't worry about me.'

In the conference room, Knight was pacing in front of the assembled officers. Bishop and Varcoe found chairs and sat down as he started speaking.

'Just to let you all know that we found the van driven by Milica Zukic's attacker abandoned in a lay by just out of town. The registration plates have been cloned and we think our man phoned one of his mates who picked him up. Chances are, he won't be very popular when he tells his boss he could have snatched her but has come back empty handed, which is why Miss Zukic is on her way to a safe house as we speak.'

'Shows she's still important to them though.' said Chris Rogers.

'Exactly, even though they must realise she's been with us since Steven Kent's death and has had plenty of time to share all she knows.'

'Do we think the attempt to grab her was planned, or did he just happen to be going to the lock up and recognise her?' Sullivan said.

'We've no way of knowing, though DS Bishop didn't notice anyone following her. As it was just one man, I'd guess it was spur of the moment; he saw his chance and tried to grab it – and her. Little did he know he'd have a fight on his hands.'

'Any chance of any fingerprints or trace evidence that could help us identify him?'

'He was wearing leather gloves, a cap and a scarf over his face. I didn't recognise him but I couldn't swear I've never seen him before, I've no way of knowing. Miss Zukic's going to be interviewed when she's safe but she didn't seem to know him, I didn't recognise any names in what she was shouting.' Bishop said.

'Plenty of Serbian swearing going on I bet,' grinned Rogers.

Knight asked Varcoe and Lancaster to update them on what they'd learnt that day, and then Rogers and Sullivan. Progress had been made and they were down to five men called Nick or Nicholas, seven Daves or Davids. Knight was quietly pleased, offering encouragement. He asked Varcoe to share what she'd learnt about the ownership of the property she and Bishop had visited, which she did to general approval. There wasn't a copper in the place who would be sorry to see Dougie Hughes or any of his family behind bars. Knight calmed them down, reminding them they were a long way from that. They still needed to find Ron Woffenden and the chances of tracking down the man who'd tried to snatch Milica Zukic were slim, though the possibility he was linked to the Hughes family would be explored. It felt as though they were moving in the right direction again. Sullivan and Rogers were going out again to attempt to track down a few more of the men on their list before heading home for the day, while Varcoe and Lancaster were going to see Mike Pollard. As the room emptied, Knight called Bishop over.

'Why don't you call it a day and finish early for a change? You've got my spare key.'

'I've got things to get on with, sir. I don't want to leave when others are still working.'

'Well, it's up to you.'

'Thank you.' She turned away from him.

Knight hesitated, then made his way to the incident room. Bishop was looking paler by the hour and though he doubted she would ever admit it, he knew she was struggling. How long before DCI Kendrick noticed it too?

Bishop stubbed her toe on the corner of her desk as she hurried around it to pick up the phone. It had been ringing since she stepped back into the CID office and she didn't want to miss the call.

'Ow, shit, bloody hell . . . Hello?'

'Is that DS Bishop?'

'Yes, speaking.'

'DI Foster. I've got a couple of names for you.'

Bishop thought fast. 'DI Foster, of course. Thank you.' She fumbled for a pen and scrap of paper. 'And how do you spell that . . . Okay, that's great, thanks very much.'

Two names at last. She leant forward, hands poised over the keyboard. Her mobile started ringing in her bag and she rummaged for it, her eyes widening when she saw the caller's name.

'Hello, Louise?'

'Catherine? I can hardly hear you.'

'Sorry, I'm in the office, you know the signal's not great.'

'I thought you were going to call?'

'I know, I'm sorry. I've had a crap day.'

'And you're still at work?'

'It's only just gone six, Louise, of course I am.'

'I only asked.'

Bishop sighed.

'I know you did.'

'So I won't see you tonight?'

'I don't think so. I'm sorry.'

'That's fine, give me a ring when you can fit me in.'

Louise hung up. Bishop stared at the phone. *So much for a new start and being understanding, Louise*, she thought. She scrolled through her emails until she found Claire Weyton's phone number and typed a text message, her heart pounding: How about that drink tonight? She quickly placed the phone face down on her desk, almost afraid to read any reply that Claire might send. *What are you doing, Catherine?* She concentrated on her monitor but found no records for either of the names Foster had given her. Picking up desk phone again, she called down to the incident room and told Knight about her conversation with Foster.

'Why don't you go home and I'll see what I can dig up on them?' Knight said.

'I've already said . . . ' Bishop glanced at her mobile as it beeped – a text message. She snatched it up, held her breath and read the message: Any time x 'Then again, sir, you might have a point. It's been a long day. You will let me know what you find?'

'If you're up when I get in.'

'I might go out for a few hours and meet a friend.'

'Oh, I see. I'll send you a text then.' Knight said hurriedly. He paused. 'I know I've said this before, but be careful.'

'I will. Thank you.'

Bishop put the phone down, already typing: On my way, where? X

35

Dave Bowles was in bed, curled on his side, his mind racing. What could he do? Nick would know, Nick would come for him. He could be outside now, walking down the path, opening the door. He listened, eyes roaming the room. Maybe it wouldn't be tonight. He should have gone to the police years ago and confessed. Maybe it would have been all right. It was too late now though. They would blame him, he knew it. He would have to wait until whoever had killed Craig and Steve found him too, unless he could think of another way quickly.

36

Bishop saw Claire immediately, sitting alone at a table in the corner sipping a glass of red wine. She stood as Bishop approached.

'What can I get you?'

'It's okay, I'll buy.'

'No, please, let me.'

'Same as you is fine then, thanks.' Bishop stammered, hardly aware of what she was saying. Claire smiled and went over to the bar. Bishop watched, her stomach churning. *What are you doing? What about Louise?* She ignored her own voice in her head as Claire came back to the table and handed her the wine. She took a gulp.

'Thank you.'

'I didn't expect to hear from you so soon.'

'I know, I finished early.'

Claire nodded, knowing better than to ask. There was a silence. *Well, this is awkward,* Bishop thought, glancing around the pub. She took another swallow of wine. It wasn't a drink she would usually have chosen, but it didn't taste too bad. She was very aware of Claire's thigh close to her own, the smell of her perfume. All at once, Bishop had an urge to tell Claire everything - the messages left by the murderer of Pollard and Kent, the photograph taken through her own window, her worries and fears, the plight of Milica Zukic and the others in the house. Louise . . .

'Catherine?'

Bishop looked up.

'Pardon?'

'You were miles away.' Claire's voice was gentle.

'I'm sorry, I just . . . '

Here goes, she thought, her hand seeking out Claire's where it rested on the bench between them. Smooth, warm, slightly larger than her own. She stroked her thumb over Claire's fingers and felt her respond, heard her quiet intake of breath. Claire moved closer, her fingers entwining with Bishop's. They sat quietly, savouring the moment. Claire drained her wineglass.

'Can I get you another?' Bishop said softly.

Claire looked into her eyes.

'Shall we go?'

Bishop gazed back. This was the moment when she had to choose to stay on the path she'd always taken, or make the leap. She knew she had no choice, that this was going to happen however much she tried to persuade herself it couldn't. She nodded gravely, and Claire smiled.

Claire was staying in a hotel down by the river, close to the centre of town. They walked quickly, not touching, not speaking. Afterwards, Bishop couldn't have said what route they took, if they saw anyone as they hurried along. Bishop's mind was still filled with all the reasons why this shouldn't happen, as well as the knowledge that it would. It was only as the door closed behind them and Claire reached for her, their mouths meeting urgently, that she felt herself relax. All her worries, temporarily at least, were forgotten.

37

In Kendrick's office, Knight waited until the DCI had closed his mouth after a huge yawn.

'Time I was at home, I'll be turning into a pumpkin at this rate. It's the end of another day, where are we?'

'I think we're definitely making progress, but . . . '

'Come on, don't play the bloody mystery man with me, Jonathan. Tell me what you're thinking.'

'It's just that the house Milica Zukic was held in is owned, ultimately, by a bloke called Richie Hughes,' Kendrick made a noise that indicated disgust, 'And more than once I came across the name Hughes in London, Malc Hughes. It just so happens he has a cousin called Dougie.'

'Our friendly local self-styled gangster. Too much of a coincidence.'

'Just what I thought.'

'Dougie Hughes is a nasty, slippery bastard. I'm presuming there's a family resemblance?'

Knight's left hand touched his right shoulder blade, then moved away 'Yeah, sounds just like Malc.'

'Involved in people trafficking?'

'I've heard rumours, but you know what it's like – no one wants to point the finger.'

'So what are you suggesting?' Kendrick shuffled in his chair, which groaned beneath him.

'I don't know. We could never bring Malc Hughes in for anything at all and from what DS Bishop's told me, you've had the same problem up here with his cousin.'

'Exactly right. All sorts of rumours, no substance. We know, but we can't prove it. We do have Miss Zukic in a safe house?'

'Yes, as discussed with the Super.'

'And we've narrowed down those lists of names?'

'Only three Daves and two Nicks left.'

'Sod's law it'll be the last ones we get to. Wouldn't it have been a good idea to have more officers on it?'

'I used everyone I could. We'll get there.'

'Fair enough. What do you suggest we do about Milica Zukic? She can't stay here indefinitely.'

'No, I think she's keen to go back to Serbia.'

'Can't blame her.'

'I'd feel happier if she stayed here for now, at least until the Pollard and Kent murders are closed.'

'The cost . . .'

'Give me a few more days.'

'Fine. A few more.' Kendrick looked at Knight knowingly. 'You want to have a crack at Hughes, don't you? The whole family.'

'Of course I do. Don't you?'

'Don't be daft, I'd love to see them all sent down, but we can't go barging in. They've got money, connections and the power to make our lives very difficult.'

'I don't doubt it.'

'So we go slowly, tiptoe around them, see what else we can find out. I'll talk to the Super, tell her what we know. Has Milica Zukic said any more?'

'She was able to tell Whelan exactly which lock up she'd been in. I'm not sure how she knew, but we'll get the fingerprint people in there first thing tomorrow morning and see what we can find.'

'How's DS Bishop holding up?'

'She seems okay. She had no idea who Kent was, so there's no link there. She's not been back to her house but I had Simon Sullivan call in there, with Catherine's permission of course. There was nothing suspicious in her post, no more messages or photos. The only thing is, another photo turned up here today, a picture of DS Bishop going into a friend's house the night before last.'

'Christ, so he's followed her? I thought the messages were left with the bodies?'

'So far, but the photo was posted to her flat, this latest to the station.'

'Of course. We don't want any more. You're sure Catherine's not in danger? Sounds dodgy to me.'

'She's very keen to stay on the case.'

'It might not be her decision. Let's play that by ear, we'll talk again in the morning, see if more photos turn up tomorrow. I've never known anything like it.'

'Catherine got two names from Intel, people they believe were involved with the house Milica Zukic was held in. A man and a woman they were expecting to find when they raided the house, except of course that the raid didn't happen. I've spoken to a few people and I think the man could be harder to trace, but the woman is interesting. I'm wondering if she could be the Ivona Milica Zukic told us about.'

'How could they have allowed them all to leave that house? Wasn't it under surveillance?'

'You'd have thought so. I don't know the details.'

'What's this woman's name?'

'Jasna Dijlas.'

'We still don't know where she's gone though?'

'No.'

'And we don't know if any of this is linked to Pollard and Kent's deaths?'

'Not for sure.'

'Let's concentrate on finding our man for those two first, keep this on the back burner for now. I want to get them as much as you do, but our priority has to be the murders.'

'I know, but this . . . '

'Afterwards.'

'Fine.'

38

Dave Bowles had no idea how long he'd been in bed. He would have to get up
soon, if only to hurry to the bathroom before his bladder exploded. He reached
for the bottle of whiskey and took a huge mouthful. One more wouldn't hurt.
Wincing as it burned, he clambered unsteadily out of bed and staggered to the
bathroom. He managed to use the toilet without falling which seemed to him
quite an achievement, then stumbled over to the medicine cabinet that a
previous tenant had fixed to the wall above the sink. A blotchy face stared back
at him from the mirrored doors, eyes bloodshot, nose and mouth surrounded
with dried mucus. Bowles could remember bawling like a baby at some point,
sobbing out the years of pain and guilt. Managing to open the cabinet, he
fumbled through the contents. Shaving foam and spare razor blades, which he
placed unsteadily on the sink. Soap and shower gel. Two packets of condoms,
unopened and probably out of date. He let them fall to the floor. The
paracetamol went next to the razor blades. Bowles turned on the hot tap,
scooped some water into his hands and washed his face. It didn't help so he
repeated the process with cold water and that felt better, he could fool himself
into thinking he was more alert, thinking straight. He would have to go out.
Tottering back to the bedroom, he lost his balance and stumbled against the
wall. Leaning there he started to giggle, a response that struck him as odd given
his situation. Eventually managing to reach the bedroom, he sat on the bed and
made several attempts to pull his jeans on before eventually succeeding. The
walk downstairs would be tricky but he knew he'd have to do it, then out into

the street to the all night garage and the twenty four hour supermarket. Then he would decide.

It was Nick Brady's round and he'd have to buy it, he couldn't admit to his mates he was worried about money. They'd already taken the piss when he'd told them he was jobless again. He leant on the bar, brooding. They all had jobs, not great jobs most of them, and they all did a fair amount of moaning, but they were working all the same. He didn't want to take up his mum's offer of asking around for work, but he might have to swallow his pride in the end. The job centre hadn't been exactly helpful so far and he hadn't seen much in the papers or online either. He bought the drinks and went back to the pool table where two of the lads were in the middle of a game, the others standing around watching. Brady thought he'd probably call it a night after this pint. He wasn't in the mood. The walk home should clear his head; it had been cold but dry when he'd arrived at the pub and he had a lot on his mind. The police were making little progress in finding who had killed Pollard and Kent according to the newspapers and Brady still wasn't sure what to do. So far, he'd chosen to keep quiet and see what happened and it had worked except for the constant stream of questions in his head, the guilt and the worry. He knew it was possible he was at risk too, but he wasn't seriously concerned. He'd moved out of town, after all and no one knew much about him here, even the blokes he was drinking with. Anyway, from what he'd heard, Pollard had been too pissed to fight back and Brady intended to be on his guard until he heard the police had their man. There was still the possibility that Pollard and Kent's deaths had nothing to do with that day on the moor, or so Brady kept telling himself. It could be a coincidence and until Brady heard otherwise, he was staying out of it. He drained his glass and set it on the bar, then said his goodbyes and made his way out into the night. Glancing up and down the street, he shoved his hands in his jeans pockets then removed them, realising it made him vulnerable. He hated feeling like this and even though it might be paranoia, he wasn't going to take any chances. At least he was fairly well built. If he'd been only as big as Dave Bowles, he'd be more concerned. Unless he'd filled out since Brady saw him last, Dave's small frame would surely make him an easier target. Brady started walking, almost slowly enough to convince himself he wasn't scared.

39

'So let me get this straight. You had her trapped and you let her go?'

Richie Hughes bowed his head.

'I've said I'm sorry.'

'A lot of good sorry is, you useless little shit.' His father's voice was quiet, his anger contained for the moment at least. Richie hated that tone. He'd rather his dad yell at him like his mum did, because the restraint was a bad sign.

'She's been with the police for hours anyway, she'll have told them all she knows by now.'

His father moved to stand directly behind where Richie sat, leaning on the marble breakfast bar in the huge house Dougie and Bernice Hughes called home. Hughes made a sudden movement, grabbed as much of son's hair as he could in his meaty fist and twisted it until the younger man cried out in pain.

'This is nothing to what Malc will do to you when he hears. How hard can it be? She's only tiny, for God's sake.'

'She was with a copper.' Richie managed to gasp.

'So what? The copper wasn't even in the car, if you'd have undone the seatbelt straight away you could have got Zukic out before she even knew you were there.'

'She fought back, you should have sent Damien with me.' Richie bleated. His father released his hair, slowly moving to Richie's side.

'Oh, I see.' The quiet voice was back and Richie panicked, realising he'd made a mistake. 'This was my fault, of course, I see it now. I ask you to go to the lock up to make sure everything's okay and while you're there you have a golden opportunity to get back what's ours, and what do you do? You lose her, and all because I was stupid enough to expect you'd be able to do a simple task like that alone.'

He lunged at Richie, who cowered. Hughes didn't actually strike his son, but the gesture was enough to send Richie scampering from the room. Hughes picked up the phone that lay on the worktop and dialled his cousin's number, stored only in his own memory, not in the phone's.

'It's me. We've got a problem. Richie tried to grab Zukic without realising she was sitting in a cop car. She's disappeared again.'

There was a silence. Dougie Hughes braced himself for the explosion.

'He didn't realise? What, the big yellow stripes and blue lights on the top weren't a big enough clue for him? Not to mention the word POLICE in foot high letters along the side?'

'It was unmarked.'

'I know, Dougie, I know. Jesus. They still stand out a mile, how stupid is that lad of yours?'

Dougie gritted his teeth. 'Fairly.'

'You're telling me. So what's happening?'

'Well, they didn't catch Richie. He phoned Damien and met him in a lay-by, then they disappeared for a few hours until things calmed down and he's just come to tell me.'

'Where did it happen?'

'Outside the lock up.'

'Shit, so they know about that? How could they? Everyone who's ever been there has been in the back of a van, including Zukic.'

'I know, but that's where they were. They must have been asking Zukic which one she thought it was but how they found them in the first place, I don't know.'

Both men paused to consider this, until Malc said, 'Kent. Has to be.'

'How do you work that out?'

'Because he's dead and the police are trying to find out why and who killed him. They wouldn't have to look that far to find a link to us with Milica bloody Zukic was still in the back of his van when he was killed. I can't believe our luck there.'

'I know, what were the chances?'

'We used him too often really, we should have found someone else. Still, too late now.'

'Doesn't explain how they found the lock up though. Like you said, Zukic wouldn't have known where it was even if she recognised it when she saw it, and she shouldn't really have been able to do that. Kent must have let her walk out to his van, useless sod.'

'True. I wouldn't put it past them to drive her to every possible place though, every row of warehouses and lock up garages in Lincolnshire, especially if Knight's involved. He's a stubborn bastard, I'll give him that. He probably drove her round himself.'

'No, it was a woman with Zukic, even Richie noticed that. Surely Knight's learnt his lesson?'

'You don't know Knight.'

'And you do?'

'Well enough, and I made sure he won't forget me in a hurry.'

They laughed knowingly until Dougie's good humour was interrupted by a fit of coughing.

'Christ . . . ' He cleared his throat energetically.

'You should give up the fags you know.'

'Bernice has already got me cutting down on the booze.'

'Never thought I'd see the day. Seriously, though – Zukic. They'll have stashed her away somewhere. Any ideas?'

'I don't understand why you want her so badly.'

'Are you joking? She owes us. We gave her a place to live, a bed, a job – and not the job we originally had in mind for her either. She wouldn't have been in that van if she'd been on the heavy work and we wouldn't be having this conversation.'

'We don't want to piss her uncle off though.'

'He wants her found as much as we do. I spoke to him this afternoon.'

'What does he want to do with her?'

'Search me. Probably ship her back home and forget all about her, but he's not the one who's put his hand in his pocket for her bed and board all these months, not to mention her wages. We did her a favour, more than one, and she repays us by going snivelling to the police.'

Dougie frowned.

'She didn't have much choice though, Malc. They found her in Kent's van, they weren't just going to let her go when they knew he'd been murdered.'

'She could have played dumb.'

'Maybe she did. We don't know what she's told them. What did she really know anyway?'

'Ivona's name for one. Probably Ron's too, he was always panting after her.'

'Not Ivona's real name.'

'It's enough. It's a bloody mess, Dougie.'

'We'll never get hold of her now though.'

'They'll have to let her go someday. Unless they charge her with Kent's murder, of course. Now there's an idea.'

'Nice try, Malc.'

'Wish I did know who killed him though, he's dropped us right in it. Keep me posted. Knight will keep going forever, but as I say, they'll have to let Zukic go before long. Keep sniffing around.'

'But how? I've no idea about any safe houses.'

'You must know the right ears to have a few words in? I'll talk to a few people as well.'

'We still won't be able to just walk in and get her.'

'No, but we can keep an eye on the place and follow when she does come out. I'm not letting this one lie, Dougie.'

'I understand that.'

'And you better not let that lad of yours anywhere near. I'll send Paul up for a while, he can keep an eye on Richie, teach him a few tricks. If he's capable of learning, that is.'

Dougie bit his lip but Malc had ended the call anyway. *Bloody hell, not Paul*, Dougie thought. Arrogant and big mouthed, his cousin's son was not a person he wanted on his turf. It seemed though, as usual, that he had no choice.

40

With his purchases lined up on the coffee table, Dave Bowles sank onto the carpet, its swirls of pink and gaudy flowers clashing horribly with the burgundy sofa as always. Bowles hated this room, hated the whole flat. Even his own home was a place where he felt uncomfortable. It wasn't somewhere you could invite friends to, or a woman. Bowles thought about his last girlfriend, one of the few if he was truthful. Leanne: light brown hair, very overweight, three children. She enjoyed watching soaps and reading gossip magazines. They'd met in a pub in town when he'd gone there to watch football and have a quiet drink. He was sitting minding his own business when she'd tripped over the legs of the bar stool he was perched on, already drunk. He'd gone home with her that night, scarcely able to believe his luck. She'd paid the babysitter then marched Dave straight upstairs and into the bedroom, stripped him off and shown him exactly what she expected from him. He'd done it before of course, but never with anyone quite so . . . demanding. He'd gone to sleep in a state of bliss, then had a rude awakening the next morning as he opened his eyes to see all three of her children staring at him. He sat with them and had breakfast, toast for him, cereal for them. By the end of the meal they were calling him Uncle Dave. He'd felt a little awkward at first, but the appearance of a strange man in their mum's bed and at their breakfast table was obviously not unusual for the children and Leanne was a jolly, cheerful sort of person - she made Dave feel safe. The relationship had lasted a few weeks, but ended when an ex-boyfriend of

Leanne's, her son's father, came to the door one day begging Leanne to take him back and she'd accepted so her little boy "could know his dad". Bowles had been heartbroken. He'd hoped to move in with Leanne and be a father to her children, had even thought of suggesting him and Leanne have a baby of their own. He couldn't remember ever being happier. Of course, it hadn't lasted, the story of his life.

The whiskey bottle was in his bedroom and he couldn't face standing up again so he half crawled, half dragged himself down the corridor and found it amongst the tangled mess of his bed. Swigging from the bottle, he made his way back to the living room. There was a ball-point pen under the coffee table and he managed to tear off a piece of card big enough to write on from the box of tissues thrown on the chair. He didn't have much to say, so it didn't take long. Looking again at the razor blades, he reached instead for the first box of paracetamol. With no idea how many he would need to take, he would just keep going until . . . what? Until he was unconscious, he supposed, when he couldn't see to take anymore. He removed the foil wrapped tablets with shaking fingers and after a couple of false attempts, managed to extract two. Another slug of whiskey and he put them in his mouth. These two were for Leanne. A couple more for the boy on the moor. Four more for him. Two for Steve Kent. He was onto the second packet, which was even harder to open than the first one had been. Perhaps he should open the other packets now so they were ready, just in case. More whiskey.

All the paracetamol out on the floor now and a handful in his mouth. More whiskey, struggling to open the second bottle.

Brady stopped, sure he'd heard footsteps behind him. He turned cautiously –
no one. *Come on, Nick.* He turned back and kept walking. Footsteps again, but
he wasn't going to stop this time. A side street joined the main road and he
hurried across, not looking right or left. Another two minutes and he would be
home. It was freezing. There was no wind tonight but the air itself was biting,
the chill numbing his ears and fingers. This was his street. Halfway down the
road . . . here. He turned left and hurried down the path, reaching in his pocket
for his keys, not daring to look over his shoulder. There was a loud thud behind
him and he jumped, dropping the keys, hardly daring to turn around. Next
door's cat meowed at him. The sound had been its paws hitting the bin as it
leapt over the fence. Cursing, he unlocked the door, went inside and slammed it
shut. As he took off his coat, he realised just how fast his heart was beating.

41

The nightmare again. Knight woke abruptly, sheets sticking to his sweat-soaked body. The clock said five twenty. His breathing gradually slowed, calming him. Talking about the Hughes family was obviously a bad idea, though it seemed there was no escaping them. Knight could admit to himself, if to no one else, that he'd heard Malc Hughes had a cousin in Lincolnshire long before he applied to transfer. One day he'd be in the court that sent Hughes down.

The second whiskey bottle seemed to be empty and Bowles couldn't feel any more paracetamol as he groped around on the floor. The pen was digging into his leg, but his hand couldn't grasp it properly. He had no idea where his note was. It probably didn't matter. Who would read it anyhow? Who would find him lying here, and when? Bowles suspected it wouldn't be for weeks. The thought was comforting somehow. His head drooped even further towards the floor. One leg twitched. Not long now, surely. He waited calmly for whatever would happen next.

42

Catherine Bishop lay on her side, her head resting on her arm, feeling more relaxed than she had in weeks. Her body seemed to still be tingling, though surely it must be imagination. Her eyes were open, a small smile on her lips. There was a rustling of sheets and the muffled sounds of a person reluctantly regaining consciousness.

'Do you always wake up this early?' Claire Weyton asked, squinting at Bishop from her own pillow.

'I don't think I've been to sleep.'

'You're joking – I have. Not for long, mind.'

'I know – do you always snore?'

Claire laughed.

'Cheeky.' She snuggled into Bishop's side. 'Are you okay?'

'Never better. You?'

'Mmmm. I could have done with some more sleep though.'

'Now you're being cheeky.'

'What time is it?'

'I don't know, there's no clock in here is there?' Bishop glanced around the room, still almost in darkness.

'I just use my phone, but I've no idea where it is.' Claire leant across and switched on the bedside light, climbed out of bed and picked up a fleecy pink dressing gown covered in white hearts from the chair in the corner. Bishop grinned.

'Now that's attractive.'

Claire threw a slipper at her.

'Matching slippers too, even better.'

Laughing, Claire went over to pick up her coat which lay on the floor by the door. The rest of their clothes were piled nearby. She rummaged in a coat pocket, found nothing and picked up her bag, saying, 'Here it is. Just before six' a few seconds later.

Bishop groaned. 'I'll have to get up, I need to be in for half seven.'

Claire walked back to the bed, hands on hips.

'And I suppose you'll want to borrow clean clothes, have a shower and go and get some breakfast?'

'I suppose so.'

'Don't ask for much, do you?'

'Not really. I'm your guest though, you're supposed to wait on me.'

'Ha, you wish. I'll make you a drink but then you're on your own.'

There was a pale wood wardrobe unit along the wall opposite the bed which housed a tiny kettle and two mugs. Claire went to fill the kettle in the small bathroom that took up one corner of the room. Bishop smiled to herself. She was very tempted just to lie here, to see how long it would be until she was missed. She was far too warm and comfortable to think about moving. If she didn't think about the case, about Pollard and Kent, Kendrick and Knight, she could believe none of it existed, just for a few more minutes. With a sigh, she swung her legs over the side of the bed. No chance. She went into the bathroom where Claire was washing her face and stood behind her, slipping her arms around Claire's waist. They smiled at each other in the mirror and Claire turned in the circle of Bishop's arms to face her. They stood for a moment, Claire stooping slightly, forehead to forehead, eyes closed. Bishop hardly dared breathe.

'I'm sorry, Claire,' she whispered eventually. 'I'm going to have to go.'

Claire opened her eyes, lifted her hand to Bishop's face and stroked her cheek, smiling faintly.

'I know. I don't want you to, though.'

Bishop moved away gently.

'You go back to bed, get some more sleep. I'll have a quick shower.'

She stepped into the bath, turned on the shower and picked up Claire's shampoo. At least she could walk to the station from here.

43

Paul Hughes got out of his car and looked around. What a dump. He knew that few places looked their best in November, but Christ. Apart from the cathedral on the hill which loomed out of the mist, he could be anywhere. That would be good, anywhere but here. His dad had phoned at some stupid hour last night when he'd been in bed with Nadia to tell him to get his arse up to Lincolnshire. He'd booked into a chain hotel using a credit card associated with one of the many company names they used. Fine for staying anonymous, not so great for luxury and comfort. What his dad expected him to do up here was anyone's guess. From what he'd said last night, he didn't even know himself. Dougie's son had always been an idiot, they all knew that, and Paul could never understand why he'd been allowed into the family business at all. There must be a useful job out there for him, just not this one.

The receptionist at the hotel looked as if she'd been there all night and though she managed a smile for Paul, she didn't respond with the instant devotion he was used to. *Snooty bitch* he thought, sneering as she slid his key card over the desk. The room was as drab and impersonal as he'd expected. Back outside, he wandered towards what appeared to be the city centre. Most of the shops weren't yet open so he ducked into a fast food outlet for a quick breakfast. He was licking tomato sauce from his fingers when his mobile rang.

'Dad.'

'Are you there?'

'Got here about forty minutes ago. Not much to write home about, is it?'

'It's not bad, there are worse places. Here for one. Have you seen Dougie yet?'

'Dad, I said I got here forty minutes ago, I've not had time to scratch my arse yet.'

Paul only felt brave enough to speak to his father in that tone when they were on the phone with over a hundred miles between them. Reading his mind, Malc said, 'Don't think you're so far away that I can't come up there and kick your backside, never mind scratch it.'

'All right, I'm sorry. What do you want me to say to Dougie when I do catch up with him?'

'I want you to find out where this safe house is. I want Zukic.'

'I know that, but how do you expect me to find her?'

'Use your initiative.' The line went dead.

Paul Hughes snorted and sipped his coffee, then cursed as it scalded his mouth.

44

'You're sure Jasna Dijlas is Ivona?' Bishop said sceptically to Knight.

'She's got a record, lots of wholesome activities like running a brothel, money laundering, GBH in her younger days . . .'

'Sounds like our woman.'

'We've got a mugshot, we can take it to Milica Zukic to check.'

'How did you find her?' asked Bishop. 'I had a quick look, there was nothing.'

'Lucky guess really. I looked up women's first names used in Serbia on the internet, then checked our systems for all the ones in the age range Zukic guessed Ivona was in. There weren't many. Nothing you or Claire in Intelligence couldn't have done this morning. Although she won't be here today, of course.'

He glanced at Bishop who was silent, looking at her shoes. She knew she could have done just what Knight had, so why hadn't she thought to? Because her mind had been full of Claire Weyton. Just why she'd never allowed her personal life near her job before.

'So we can bring her in if and when Miss Zukic confirms it's the right woman?'

'The DCI and Super want us to concentrate on Pollard and Kent.'

'We're doing that as well, surely?'

'They want the case closed.'

'Don't we all. Are you going to take the mugshot to Zukic then?'

'I could always email it, quicker and safer probably. You're going to talk to the last names on the list with Anna Varcoe?'

'Yep.'

'Meet at noon then.'

Bishop watched as Knight left the room. For the first time, she'd felt uncomfortable with him, as if he somehow could tell where she'd spent the previous evening. In fact, she had a strange idea that the whole station would be able to see straight through the professional relationship she and Claire had agreed to maintain in working hours. Bishop knew she should have been able to find Jasna Dijlas as Knight had done and was grateful for the way he'd shared the information he'd discovered without making a fuss about her not finding it first. She had to concentrate, try to forget about what was happening between herself and Claire and focus on whichever Nicks and Daves remained on Varcoe's list.

Anna Varcoe was waiting, sitting at her desk but with her outdoor coat still on, takeaway coffee in hand. Bishop took a deep breath and strode over to her. Varcoe stood.

'Morning, Sarge.'

'Morning, Anna. How are you?'

'Fine, thanks.' said Varcoe, giving Bishop a curious glance.

'Good, good.' said Bishop, rubbing her hands together. She cleared her throat. 'Where are we heading first?'

Varcoe consulted her notebook.

'Other side of town, Sarge. Do you want me to drive?'

'That would be lovely.'

Bishop marched off, leaving Varcoe looking puzzled. *Lovely?*

Bishop stalked back to the car, with Varcoe hurrying after her.

'What a cocky little shit.' she said, fastening her seatbelt aggressively.

Varcoe started the engine.

'I know. All had he had to say was that he was working offshore when Pollard was killed, no need for all the fannying around.'

'We had to get the confirmation though. Anyway. On to the next one.' She consulted the list. 'David Bowles.'

'And he lives . . . ?'

Bishop gave the address. 'Just around the corner. I knew there was method in the madness.'

They arrived at the house in less than five minutes. Varcoe's face showed exactly what she thought of the place – not a lot.

'What a bloody dump.' she grumbled, carefully stepping over a half eaten kebab that had been dropped on the pavement as she climbed out of the car. Bishop couldn't disagree. It seemed Bowles lived in the top half of a crumbling semi midway down the street. The front gate stood half attached to its post. It had once been white but now was a dirty grey. A dingy lawn was surrounded by litter filled borders. A few evergreens struggled on but failed to make an impression. No doubt in a different season, weeds would be rampant. A pile of black dustbin liners were piled at one side of the lawn. Some had been ripped open by cats or vermin and their contents were strewn across a patch of grass – chicken bones, pizza crusts, some mouldy slices of bread. A clear plastic bag bulged with beer cans, a few takeaway boxes and some wine bottles.

'At least they're trying to recycle.' Bishop said.

'Yes but taking it further than the garden would help.'

They approached the front door. There were two doorbells, one labelled 14, the other 14a.

'It's 14a.' Bishop announced. 'What's the betting neither bell works?'

Varcoe shrugged. She pressed the bell for 14a firmly, then wiped her hand on her trousers. Bishop grinned and nudged her.

'Haven't you brought some antibacterial spray?'

'If the inside's anything like the garden, we'll need biohazard suits.'

They stood for a few seconds, then Bishop pressed the doorbell again.

'Come on, you lazy sod.'

'He's probably seen us through the window, he'll be hiding behind the settee.'

'He'll be lucky to see anything through those windows. Anyway, do we look like bailiffs?'

'Not sure I've ever seen one.'

There was still no movement behind the dull panes of glass that were set into the front door.

'Right, I've had enough.'

Bishop pressed the doorbell for number 14 instead, holding it down for a good thirty seconds with her thumb. There was no response for a minute or so, then they heard footsteps and keys jangling.

'Bingo.' muttered Bishop, warrant card at the ready.

The door was wrenched open by a stocky, unshaven man wearing boxer shorts and a well worn T shirt that had originally come free with a case of cheap beer, judging by its logo. His hair was a mess, his eyes bloodshot. He looked the two women up and down.

'Who the hell are you?'

Bishop eyed him back. She held up her warrant card but he was too busy rubbing his face to notice it.

'Detective Sergeant Bishop and Detective Constable Varcoe. We're here to see Mr Bowles.'

The man scratched violently at his hair. Varcoe grimaced and took a step back.

'Bowles? You mean Dave upstairs?'

'Yes, 14a.'

'Why didn't you ring his bloody bell then?'

'We did, he didn't answer. Do you know if he's in?'

'He's always in, except when he creeps off to the corner shop.'

'Can you let us through then please?'

'If it means I can get back to bed I will with pleasure, I'm at work in a few hours.'

'Thank you, Mr . . . '

'Munroe. I suppose I should ask for some ID first, shouldn't I? You don't look like thieving types, but you never know.'

Bishop showed him her warrant card again and he stepped back, allowing them to follow.

'When did you last see Mr Bowles?'

'Yesterday morning. He was coming down the stairs as I came in. I said hello but he scuttled off like a frightened rabbit as usual.'

'Not very chatty then?'

'Dave? I don't think he's ever had a chat with anyone except himself. He's a bit odd, you know? Very quiet though.'

'The sort of person you want living above you then really?'

'I suppose so. I never thought I'd end up in a place like this, I've got a nice house a couple of miles away but the wife's moved her fancy man in and I'm stuck in this hole. Landlord keeps telling me he's going to get a bloke round, clear out the garden and do some repairs but he never does. Still, it's cheap and that's what I need these days.'

'Mmmm.' agreed Bishop, moving towards the stairs. 'Well, thank you, Mr Munroe.'

Munroe took the hint and wandered back towards the open door of his own part of the house, calling 'Tell Dave to answer his door in future.' as he went.

Bishop kept walking, Varcoe close behind.

A tiny landing had been created at the top of the stairs and there was a flimsy looking door with '14a' painted on it in wonky black letters. Paint had dripped between the numbers. The place was starting to get to Bishop, and she thumped on the door.

'Mr Bowles? Open up, please, it's the police.' Silence. She hammered again. 'Mr Bowles? Police!'

Varcoe said, 'This is starting to look bad.'

Bishop nodded, pulling a pair of nitrile gloves from her bag and slipping them on before passing a pair to Anna. Bishop reached out and tried the door handle. It moved easily, unlocked. Cautiously, Bishop stepped forward. The door opened onto a short hallway with three other doors leading off it, two open, one closed. Bishop felt the skin on her arms prickle. The place smelt musty, damp. The carpet underfoot was stained and worn with years of the dirt of everyday life trodden in to it. After bellowing Bowles' name a few more times, Bishop gave up. Glancing left and right, she headed for one of the open doors, her stomach a knot.

'Bathroom.' she said to Varcoe, who leaned around her to have a look.

'Christ.'

The bathroom was in desperate need of a clean, if not fumigation. The doors of the cabinet above the sink hung open. Bishop peered at a couple of packets of condoms that had seemingly fallen out of it onto the floor.

'Even I've got some newer than those.'

Varcoe laughed, then wrinkled her nose.

'Looks like vomit in the sink, Sarge.'

'If you say so, Anna. I'd never have taken you for someone who vomits in bathroom sinks.'

She blushed.

'You'd be surprised.'

'I'd be amazed. He's not in here anyway, so where next?'

Varcoe led the way to the next open door, hesitantly poking her head around to see inside.

'Bedroom. He's not in there either.'

The room was almost filled by a double bed with a coverless duvet screwed into a ball thrown on it. One pillow was on the floor, the other still on the bed, bearing the imprint of a head. Reluctantly, Bishop sniffed the air.

'Smells like . . . '

'Whiskey.'

'I'll be changing my opinion of you at this rate, Anna.'

'My dad used to drink a lot of it.' Varcoe said, her face expressionless. Bishop touched her arm gently, then stepped away.

'He must be in the other room if he's here at all.'

They went back down the short hallway and approached the closed door. Bishop glanced at Varcoe, who shrugged. Swallowing, Bishop eased the door open.

'Oh, yes, he's here, get an ambulance, Anna.'

Hurrying forward, Bishop dropped to the prone man's side. There was more vomit here, a pool of it on the sofa, another by his head. Bishop found a pulse but it seemed weak. Two huge empty whiskey bottles caught her eye and foil packets that had contained tablets were strewn across the floor. On the coffee table, its surface pitted with scratches and stained with spilt food, a torn piece of card was covered in spidery scribble. Bishop leant forward, trying to make out what it said:

"I'm not going to wait for him to come to get me like he did Craig and Steve. I know I won't be missed and I'm sorry for causing any trouble. I'm sorry for it all."

Bishop looked down at the figure on the floor. 'Hang on, David.' she said softly. Varcoe reappeared.

'Ambulance is on its way, Sarge.' Sharp eyes scanned the room. 'No prizes for guessing what's happened here then.'

Bishop got to her feet, knees cracking.

'No prizes.'

Varcoe spied the card covered in handwriting.

'Suicide note?'

'Something like that. Will you go downstairs and wait for the paramedics please? I don't want to rely on Munroe, we'll probably all be dead of old age by the time he lets them in, never mind Mr Bowles here. I better let DI Knight know.'

Varcoe nodded and left the room again. Bishop took out her phone.

'Hello, sir. We've found David Bowles and it's looking like he's definitely involved.'

45

After asking Bishop to travel with Bowles to the hospital and Varcoe to go on to the next name on her list, Knight sent Sullivan out to meet Varcoe and accompany her. The stakes had just been raised even higher. Not only did they now have two murdered men, they had a suicide attempt by someone who could potentially be either killer or victim. From what Bishop had said about the note she had found with Bowles, he seemed more likely to be a victim. If he had killed the others though, wouldn't he have admitted as much in a note he had only expected to be read after his death? Knight didn't know. He'd never claimed to understand how people's minds worked. It was now more important than ever that they track down 'Nick', though again, they had no way of knowing whether he was the killer or another potential victim. Either way he had to be found, and fast. Knight trudged towards the lair of DCI Kendrick. This case got more complicated by the hour.

Paul Hughes was meeting Dougie for what he called lunch. Dougie called it dinner. Paul hadn't been expecting much of the food in a pub miles from anywhere called 'The Lamb', but his steak was perfectly cooked, the chips chunky and crisp, the salad as fresh as if it had just been picked. Dougie picked at a dish of lasagne. Paul gestured at it with his knife.

'Something wrong with your meal?'

'It's not that, the food's always fantastic here, that's why I come. It's quiet in the week too and they leave you alone. It's manic at the weekend.'

Paul speared another mouthful of steak with his fork.

'So what's the problem?'

'It's this obsession your dad has with Milica Zukic. How does he expect us to get her back?'

'No idea. I was hoping you could tell me.'

'The police have her. Wherever she is now, it's not going to be somewhere you can just wander in and take her by the hand.'

'Pity Richie screwed up when he had the chance to grab her then, isn't it?'

Dougie closed his eyes briefly.

'We're agreed on that. He said she fought like a lunatic.'

'Any excuse. From what I remember, she's as skinny as anything, not to mention she was sitting in a car. How much could she struggle?'

'I don't know. I'm not defending him.'

'Sounds like it to me.'

'The point is, we've not got a hope.'

Paul finished his meal and wiped his mouth, setting his cutlery neatly on the empty plate.

'Dad said Knight's in charge?'

'We think so.'

'So he'll be going to see her. We can follow him and find her that way.'

'Why would he? They must have given her a phone, it's not like she's under arrest.'

'How do you know? She could be sitting in a cell somewhere, not many places safer than that.'

'What would the charges be?'

'Apart from coming into the country illegally?'

'She didn't know that.'

'Didn't she? Anyway, I don't want to be the one who has to tell Dad we've failed, do you?'

'But it's impossible, he must see that, you must see it. Trying to snatch a witness from police protection? Come on, Paul.'

The waiter was hovering a few tables away and came to take their plates when Dougie nodded to him. Both men refused pudding but accepted coffee.

'I know it'll be . . . difficult.'

'Difficult?' snorted Dougie.

Paul studied the tablecloth and then met Dougie's eyes, a crafty smile flickering over his face.

'Maybe we don't need to actually grab her.'

'What do you mean?'

'I don't think my dad's ever seen her.'

'How do you work that out? He told me how much she weighed.'

'Doesn't mean he's seen her, Ron or someone could have told him that. I can take any girl back to him, give her a few quid to pretend she's Zukic. Dad will rant and rave and then let her go. He wouldn't hurt her, not the niece of the big boss. When the real Zukic goes free, she'll be on the first plane back to Serbia and if she's got any sense, she won't set foot in the UK again. It'll work.'

Dougie shook his head.

'No way, Paul. There's no chance I'm getting involved in a scheme to pull the wool over Malc's eyes. He'd kill me.'

'He'll never find out.'

'He will, I know him.'

'So do I and I'm telling you . . . '

'I'm telling you no.'

Paul stood, towering over Dougie.

'What do you think you can do about it?'

He turned and marched out, leaving a grim faced Dougie with two cups of espresso and the bill.

46

Bishop had to admit that there was something fascinating about a celebrity wedding. How people with so much money could be so utterly tasteless was beyond her. The magazine was well thumbed; other people must share her grudging interest in the lives of the rich and famous. She would never buy one but she couldn't help picking the magazines up when she encountered them in hairdresser's salons or in poky waiting rooms such as this one. There was a water cooler in one corner of the room and she went over, filled a plastic cup from the dispenser and took a sip. Warm. Wrinkling her nose, she forced the rest of it down, not able to remember the last time she'd had a drink. Probably tea with Claire that morning. She was trying not to think about Claire, but it was almost impossible. She took out her phone, and sure enough there was a text from her: Wish you were here x Their night together had been everything she'd imagined it would be, but the text she'd received that morning from Louise had been a shock: Working late? Sitting in the pub with some woman don't you mean, holding hands, cuddling up and leaving together? Don't bother contacting me again, Catherine. You can post my clothes back. Bishop had no idea how she had found out, perhaps one of her friends had been in the pub, but it meant Louise was hurt and Bishop had never wanted to do that, it wasn't what she deserved. Sleeping with two different people in the same week wasn't usually Catherine's idea of acceptable behaviour, but her present situation was anything but normal. She was only glad there had been no more bodies, no more messages cryptically pointing in her direction. Finding David Bowles in a pool of his own vomit had been a shock too. She'd seen much worse in her career of course, but this case was beginning to affect her as no other had done. The messages, the photograph, then the discovery of Milica Zukic and her story . . . it was like a nightmare. Her only hope was to see this case solved, only then would she feel safe to go back to her own home. There seemed no hope of understanding what motivated the killer until he was caught and could tell them himself.

Bishop turned at the sound of soft footsteps. A man entered the room, white coat, weary expression. A doctor. *You should be a detective.*

'You're Sergeant Bishop? You found Mr Bowles?'

'Yes. How is he?'

The doctor passed a hand across his brow.

'He's had a lot of whiskey, plenty of tablets. We're doing all we can.'

'At least he's alive, I'd thought . . . well, I'd thought he might not recover.'

The doctor nodded.

'I know he looked bad but we're fairly confident he'll make a full recovery.'

'I'll need to speak to my boss. He'll probably want a guard with Mr Bowles.'

'A guard? Is he suspected of a crime?'

'It's complicated.'

With a rueful smile, the doctor said, 'Most things are in here.'

'Is there a place I can use my mobile?'

'Follow me, you can use the phone in my office.'

For the second time that day a neighbour had come to the rescue. Varcoe and Sullivan had hammered on the door of the terraced house that Nicholas Brady rented until the woman next door had wandered out to tell them he'd gone out early that morning and she'd not seen him come back in. When they asked for a work address, she said she'd heard from his aunt he'd been made redundant again so who knew where he'd been rushing off to earlier? After some persuading, she invited them in while she called Brady's aunt to see if she had any ideas.

They went back to the car with Brady's mum's address.

'Worth a try.' Sullivan commented, rejoining the traffic.

'I think it's called clutching at straws.'

'She might be able to help.'

'Maybe so, but why would his mum know where he'd gone? Do you tell your mum your every move?'

'No, but she'd probably like me to. Brady could be a proper mummy's boy.'

'He could also be lying somewhere with his head smashed in.'

Sullivan glanced at her.

'Do you think so?'

'The way it's going, I wouldn't be surprised. Bowles could be our man, he could have had a fit of remorse after killing three of his old mates and decided he should be next, then chucked a load of tablets down his throat.'

Sullivan indicated and turned right.

'I thought you said the note he left sounded as if he was scared of someone?'

'It did, but he could have been trying to throw us off the scent.'

'I think you've been watching too many films.' Sullivan said, shaking his head. 'Convenient if it was Bowles though. Case closed.'

'Too easy, we wouldn't be that lucky.'

'If he dies, we may never know.'

The rest of the journey passed in silence. Sullivan parked on the side of a road that was terraced houses on one side, bungalows the other. They approached the Brady's bungalow and the door opened immediately.

'You'll be the police? I'm Helen Brady. Come in, my sister phoned and said you were on your way.'

They followed her into a homely kitchen with wooden units and the smell of baking filling the air. Sullivan sniffed appreciatively.

'Fairy cakes. They're not ready yet, but I can offer you a drink? Tea, coffee?'

'No, thank you.' Varcoe and Sullivan chorused.

'Mrs Brady, have you heard from your son Nicholas today?' Varcoe asked.

'Nick? No, not today. Why? Is he okay?'

'We're investigating the deaths of two men we think may have been friends of your son when he was younger and we need to speak to him. Have you any idea where he could be?' Sullivan tried to keep the urgency out of his voice, but it wasn't easy.

'Do you mean Craig Pollard and the other one, somebody Kent wasn't it? Nick did know them, he told me that. He was quite upset about it. You don't think he's in danger?' She moved to the kitchen table and picked up a mobile phone. 'I'll ring him.' She listened intently, her expression becoming panicked. 'It says the number's unavailable, what does that mean? It's never said that before.'

'It means his phone's switched off, or he's in a place without a signal.' Varcoe tried to ignore the feeling of dread that was crawling through her.

'He's never switched his phone off before, why would he? What would be the point? Even when he's been fishing on some lake in the middle of nowhere I've been able to reach him. Something must have happened, can't you go and find him?'

Wordlessly, Varcoe stepped out of the room leaving Sullivan trying to placate Mrs Brady. She called Knight, who agreed it was imperative Brady was found and said he would put an alert out. He wanted Sullivan and Varcoe back at the station and they eventually managed to extricate themselves from Mrs Brady who had luckily been distracted by the smell of burning coming from inside her oven. With a squeal, she leapt over to retrieve the ruined cakes, leaving the two detectives to make their escape after promising to keep her informed. She was making a breathless phone call to her husband as they closed the door behind them.

47

Nick Brady still couldn't shake the feeling that he was being followed. Even
here, out in the wilds, he could feel eyes watching. He kept telling himself he
was imagining it, that he should relax and enjoy the views but it wasn't that
easy. The bleakness of the moor, especially at this time of year, suited his mood.
Memories filled his head; the heat of the sun on his back as they walked, the
casual boasting, the teasing, the cans of lager Craig had brought that had grown
steadily warmer but were still so welcome when they eventually sat on the bank
side. Brady didn't want to remember any more. He stood lost in the past, eyes
searching the opposite bank for the exact location. This was the spot, he
thought. There should be a marker, a shrine, but there was only pale grass, mud
and the ever moving water.

A figure approached slowly, stealthily. Brady didn't turn.

48

Knight ran his hands across his face. David Bowles was still unconscious, Nicholas Brady was missing, journalists were circling and Kendrick and Stringer were on the warpath. The only bright spot in the day so far had been Milica Zukic's confirmation that Jasna Dijlas was indeed the Ivona she'd known. Since Knight had been told to rein himself in on the people trafficking case until the killer of Pollard and Kent had been found, he could do nothing with the information. It frustrated Knight, but he understood. The Hughes family had been under surveillance more times than Knight could count, yet still they were free to do more or less as they pleased. Knight wanted to be sure that when he brought the empire down, it would be destroyed for good and that would take time, patience and cunning. He'd been accused before of being obsessed with Malc Hughes, of allowing the fierce desire to bring him to justice to cloud his judgment and blind him to the facts. Knight had to grudgingly admit that there was some truth in the claim. He still bore the scars of his previous attempts to teach Hughes a lesson and had no desire to repeat his mistakes.

Bishop tapped gently on his open office door, came in and sat down.

'That's what you call an interesting morning.' she said.

'We've still not found Nicholas Brady.'

'We will.'

'Hopefully he'll be in one piece when we do.'

'You don't think . . . '

'Who knows? He's the last on the list and he's disappeared.'

'Bowles thought he was next.'

'We need Bowles to wake up and start talking. His note confirms the link between him, Pollard and Kent and he seems to know who would want to kill them.'

'Bowles could have killed them both, of course.'

'So could Brady.'

49

Nick Brady heard a small noise behind him that broke his reverie and half turned. He was too late. The first blow struck him before he could fully register the figure he had glimpsed. The second fell just as he hit the ground, the churned mud where he'd been standing splattering the side of his face. Brady was still aware of the figure standing over him, the black coat with the hood drawn tightly around the face. Narrowed eyes stared down at him. He couldn't read their expression – fear certainly, apprehension, triumph? He thought so. A black scarf blanked the other features so he could gain no clues from the mouth. A satisfied smile, a grimace, a snarl? Surprisingly, he felt no pain. The figure bent closer, raising its arms again.

'Please . . . ' Brady mumbled.

Brady didn't see the weapon but he felt the impact and this time agony, light exploding in his skull, eyes losing focus, blackness. Again, his attacker bent over him, waiting. Seconds passed, the only movement the rustling of the wind through bare branches and the murky water of the stream just in front of them. Then, a flash of white as a dog came racing up out of nowhere, barking excitedly. There was a distant shout as the dog's owner lost sight of it. The black hood turned towards the sound. No time for the check, just a second to shove the laminated paper under Brady's mud clogged boot and then run. The dog, frenzied now, kept barking and racing around Brady's body, pawing at his legs. Eventually its owner, a broad shouldered man in his sixties, arrived at the scene out of breath and red-faced. His eyes widened at the sight of the man on the floor.

'Oh, Christ.' he said, pulling his phone out of his coat pocket.

The call came through to Knight as he was still discussing the case with Catherine Bishop. She watched his face as he listened intently to what was being said, thanked the caller and softly replaced the receiver.

'Good news is, we've found Nicholas Brady.'

'And the bad news?'

'He's unconscious. Come on.'

He was up and out of his chair, Bishop rushing after him.

'How do you mean, unconscious?'

'He was found out on the moors, he's been smacked over the head but looks like our man's dropped a clanger. Brady was still breathing when he left him.'

'Disturbed then?'

'Possibly, though he had enough time to leave his message.'

'Catherine of Aragon again?'

'Exactly the same.'

Bishop shuddered.

'Who found him?'

'Bloke walking his dog. What would we do without dog walkers? The dog got to Brady first and barked its head off. The problem is there's no phone signal up there, so the man who found him had to leave Brady for twenty minutes before he could actually ring for help. They got the air ambulance to him and he's now in the same hospital as David Bowles.'

'So we need one of them to wake up soon. Unbelievable. Did the man that found Brady see his attacker?'

'Doesn't sound like it.'

'Typical.'

50

The journey to the hospital was quiet. Bishop was valiantly trying to keep her mind on the case, on Bowles, Brady, Kent and Pollard, but Claire kept creeping in. Bishop wondered if she'd gone back to bed, if she was lying there now, catching up on her sleep. Perhaps she was watching TV wearing the fleece dressing gown and slippers, sipping tea and eating biscuits. Bishop forced herself to concentrate. The attack on Brady was again causing them to rethink. Bowles could have killed Pollard and Kent then tried to take his own life in a fit of remorse, but he couldn't have attacked Brady. Brady could also have been the murderer, but obviously hadn't hit himself over the head. Who the hell was leaving the pictures and posting the photos? Why? She felt the creeping sensation along her arms and the back of her neck again. Knight's face was grim, his jaw tight. Bishop checked her phone and found another text from Claire. Thinking of you. See you later? xx Bishop quickly typed Definitely xx

They arrived at the hospital's main gates, Knight swung the car into the nearest place approximating a parking space he could find and they hurried into the building. One look at their warrant cards and expressions was all the receptionist needed to give precise instructions as to where Nicholas Brady could be found. His mother was with him, his father on his way. A uniformed officer nodded as they approached, recognising them. As they rounded the corner onto the ward, Brady's mother glanced up from her seat at his bedside. She stood, still gripping her son's hand.

'Let me guess,' she said, glaring at them. 'you're the police? Well, you're too late. I told the other two earlier it wasn't like Nick to turn his phone off and now look at him. Why didn't you find him before? Why wasn't he warned? I told him to be careful. I was only joking, but it seems I was right.'

Knight and Bishop exchanged a glance. Bishop stepped forward.

'Can I get you a drink, Mrs Brady?'

'I don't want a bloody drink, I want to know why my son's lying here!' Tears started to fall. 'I'm sorry. Tea, please. Tea will be fine. No sugar.'

Bishop nodded and left the room.

'Are you close to your son?' Knight asked gently.

'Yes. He's just been made redundant, so he was spending more time at our house. I think he wanted to be looked after a little, if you know what I mean, made to feel everything would work out in the end.'

She attempted a smile.

'Did your son mention Craig Pollard and Steven Kent to you?'

'I saw about Craig Pollard's death and mentioned it to Nick because I vaguely remembered the name. Nick had known him years ago, then when Steven Kent's death was in the paper, Nick said he'd known him too. It upset him, I could tell. That's when I told Nick to be careful. Turns out I was right.'

'Was Nick at school with Craig Pollard then?'

'Different years, but they knew each other. They were quite matey for a while, but Nick eventually stopped mentioning Craig. We weren't sorry, to be honest. I know he's dead but Craig Pollard wasn't the sort of person you'd want your son to be friends with.'

'Why not?'

'Haven't you talked to people that knew him? Full of himself, bad mannered, rude. Not above stealing either.'

'Did Nick and Craig argue?'

'He didn't say so. I'm not sure what happened, his dad and I kept telling him Pollard was no good but I don't think that's what did it.'

'Did you ever hear him mention the name David Bowles?'

Bishop slipped unobtrusively back into the room and offered a mug to Mrs Brady, who took it with a watery smile.

'A proper cup, I could only get plastic. Thank you. Sorry, what did you say?'

'Did Nick ever talk about a friend called David Bowles?' Knight repeated. Mrs Brady frowned.

'Bowles? Not that I remember. It's a while ago though, you understand. He might not have mentioned a surname anyway, he didn't always.'

'You know Nick was found on the moor, Laughton Moor? Do you have any idea why he might have been up there?'

'None at all. He used to like fishing when he was younger, he went with his dad a few times but I don't think they fish up there do they? It's the wrong time of year to be sitting fishing all day anyway. He didn't like bird watching or walking or any of that. I really don't know.'

Knight seemed lost in thought and so Bishop took over.

'You can confirm that Nick knew Steven Kent too?'

'Oh yes, he told me so himself.'

A nurse bustled over, telling Knight and Bishop they'd have to leave as the doctor was on her way. Knight protested that they wanted to speak to the doctor too, but the nurse wouldn't hear of it, telling him they would have to wait outside.

They made their way instead to David Bowles' bedside and stood looking down at him, pale and thin.

'The nurse told me he should be awake before too long.' said Bishop.

'Good. We need one of them to be and Bowles is looking the most promising at the moment.'

The uniformed PC in the corner shuffled his feet, eager for his shift babysitting Bowles to be over.

'We should get back to Brady and see if we can talk to the doctor since it doesn't seem Mr Bowles here is up to being interviewed just yet.'

A tall woman wearing a white coat was still bending over Brady when they approached, but the nurse wasn't in sight. The doctor turned at their footsteps and Knight introduced himself, the woman taking a cursory glance at his proffered ID.

'You'll want to know when he'll wake up so you can question him?'

'In an ideal world, but I doubt you'll be able to tell us.' said Knight.

'You're right, I'm afraid. No idea. Hours, a few days?'

'Not long term then?'

'I wouldn't say so, but I wouldn't say it was impossible either. I just don't know. I'll tell you the same thing I told his mother, he'll wake in his own time.'

'Thanks.' said Knight miserably.

Back in the corridor, Bishop suggested a quick drink in the hospital's cafe and Knight trailed after her like a scolded schoolboy, seemingly unsure of what to do next. They found a quiet corner and Knight sipped at his coffee.

'We know there's a link between them. Brady's mother confirms Brady knew Pollard, Kent and Bowles, which means we need Pollard's family and Kent's sister to tell us if they ever spoke about Brady and Bowles, or if any of them can remember anything that will help us. I think we can discount Bowles and Brady as our murderer, which means there's another person who also knew or knows them all. That person could be what links the four of them, or they may know what the link is. This is what we've been missing all along.'

'I'll phone Anna Varcoe, get her and the others onto Pollard's parents and Jodie Kent. They were still trying to trace Bowles' family.' She paused, frowning. 'It's bothering me why Brady was up on the moor.'

'Me too. It's not the sort of place you'd go for a wander, not in November. Perhaps he was trying to clear his head, get away from people.'

'He obviously didn't believe he was under threat though. Bowles seems to have been terrified according to the note he left, but Brady goes off by himself into the loneliest place around here.'

'And meets our man.'

'Do you think it was deliberate? That he was lured there somehow?'

'It would explain why he would go there out of the blue. His mother seems to know his habits and walking on the moors isn't one of them.'

'Varcoe said the neighbour told them Brady had gone out very early.'

'It's possible. His mobile was left with him, unlike Pollard and Kent. That could be handy, let's check the calls he's made and received lately. We need to get into his house too.'

'I'll find out where his possessions are. It'll be interesting to know what he was wearing when he was found too, see if he was kitted out in walking gear or jeans and a jacket. His mum can't know everything.'

Knight drained his cup. 'I'm going to see what Mr Ellis can tell us.'

'Ellis?'

'He found Brady. I've got his address, it's not far. You stick around here, talk to Brady's dad, see if he can remember more than his wife. Keep going back to Bowles and giving him a pinch too.'

Ray Ellis lived in a tidy bungalow on a quiet side street. He opened the door to Knight himself, perfectly composed. As he followed Ellis down a long hallway and into an airy kitchen, Knight reflected that he didn't seem the type of man to allow himself to become flustered. Ellis told Knight he'd been a lorry driver and that he and his wife spent as much time as possible travelling now he was retired.

'You'd think I'd be sick of being on the road but we sold our house, bought this place and a camper van and we can do as we please.'

'Sounds good to me.' said Knight, accepting another cup of coffee. He couldn't really complain about insomnia when he drank this much of the stuff. Ellis sat, placing his own mug on the dining table in front of him.

'I didn't expect a detective inspector to turn up, more a young lad still wet behind the ears.'

'I wanted to talk to you myself. You're the first real witness we have.'
Ellis sighed.

'I wouldn't call myself a witness, I just saw him on the ground. It's Alfie who's the witness but you won't get much out of him.'

'Alfie's the dog?'

'That's right. My wife's taken him for a walk, she thought he'd be best out of the way. He gets a bit excited around visitors.'

'So what can you tell me, Mr Ellis?'
Ellis spread his hands helplessly.

'Not much, I'm afraid. I took the route I always do, ending up alongside the stream. It's more than a stream really, not a river but quite wide. I walk back along it to the road. Anyway, Alfie had run ahead a little but I could still see him so I didn't worry. He usually comes back when you call. I was wandering along when he started barking and ran off. I shouted, but this time he didn't come back and he kept yapping. I couldn't see him, I just followed the noise. I could see the man on the ground from quite a way off and ran to him. When I saw he was still breathing, I got out my phone but there wasn't a signal. I didn't want to leave him, but I didn't have much choice so I put him into the recovery position, covered him with my coat and then went as fast as I could back towards the road. I thought even if I didn't get a signal before I reached the car, at least I'd be able to drive for help. That's about it I'm afraid.'

'You didn't see anyone?'

'No. He could have been lying there for hours for all I know. How is he, by the way?'

'Still unconscious. I don't think he's in any danger, the doctor seems confident he'll recover.'

'Would you mind keeping me informed please? I know it's a lot to ask, but I just feel responsible somehow. I know I didn't do it, but finding him like that . . . I'd just like to know he's okay.'

'I can understand that. I'll make sure you're kept up to date.'

'Thank you.'

'Were there any other cars parked near yours?'

'No, none. I didn't see another soul except the lad on the ground.'

Knight thanked Ellis and left. He wasn't sure why he'd thought Ellis might be able to give him a clue as to who they were searching for. Wishful thinking, probably. He phoned Bishop from his car and asked her to find out if Brady drove. He sat for a moment, eyes fixed on his rear view mirror. The same car had appeared there a few times now and Knight was sure it wasn't coincidence. He hadn't seen the driver yet, but couldn't think who would follow him. The old panic was threatening to bubble to the surface and Knight fought it as best he could. The car was no longer in sight. Knight smiled wryly. Had he imagined it? He opened the door and got out, went around to the rear of the car, rummaged around in the boot for a few seconds then slammed it shut and discreetly glanced around. The only person in sight was an elderly lady hauling a couple of bags of shopping. Knight climbed back into his car feeling silly.

In the next street, Paul Hughes watched the junction at the top of the road intently. He'd been following Knight all morning and it hadn't been very productive so far, but he didn't want to miss his quarry. He knew Knight was in the middle of a murder investigation but he'd only been to the hospital and some bungalow so far today, neither of which helped Hughes with his quest. The bungalow certainly didn't look like a safe house, not that Hughes had ever seen one. He imagined it would be a top floor flat with hundreds of bolts on the doors and windows, at least one armed guard and cameras everywhere. Hughes wasn't sure what he was going to do if Knight didn't lead him to the safe house soon. Then again, he had no idea what he was going to do if Knight *did* lead him to the safe house. His dad had been on the phone again nagging at him and there were only so many excuses Malc Hughes would listen to before he exploded. Paul knew his dad had always had a grudging respect for Knight, though why he couldn't say. He'd never seemed to have achieved anything particularly amazing to Paul, either before or after the night in the garage. Still, the way Knight had picked himself up and moved North to seemingly start again was impressive, even Paul Hughes had to admit that. He'd seen people go completely to pieces after an evening in one of his dad's lockups. There was Knight's car. Hughes eased out of his parking space and followed.

51

I've been forced into a mistake and I promised myself that would never happen. I shouldn't have followed Brady there, I wasn't properly prepared and seeing one of them in that place . . . I couldn't help myself. Even if a car full of police officers had been watching, I would still have done it. I'm not even sure Brady is dead since that stupid bloody dog turned up. Where there's a dog, there must be an owner. It had a collar on and looked well fed, so I doubt it was a stray. At least I had time to leave the message. Brady might still survive though and all I can hope is that he can give no proper description. I wasn't wearing the suit, it would have made me too conspicuous and I didn't really intend to do it then, I just wanted to see what he was doing, if he was really going back there. He could have gone there often, I don't know. He might feel some guilt. None of the others seemed to, but he might. He should do. In my eyes, they're all as guilty as each other. My message was there and surely it will all be linked together in the end, even if I have to spell it out myself in words of one syllable. Bowles is next, the last. Little Dave Bowles. It will have to be soon. I need to find out what has happened to Brady. There's been nothing in the news yet, though it's early. If he's dead, it will be made public soon enough.

52

Bishop skulked around the hospital, waiting for her phone to ring. Brady's father hadn't been able to add anything to his wife's answers to their questions. Brady had a driving licence they'd told her, but hadn't owned a car since his last one failed its MOT and was deemed not worth repairing. It was languishing on a garage forecourt nearby, hopefully to be sold for parts. Bishop hated waiting around and wanted to be busy but Knight had again asked her to stay at the hospital. She wasn't even sure why. She was a DS, surely there was more she could be doing than killing time here? She could speak to neither Brady nor Bowles. Brady's parents had taken both the chairs near their son's bed and hadn't offered her one of their boiled sweets. Feeling a little sorry for herself, Bishop made yet another trip to the hospital cafe, ordered a cappuccino for a change and settled back in her chair. Claire answered on the first ring.

'Catherine?'

'I just wanted to give you a call.'

'I wasn't expecting to hear from you, I thought you'd be too busy.'

'I'm having a bit of a break.'

'Where are you? It doesn't sound like the station.'

'No, I'm . . . I'm out. We've had a few developments.'

'Really?'

'Yes, I'm just waiting around while we follow up a few leads.'

'Can't you come back and wait around with me?'

'I'd love to. Not sure DI Knight would agree though.'

'We will meet up later? If you can?'

'Definitely.'

There was a pause.

'I really enjoyed last night, you know.' Claire said softly.

'I did too. Claire, I'm really sorry, I'm going to have to go, I'm expecting some calls. I just wanted to say hello.'

'I'm glad you did. I'll see you later then.'

Bishop sat smiling to herself.

53

Kendrick was pacing. Knight was surprised to see the dark blue carpet tiles in his office didn't have a path worn through them.

'You're telling me we've still no suspect?'

'We've lots of suspects, it's narrowing them down that we're struggling with. We've still nothing on Mike Pollard, Kelly Whitcham, anyone.' said Knight. Kendrick rounded on him.

'That's right, Inspector, make a joke. It's just the time to try to be funny. Christ, you've been telling me the same thing since Pollard was killed. Following leads, questioning people and here we are, days later and all you've got to show for your efforts is another dead body and two of his mates flat on their backs in the hospital. Not exactly Sherlock Holmes, are you?'

'I never said I was. You know as well as I do that this case was never going to be easy.'

'Have we made any progress at all? That's what the Super's going to want to know and that's what the press will be asking. It's only a matter of time before Bowles' suicide attempt and the attack on Brady are front page news. We've had some calls already.'

'Only to be expected.'

Kendrick exploded.

'For God's sake Jonathan, do you actually care that this whole investigation is well on its way to becoming a national joke? We'll probably be held up as an example of how not to run a murder enquiry to new recruits. If you came up here to resurrect your career, you've a strange way of going about it.'

Knight's eyes narrowed.

'I wasn't aware my career needed "resurrecting", as you put it. I came here as a transfer, not a demotion.'

'Come on, I bet you thought life up here would be a piece of piss compared to London. Well, you were wrong. You've been thrown in at the deep end and it seems to me that at the moment you're struggling to stay afloat.'

Staring at him, Knight got to his feet. *Does anyone really talk like that?* he thought. Kendrick sighed, gestured to Knight to sit back down. When he spoke again, his voice was soft.

'I know this case is a bastard. These messages that have been left . . . I don't see what they're supposed to tell us. That's probably the point. Either way, you know how it is. The Super's on at me for progress because she's being pressured from higher up and the press are haranguing everyone. We've got nothing to show for all our man hours, we've uncovered a people trafficking gang that we've so far no chance of breaking and to top it off, somehow we've got mixed up with the Hughes family, which isn't where we want to be. We need to close this case soon before the whole force becomes a laughing stock.'

'I know that.'

'Catherine Bishop?'

'She's fine, coping well.' Knight had his own ideas about what Bishop had been up to, but he wasn't going to share them with Kendrick.

'We're expecting Bowles at least to be ready to talk soon?'

'Hopefully.'

'I'll want an update later on.'

Knight realised he was dismissed. As he left Kendrick's office and headed to his own, he stopped by a window that gave a view over the street below. It was a grey day, murky and miserable. Through the gloom, Knight could see the car that he'd thought was following him earlier. He could even make out a figure in the driver's seat, but as the car was parallel parked there was no chance of seeing the number plate. His usual caution deserting him, Knight strode down the stairs and out into the car park. Taking the narrow path between the police station and the old post office building next door led him back onto the street, just behind the car. Stepping back into the alleyway, he gave the number plate to a colleague in control, who told him the car belonged to a national hire company. Back upstairs, Knight found the phone number of their head office and after a few more minutes was staring down at the name of the company who'd hired the car out in London. It was one he knew well; he'd seen it several times during his life in the capital. Huggy's Cabs. It didn't take much imagination to substitute Huggy's for Hughes' and then the picture became clearer. One of Malc Hughes' many taxi companies. It was no surprise to find his new friend was part of the Hughes gang. In the corridor, Knight took another peek out of the window. The car was still there. Retracing his steps down through the alley and around to the back of the car, Knight crept as close as he dared. A woman waiting for a bus on the opposite side of the road watched curiously. Standing at a bus stop seemed a good idea, less conspicuous, so Knight made his way across to stand in the bus shelter, making sure the occupant of the car could only see his profile.

'It's okay, I'm a police officer.' he told the woman, showing his warrant card discreetly. She visibly relaxed.

'You just never know these days, you hear such stories.' the woman said. He still couldn't see the figure in the driving seat clearly.

'Fuck it.' said Knight audibly, causing the woman beside him to gasp, 'Charming!'

He marched across the road, up to the car and hammered on the driver's window. The man inside had a baseball cap pulled low over his brow, but Knight caught a glimpse of his face as he instinctively turned towards the noise.

Paul Hughes. Hughes, panicking, wrenched the car into gear and sped away. Knight stood in the road, hands on hips. Interesting. No doubt here to do some dirty work for his dad. A car slowed to pass him, the driver angrily gesticulating and Knight made his way back to the pavement. As he reached it, his phone started ringing. Catherine Bishop.

'You better get back here, sir, Bowles is awake.'

'Lucid?'

'Chattering away to the nurses. He doesn't know I'm here yet.'

'Don't let him find out.'

54

David Bowles was sitting up in bed flicking through a dog-eared magazine as Knight and Bishop approached.

'Any good knitting patterns?' asked Bishop, nodding at Bowles' reading material. He threw it down, blushing.

'One of the nurses brought it for me. Who are you?'

Bowles was still pale, his voice slightly husky. Bishop wondered if it was a result of whatever they'd had to do to get all the whiskey and paracetamol out of his system. Perhaps he always sounded like that. Bowles looked tiny in the hospital bed. Bishop bet he was about the same height as herself, on the small side for a man.

'Detective Inspector Knight and Detective Sergeant Bishop.' Knight said, observing Bowles closely to gauge his reaction. It wasn't subtle. Bowles grew even paler and shrank back against his pillows.

'Police?'

'Well done.' Bishop replied.

'But trying to commit suicide isn't illegal . . . is it?'

Knight didn't reply, just settled himself in the chair at the head of Bowles' bed. Bishop plonked herself down next to him, set the carrier bag she'd been holding on the floor and opened her notebook. Bowles' eyes flicked worriedly between them.

'Why are you here? Do I need a solicitor?'

'We just want to have a chat, Mr Bowles.'

'A chat? About what?'

'Why don't you tell us about Craig Pollard and Steven Kent?'

Bowles' face crumpled like that of an unhappy child. Tears ran down his cheeks and he did nothing to hide or stop them.

'They're dead.' Bowles managed to say.

'We know that, Mr Bowles. Why?' Bishop was curt.

Bowles glanced quickly around the ward. Of the four beds, only two more were occupied, one by an elderly man who was snoring. In the other, a younger man read a thick paperback.

'I don't want to talk here. Can't we go somewhere else?'

'We can have a trip to the police station if that suits you better.' said Bishop, making as if to stand.

Bowles protested, 'I'm ill, I've got to stay in the hospital.'

'Your doctor's just told us you can leave when you're ready.'

Staring, Bowles said, 'But that's rubbish, I've only just woken up, how can I go home?'

'Think of it as a miraculous recovery.' Bishop deliberately sounded bored.

'I've got no clothes . . .'

Bishop bent down to open the carrier bag, then threw a black tracksuit and plain white T shirt onto the bed.

'Put these on. We'll wait.'

She and Knight stood and a nurse stepped forward to pull the curtains around a stricken David Bowles' bed. After a few minutes, Bowles reappeared dressed in the tracksuit.

'It's too big.' He flapped his arms pathetically, the sleeves hanging over his hands.

'Beggars can't be choosers, Mr Bowles. Haven't you heard that one?'

Bishop strode away from the bed, Bowles scurrying along behind her and Knight bringing up the rear.

'I don't understand why you're being so awful. I'm ill, I'm . . . '

'You're coming with us.' Bishop said grimly.

In the interview room Bowles looked terrified, glancing around him as if he expected to be attacked at any second. Perhaps he did. Knight sat quietly opposite Bowles, content to let Bishop do the talking. She entered the room and placed a plastic cup of water on the table in front of Bowles.

'Thank you.' His hand shook visibly as he lifted the cup to his mouth. 'Am I . . . have I been arrested?'

'No, Mr Bowles. You're just answering some questions.'
Bishop took the seat next to Knight. Bowles licked his lips.

'Helping with enquiries?' He risked a smile.

'If that's how you want to describe it.'

'About Craig and Steve?'

'That's right.'

'I didn't kill them.'

'Can you help us find who did?'
Bowles looked wretched.

'I don't know.'

'Why don't we start at the beginning? How did you know Craig and Steve?'
They knew Bowles was the man who'd made the anonymous phone call asking for details of Pollard's death. Even from the grainy image they had there was no mistaking him.

'I lived near Craig. He knew Steve from somewhere, I don't know how.'

'So you were friends with Craig?'

'I wouldn't say friends, he wasn't really the sort of person you were friends with. He was the leader around where we lived, people followed him.'

'You followed him?'

Bowles' head went down.

'I suppose so.'

'Did you like Craig?'

'How do you mean, like? I just hung around with him sometimes.'

'When Craig asked you to?'

'I didn't go with them very often. He . . . they liked to tease people.'

'They teased you?' Bishop's voice was gentler now.

'Sometimes.'

'Craig especially?'

Bowles glanced at her.

'Yeah. Everyone joined in, but he always started it.'

'A bully.' Knight added.

'Yeah.'

'You were in hospital because you took an overdose of paracetamol, Mr Bowles. Could you tell us why you did that?'

'I'd had enough.'

'Enough of what?'

'Of everything. I left a note . . . '

'I know. I read it.'

He frowned, confused. 'How could you have?'

'A colleague and I went to your flat to question you and found you unconscious.'

'So you called the ambulance?'

'My colleague did.'

'Oh. I suppose I should thank you.'

'You're welcome. In your note, you said "I'm not going to wait for him to come and get me like he did Craig and Steve". Who were you referring to?'

'I thought it might be Nick, but now I think it's the boy from the moor.'

Bishop paused, startled. 'Which boy from the moor?'

Bowles raised his head to meet her eyes.

'The one whose little brother we killed.' he said quietly.

55

As Bowles was led to a cell, Knight and Bishop ducked quickly into the room usually reserved for legal representatives to wait in.

'Well, I wasn't expecting that.' Bishop said, feeling shaken.

'Seems we're going to get the full story at last. Is Anna around?'

'Not sure, she went out earlier to talk to Pollard's parents again.'

'I'll find her and get her onto checking the records, see if we can start piecing this together. There can't have been that many people killed on the moor. How have we missed this?'

'No idea, sir, I don't remember hearing about it before. We don't know though, the body could never have been found.'

'I don't want Bowles telling us any more yet.'

'Understood.'

'Can you make sure the duty solicitor's on the way? Not that Bowles seems to care, I think he just wants to get it off his chest now. I'll find DCI Kendrick, bring him up to date too. He'll probably want to observe. I want you to lead the interview, Catherine.'

Bishop stared.

'Okay, sir, if you're sure.'

'I am. We need to handle Bowles carefully, remember he's just recovering from taking an overdose and we don't want to upset him or traumatise him anymore than his story's going to. Kid gloves all round, unless it's necessary to change the strategy. I don't think it will be, I'll think the floodgates are about to open. I'll be back as soon as I can.'

Knight rushed out of the room and Bishop ran her hands through her hair. This was it, the breakthrough they had been waiting for, and yet it seemed almost an anticlimax. Bowles was sitting there ready to spill his guts and it was a result of his own suicide attempt, not the hours of work they'd put in. She supposed it was their investigation that had led them to Bowles; if she and Varcoe hadn't found him they wouldn't have him here at the station now. She didn't think he was the man they were looking for though and she knew Knight didn't either, but at the same time, he'd just confessed to a crime they hadn't even known about until this point. There was the possibility of closing three cases here; the Pollard and Kent murders and attempted murder of Brady, always supposing he did survive, the crime Bowles had just admitted to, and the people traffickers if Knight had his way. She felt expectation building, as well as the hope that the case would soon be over. The messages and photos would stop and the house would feel like her own again. The image of Milica Zukic's shy smile appeared in her mind. She imagined the faces of Pollard's children, thought of Kent's sister, Brady's parents. There were so many victims in this case and from what Bowles had said, more to come. Her own mother's face when she spoke of the child she'd lost . . . Bishop took out her phone. No messages. She was suddenly desperate to hear Claire's voice, for reassurance, for her to say that however long it took, she would be waiting, that whatever state Bishop was in after this was all over, Claire would still be there. It was so early in the relationship and although the feelings she had were the most intense she had ever experienced, Bishop knew she couldn't ask so much from Claire this soon. She'd have to do without the pep talk.

With Varcoe and Sullivan trawling the system and Kendrick watching through the two way mirror the interview resumed, more formal now, Bowles having been cautioned and with the duty solicitor sitting by his side. Bowles was calm, almost serene, ready to tell his story. The solicitor was a woman about Bowles' own age, neatly dressed in a navy suit and white shirt. Bishop, now entirely focused on the task in hand, went through the official preliminaries for the recording and began the interview.

'Mr Bowles, when we spoke to you earlier, you mentioned a boy that was killed on the moor. Which moor were you talking about?'

'Laughton Moor. You know, just out of town. We went up there a couple of times. I think Craig and Steve and a few of the other lads went there quite a lot back then. It was somewhere to have a few drinks, a swim if the weather was warm enough.'

'You're referring to Craig Pollard and Steven Kent?'

'Yes.'

'So you, Craig and Steve went up onto the moor?'

'I was at home, messing around in the garden, I think. Mum came and said there were some lads asking for me, so I went round to the front and Craig was there, he said I could go with them. I was pleased to be asked, to be honest. I don't know what it was about Craig but you just wanted him to like you, take notice of you. It was like he was a celebrity round here. I know that sounds stupid, but that's how it felt. He told me where they were going, that they had some cans of beer and I took a few bags of crisps from the cupboard as well. It was really warm, I thought it would be like a picnic.'

'Can you tell me when this was?'

'Summer. Mid July, twelve years ago. It was hot and I was sunburnt when I got home, I remember that.'

'Did you walk up to the moor?'

'Yeah. We called for Nick on the way.'

'Nick's surname?'

'Nick Brady, Nicholas Brady. He lived nearby too. He was another mate of Craig's, though I don't think Nick liked Craig much really, he always seemed to be laughing at him behind his back, being sarcastic or muttering about him.'

'But Nick still came with you that day?'

'Yeah, like I said, Craig was God where we lived. Even if you didn't particularly like him, it was still good to be seen with him, people would respect you. Nick wasn't above knowing that.'

Bishop thought of Nick Brady lying in hospital, his parents by his side not knowing when or if their son would wake. Craig Pollard and Steve Kent were both dead and Bowles himself had seen suicide as preferable to coming to the police. Bowles had said they'd killed, presumably a child. Bishop took another deep breath.

'So the four of you arrived at the moor. Can you remember the time?'

'Late morning. Before twelve, because we'd gone by the church as the clock struck eleven and it wouldn't take that long to walk up there. Around eleven thirty. We walked slowly though, talking, messing around. Craig was telling us about some girl he'd been with the night before, I can't remember the name but . . . It was always like that with him, a different girl every night if you believed him.'

'And did you?'

'Why not? All the lads wanted to be around Craig, so no doubt the girls did too. I didn't like the way he talked about them though. He wasn't very nice, not respectful. Laughing at what they'd done, things they'd said. It didn't seem fair for him to tell us. I think Nick felt the same because he wandered off in front but Steve wanted to know every detail and Craig loved boasting. We were walking alongside the stream by then, that's what everyone calls it though it's bigger than a stream really. Nick was skimming stones, Steve and Craig sat on the bank. I wasn't sure what to do. I watched Nick for a while then had a go myself but he was much better at it than me. Story of my life really.'

He looked to Bishop for sympathy but found none. Her face remained impassive.

'And then?'

'Eventually, Nick went and sat down too. I followed and Craig gave us a can of lager each. It was warm, but we drank it down and then had another can each. I was feeling a bit drunk by then, I wasn't used to drinking like Craig was. He could get served in pubs and everything. He went out at the weekends and in the week too, he told us. Beer or vodka. Then Craig said he bet he could jump over the stream but Nick laughed and said no way, he'd fall in. Craig stuck to his guns, but so did Nick. Craig started to get annoyed, told Nick he didn't know what he was talking about. Craig had to prove it of course, so he took a run up and jumped. He just made it and then came back and sat down, cocky as anything. He told Nick he owed him a tenner. Nick said if he could do it too they were even and Craig agreed, so Nick had a go. He nearly fell in on the way back and had to scrabble with his feet, but he got across.'

Bowles paused, took a sip of water and then another. He held out the empty cup.

'Could I have some more, please?'

More water was brought in, Bishop grateful for a cup too. Knight stretched in his chair then settled back. Bowles drank, fidgeting. Bishop waited patiently.

'When you're ready, Mr Bowles.'

'Steve went across too eventually and of course Craig was going on and on about me having a go but I knew there was no way I could do it, they were all miles taller than me. I just said no way and they let it drop eventually. We sat around for a while and then we saw these two kids heading our way. One had a fishing net in his hand, he was the youngest. He was about the same size as my cousin so he must have been about six, I'd say. The other was older, thin, eleven or twelve maybe.'

'Boys?'

'Yeah, they went down to the water and the younger one started trying to catch fish. I don't think there were even any fish in there. The older one was watching. It didn't take long for Craig to start showing off. He jumped across the stream again and stood on the other side, opposite where they were fishing. He asked them where they lived. The younger one said they were travellers, staying down the road somewhere and that their dad was doing some work for one of the farmers. Craig thought that was hilarious. He called them gyppos.' Bowles' unseeing gaze was fixed on the table as he relived the events that had haunted him, replaying the scene in his mind.

'I thought you looked like peasants,' Craig sneered, hands on hips. 'How many times have those clothes been handed down then? Bet your dad wore them first twenty years ago. You'd think someone would have washed them in the meantime. You stink, I can smell you from here.'

The younger boy glared at him.

'Ignore him.' the older one said.

'That's right, ignore the nasty man,' Craig mocked. 'What are you doing then, trying to catch some fish for your tea? Can't you afford anything else? Not sold enough pegs lately, or hasn't your mum had enough customers? Maybe Steve, Nick and Dave here could come over and have turns with her, God knows they have to pay for it.'

The older boy stared across at Craig.

'Come on, Tommy, let's go.' he said softly.

'No.' Tommy said. 'I want to catch some fish.'

Craig laughed nastily.

'That's right, you can't go back to your hovel with no fish, what will your mummy and daddy say? What will you have to eat? Maybe you'll be lucky and your dad will have found a turnip at the side of the road, you can take it in turns to have a chew on that.'

The older boy said again, 'Come on, Tommy.'

'No, I'm staying here, he doesn't scare me.'

The older boy stared at him in frustration, then walked away. He disappeared over the bank. Craig shook his head.

'You're a brave boy, Tommy. Not like pathetic scaredy cat there, running off home.'

'You're not clever,' said Tommy, dipping his fishing net into the water again. 'You're just a bully.'

Craig narrowed his eyes.

'A bully? What do you mean, a bully? We're just having a chat, you're lucky I'm even bothering to speak to you, you filthy fucking gyppo.'

Nick looked uncomfortable.

'Come on, Craig,' he said. 'He's only a kid.'

'Shut up, Nick, or fuck off home.' Craig snapped.

With a snort of derision, Nick got up and began to walk away.

'So,' Craig addressed the child again, 'How much scrap have you collected this week?'

'Scrap?' the boy looked bemused.

'Yeah, you know, scrap. What your dad brings home when he's finished stealing for the day. He brings it back and leaves it outside your shitty caravan where your mum's sitting making pegs and bunches of lucky heather, then you all go inside and look at the pictures in the newspaper, 'cos none of you can read.'

The boy glared, annoyed at last.

'I can read.' he said.

'Yeah, 'course you can.' laughed Craig.

'I can read!' the boy yelled, trying to launch himself across the stream towards Craig, who stepped back, laughing.

'Stupid little bastard, he'll never make it.'

Tommy was in the water, struggling and splashing. Nick ran back and started pulling off his shoes.

'Don't be daft, Nick, he'll be all right.' Craig said, turning away.

'I'm going in, he'll drown . . .'

Even Steve looked concerned now. Nick had his shoes and socks off and Bowles was wringing his hands. Craig leapt back over the stream and grabbed Nick by his T shirt.

'Don't you fucking dare. It's not that deep, he'll be able to get out further down. His brother's somewhere about, he'll get him. Come on, let's get out of here before somebody sees us.'

Bishop and Knight were silent. After a few seconds, Bishop scribbled furiously in her notebook and handed it to Knight: "RE. Messages left by killer: My brother died before I was born. Killer feels a link between himself and me?" Knight's eyes widened. He nodded and wrote a note of his own: "Has to be. We need to find the older brother, he's our man."

'What happened next?' said Bishop. Bowles stared at her tearfully.

'We ran. I still can't believe we did. We didn't even try to help him, any of us. We ran. All the way back Craig was telling us we had to keep it a secret, that he would kill us if we told anyone. We all swore not to, because we knew we'd be in so much trouble. His body was found later in the Trent, the stream must join it somewhere. We knew it was the same boy, his photo was in the paper. I think his death was put down to misadventure, something like that. I felt so terrible, like I'd pushed him in myself. Even now, all these years later I can't believe it, how we could all just have stood there and watched him wash away. I read in the newspaper that he'd hit his head while he was in the water and drowned. Tommy Heron. Six years old and dead because of us, because of me, because I just stood there and let Craig bully him into jumping, like he bullied us all . . .

Twelve years and every day it's all I could think about.' Bowles was sobbing now.

The duty solicitor, who had sat as if carved from stone while Bowles had told his story, sprang into life and rummaged through her bag for tissues. Bishop announced the interview was suspended for the benefit of the tape and she and Knight hurried out. Kendrick burst into the corridor then hustled them up his office.

'Brilliant, bloody brilliant. We need to find the records on this poor lad who drowned, find his brother's name and bring him in. Case closed by teatime.' Bishop looked dazed and Kendrick pointed a meaty finger at her.

'What's wrong with you?'

'It's just all making sense now. Pollard being killed first, hit more times than the others because he was the ringleader, then Kent . . . '

'All the victims were killed by blows to the head too. Bowles said the boy hit his head in the water and drowned.' Knight added.

Bishop quickly explained to Kendrick about the death of her own brother and the possibility that the killer had been referring to that in the messages.

'Bloody hell.' said Kendrick. 'How would he have known about it though?'

'I've no idea. It happened before I was born, he fell into a neighbour's pond when the ice broke. It was in the news but I don't think that many people know about it. My parents never came to terms with it, blamed themselves, blamed each other . . . '

Kendrick made an impatient gesture with his hand. 'Let's get on with it.'

56

Paul Hughes hurled his suitcase into the back of the hire car. He'd had enough. How his dad had thought he was supposed to find a woman who was being protected by the police he had no idea, but it had been a stupid plan from the beginning. He fully intended to drive back down south and tell his father so. Dougie had been worse than useless and he'd not even seen Richie, for all the good he was. It was time his father cut all ties with the bunch of Lincolnshire freaks he called family. He revved the engine, screeched out of the hotel car park and sped onto the ring road. He was soon on the M1, flying along and feeling more furious with every mile he travelled. His dad obviously had him down as some sort of mug, a tame monkey he could send off here and there at will. Surely he'd done more than enough to prove himself by now?

He pulled into some services, not even sure where he was. About halfway home, he thought. Abandoning the car at a jaunty angle, he strolled through the main building and into the toilets. As soon as he walked past the first cubicle door, it flew open to reveal a huge man wearing a black cap pulled low over his face. Hughes didn't have time to react as the man seized the front of the expensive leather jacket he was so proud of and dragged him towards a service door.

'What the fuck are you doing?' A huge hand clamped Hughes' mouth closed. He continued to struggle, but his captor was incredibly strong. The door clanged open and he was outside, drizzle just beginning to fall. Another man appeared and he was lifted off his feet, a black space looming in front of him. Disorientated, he took a second to realise it was the open back doors of a van. Unceremoniously, he was flung into the back, crying out as his knees and hands hit the metal floor. The doors slammed behind him and Hughes hunched his knees to his chest, terrified. He had no idea who had grabbed him or why, but he knew that he and his father had made a lot of enemies over the years. As the vehicle began to move, he was uncomfortably reminded of all those, like Milica Zukic, whose unhappy journeys in vans just like this had helped to pay for his jacket.

57

Kendrick led them into the CID room. At her desk, Bishop discreetly checked her mobile. Nothing from Claire. She turned on her monitor and began the search. Kendrick had gathered the rest of the team around him and was summarising Bowles' revelations. Reactions ranged from horror to anger, disgust to disbelief. They'd heard and seen worse of course, much worse, but the passivity of Kent, Brady and Bowles was shocking in itself. The noise level increased as Kendrick sent them back to their desks, the whole room fired by the desire to bring the brother of the dead boy to justice, whatever his motivation. Knight stood quietly by Bishop's desk.

'Here's a report on Tommy Heron's death.' Bishop said. Knight bent to study the screen.

'He did definitely die then, I wanted to clarify that first. We could have been looking for the brother when the boy himself might have survived, deciding to come after Pollard and the gang when he was old enough to fight his own battles.'

'I hadn't thought of that.'

They read silently. Sure enough, the boy had come from a travelling family and his death had been judged accidental. Bishop frowned.

'So why didn't the brother come forward at the time? Why didn't he tell his parents or the police that the only reason his little brother had fallen in the water was that a gang of yobs about three times his age had goaded him into it?'

'It doesn't make sense.'

Bishop kept searching, the minutes ticking away. Kendrick bustled over.

'There's a problem.' Bishop looked up at him. 'Why didn't Tommy Heron's big brother tell someone what happened? And why is there no mention of him in any of these reports?'

58

Kendrick's face was red as he clumped around Bishop's desk to stand behind her chair and peer at her computer monitor.

'What do you mean, he's not in the reports? He must be, wasn't he interviewed?'

'Doesn't seem like it. The boy's body was found before he was reported missing and the news was broken to his parents who said they'd told him hundreds of times not to go on the moors. The verdict of accidental death was given. If they were a travelling family, they probably moved on as soon as they could. Why would they want to stay in a place where their son died?'

'It doesn't make sense. Is Bowles sure they were brothers?'

'He seemed to be, but I suppose he could have just presumed . . . '

'Get back down there and find out!' Kendrick roared.

Bowles looked worse than ever. His tear stained faced was gaunt, as if he'd lost weight since they'd brought him to the station. He shuffled back into the interview room. Bishop restarted the recording and snapped at Bowles: 'Are you sure the other boy was Tommy Heron's brother?'

Bowles blinked at her, confused

'Who else could he have been?'

'His friend, his cousin, his nephew, his neighbour, his school mate, some kid he'd just met and decided to hang around with for the day? Am I making myself clear?'

Gawping, Bowles thought it through.

'So they might not have been brothers?'

'Did they do or say anything that made you think they were, or did you just presume?'

'I suppose I presumed, we all presumed. They didn't say anything when Craig talked about their mum and dad. It was just the way the older boy looked after the younger one, made sure he didn't stand too close to the water.'

Bishop didn't bother to comment, knowing they should have asked Bowles before whether he'd heard the boys speak to each other, whether names were mentioned. Back upstairs, Kendrick was working himself into one of his rages.

'If they weren't brothers, what chance do we have of finding him? He could be anybody, if they were travellers he could be anywhere. Can Bowles even describe this boy, not that it'll help us twelve years later, I expect he's changed slightly. Well?'

Bishop admitted that Bowles couldn't, not properly, nor could he give them a name. As Kendrick took a breath to refill his lungs in preparation for his next onslaught, Varcoe half stood and beckoned to them.

'Tommy Heron's parents are named as Annie and Christian Heron.' She pointed to her screen.

'And?' Kendrick barked.

'Annie Heron died six years ago, she jumped from the top of a bridge. Christian Heron died this summer, July, seems as if he was a heavy drinker. Do you think this could be what triggered the murders?'

'How do you mean?' asked Kendrick, calming slightly.

'Well, the mother of the drowned boy killing herself, his father drinking heavily and eventually dying as a result of it?'

'The whole family destroyed.' said Knight.

'Exactly.'

'It would make sense if we were still looking for the brother, but so far there doesn't seem to be one.' said Bishop, frustrated.

'I just thought it could be a motive.' Varcoe explained.

'You're right, and the timing works. The death of the father in July, a few months to track down Pollard, Kent, Brady and Bowles and start planning, following their movements. How would he know who they were though, the four of them?' Knight puzzled.

'If they mentioned each other's names when they were out on the moor, it wouldn't be too hard to track them down, would it?' Bishop asked.

'It took us a while, and he wouldn't have anything like the resources we have.' Kendrick wasn't going to let them forget that.

'We don't know how long he was planning this for. If he was determined enough, he'd find a way.' said Knight.

'True. We need to keep searching. I'm late for a meeting with the Super, I'll be back soon. Keep at it, we're almost there, I can practically smell him.' Wrinkling her nose at the DCI's imagery, Bishop turned to Knight.

'Still missing it, aren't we? Even though Bowles has given us all he can.'

'For now. We'll get there.' Knight spoke with more conviction than he felt.

59

Brady isn't dead, I knew it. That bloody dog, I should have killed it too, then made sure Brady was definitely gone. The newspaper says he's in a coma and from the miserable tone of the piece, it doesn't seem likely he'll be waking up in a hurry. As good as dead. Bowles has judged himself apparently and made an attempt at suicide. There was no mention in the paper. I suppose the police will be trying to keep it quiet just in case the nasty old murderer turns up to finish the job for him. They've served their purpose anyway. I followed one of Bowles' neighbours into the newsagent and heard her gossiping about it in there. She'd seen the ambulance take him away, and the man who lives in the flat below Bowles told her two policewomen had found him and called the ambulance.

It will soon be over. Such a relief.

60

Paul Hughes swore to himself that if he survived this day, he would try to persuade his father to concentrate on trafficking drugs, not people. It was so much more impersonal, less involved, and there was still plenty of profit to be made. They'd done all right out of drugs before after all. Perhaps this was the lesson his captor was teaching him; the terror and discomfort of the confined space, the unknown, the images dancing through your mind, each imagined version of your fate worse than the last. Hughes had a nasty sense though that the real lesson would be much more violent than a ride in the back of a van, however uncomfortable. Sure enough, before too long the van apparently left the relative smoothness of the road behind, turning left onto what seemed to Hughes to be the roughest track on the planet. Pothole after pothole, bump after bump, the speed the vehicle was travelling at worsening the ordeal. Eventually, to Hughes' relief but also to his horror, the van stopped and the doors were flung wide. Two men stood grinning at Hughes, their eyes registering his discomfort.

'Comfortable?' the taller man asked, his English heavily accented.

'Who are you? What do you want? You're making a big mistake here.'
The shorter man shook his head slowly.

'So many questions. There is no mistake, Paul Hughes. You are our guest.'
This man's English was more fluent, though still accented. Hughes stared from one to the other.

'Guest?'

'Oh, yes,' the shorter man said, reaching into his coat. His hand reappeared holding a gun. Hughes' eyes widened. 'You will learn what it feels like to be taken to a place where you have no identity, where you have no personality and are just there to be used by others who have no regard or respect for you.'
He waved the gun at Hughes, indicating he should get out of the van. Hughes scrambled forward, terrified, wide eyes searching his new surroundings. There was a barn and a yard but no further buildings in sight and no other vehicles.
The taller man had taken Hughes' mobile phone from him when they'd first bundled him into the van and had turned it off then. He now made a show of removing the sim card and battery, snapping the sim in two and stamping on the handset until it was no longer recognisable as a phone, just a pile of debris. The smaller man grinned.

'Much better. No interruptions. Now,' he shoved Hughes so he had to start walking, 'Move.'
Hughes stumbled towards the barn, following the taller man who had by now overtaken them. Nausea gripped his stomach and bile rose in his throat. He swallowed it down, not believing he'd get much sympathy from these two.
Trying to think clearly through the panic, he stammered:

'You don't need to do this. I've got money, I can . . .'

'What? A bribe?' sneered the man with the gun.

'Think of it as a gift . . .'

Both men laughed.

'No thank you, Paul. We don't want your money.'

'My dad will murder you.'

'I don't think so.'

They reached the huge double doors of the barn, which were padlocked. The smaller man kept the gun trained on Hughes while the tall one unlocked.
Hughes was then shoved inside. Dingy straw was scattered here and there on the

floor. The smell of animals remained but there were none here now unless you counted the two men, which Hughes supposed he did. Against one wall, a scarred pine chair stood waiting. A wave of the gun indicated that Hughes should sit. He moved slowly towards it, wondering if he should just try to run. If they shot then, at least it would be quick. The smaller man seemed to read his mind.

'Sit down, Paul. We want to talk to you.'
Hughes lowered himself gingerly onto the chair. The smaller man handed the gun to his friend, who levelled it at Hughes. Standing out of the line of fire, the smaller man stood relaxed, hands in his trouser pockets.

'So, Paul.' he said, tone friendly. 'Have you guessed who we are?'

'How should I know? Amateur gangsters from some shithole country in Eastern Europe I suppose.'
Both men narrowed their eyes.

'Be polite, Paul,' warned the smaller man. 'We can just shoot you now.'
Hughes swallowed. He knew they would. They'd not bothered to hide their faces from him, which couldn't be a good sign.

'So, again, do you know who we are?'

'I've no idea.'

'You will have many enemies.'

'I wouldn't know.'

'No, because your victims never have the opportunity to accuse you. We are here to represent them.'
Hughes wriggled in the chair.

'To represent who? What are you talking about?'
The taller man gave the gun back to his colleague, then took a length of clothes line from a reel on the floor and tied Hughes securely to the chair. Hughes struggled but the smaller man waved the gun at him and he contented himself

with shouting abuse instead. The smaller man came close and slapped him hard across the face.

'I told you to be polite.'

Hughes stared back, blood running from his nose.

'You are part of a group who has brought people, women and girls and some men, with promises of work and money into your country as slaves. Is it true?'

'No.' Hughes said firmly.

'A reminder, then.' said the smaller man. He nodded to his companion, who took a photograph from his pocket and held it in front of Hughes. A girl smiled out. Her hair was dark, her eyes huge and expressive.

'Who is she?'

'My sister,' the taller man said without expression. 'Now dead, because of you, your father, your friends.'

'Dead? But . . .'

'A drug overdose. Taken after eighteen months working as a prostitute in one of your filthy houses.'

The man breathed heavily through his nose then spat at Hughes' feet. He stepped back and reclaimed the gun.

'My cousin also came to this country to work for you. We rescued her from the place she'd been held for almost two years, forced to service men, hundreds of men, perhaps thousands. You dare to ask who we are?' He moved closer, leaning toward Hughes until their noses were almost touching, staring into Hughes' wide eyes. 'You will be punished and then you will be killed, though your suffering will still not be such as theirs. You will not exist for long in the hell they did, where not even their body was their own. Perhaps then your father and his friends will see the wrong they have done.'

I doubt it, Hughes almost said, but he thought better of it. Under no illusions, he knew his dad saw him less as a son, more as an employee. His father didn't seem to have the emotions other people had, either for his family or anyone else.

Hughes knew he was entirely dispensable. His captors exchanged a glance and the smaller man left the barn, soon returning with what looked to Hughes like a tool box. He set it down at Hughes' feet, then fetched several large petrol cans. Hughes stared at the box warily.

'What's that?'

'Tools, of course. The tools we need for our work.'

Bending, the smaller man opened the box. Slowly, he removed pliers, a hammer, a chisel, a few screwdrivers and a Stanley knife. He held each item up, making sure Hughes got a good look at them all. Hughes' eyes bulged, panic hurtling through him, one word racing through his brain. Torture. They were going to torture him to death. The smaller man grinned, picking up the hammer and weighing it in his hand.

'I see you guess our intentions, Paul. We will have fun, just like your customers had with our sisters, our cousins, our friends, our compatriots. Now,' he bent over the box again and retrieved a digital camera, 'Smile for your daddy.'

In the glare of the flash, Paul Hughes screamed.

61

'So what do we do with Bowles?' Bishop asked Knight, who shrugged.

'He can go back to the hospital for now. The DCI will probably ask the Superintendent Stringer about it.'

'What could we charge him with?'

'I'm not sure. Finding the boy from the moor has to be our priority, we know where Bowles is.'

'Yeah, crying like a baby in his cell apparently.'

'Poor thing.'

Bishop turned back to her monitor and Knight moved over to Varcoe's desk. The DC shook her head despairingly as he reached her.

'Nothing, boss, I can't find anything. How can we have no records on these people? Tommy Heron and his parents seemed to have arrived from nowhere and after Tommy's death, his parents must have gone back there.'

'It's difficult with no permanent addresses. Where did the parents die?'

'The mother in Birmingham, the father in Newcastle. Seems he'd been on the streets for some time.'

'Get onto Northumbria then please.'

Knight went to his office, half closed the door and turned on his monitor. He knew they were close, yet the man they sought still seemed to be in control, out of their reach. An email from Caitlin had arrived since he was last at his desk and feeling guilty, he quickly read through it. She was well and the baby was fine, that was all. He'd hardly thought about the unborn child, possibly his own son or daughter. There was already a stirring of emotion, a sense of wonder, almost a longing and Knight knew to protect himself he would need to take care. There was no point allowing himself to become attached to a fantasy. He might never see the baby, might never hear it mentioned again after its birth because he was not after all its father. He swore and deleted the email, then immediately regretted doing so. Caitlin should never have told him, not until she knew the truth herself. She would find out the sex of the baby, regardless of what she had said before. She would want to start shopping and if Knight himself heard whether the child was a boy or a girl, it would be harder still. The child would become even more real than it was now, a person in its own right with the beginnings of an identity. He would ask Caitlin not to tell him, not to contact him again until after the birth and the paternity test. Jed could do that. A test before the child was born was apparently possible Caitlin had said, but she wouldn't consider it. Knight wasn't sure why. A risk to the baby, perhaps? Or a risk to Caitlin's power?

An hour or so later, there was a thud as his half closed office door was barged open by Varcoe, closely pursued by Bishop, Sullivan and Rogers. Varcoe triumphantly waved a piece of paper at him.

'Jamie Fletcher, boss, he's our man. Look.'

She slammed the paper down on Knight's desk and he scanned it. Fletcher was the son of Annie Bacon, born before she married Christian Heron. Tommy's half brother and there was a half sister too. The age seemed to fit what Bowles had said. Jamie had been six when Tommy was born, making him twelve when Tommy died.

'We need to find Fletcher.' Knight said. 'Great work, Anna. Well done all of you.'

He picked up his phone and called DCI Kendrick, who shot through the door from his own office in record time.

'Where does this Jamie Fletcher live?' Kendrick demanded.

'There's an address over the other side of town.' Varcoe said.

'Right. Let's get some transport organised and bring him in. No messing this time.' He glanced over at Bishop, who was shutting down her computer. 'Sorry to break it to you, Sergeant, but you're not going.'
Bishop turned to stare at him.

'Not going? What do you mean?'

'I mean what I say. You are not going to bring Jamie Fletcher in.'

'But . . . '

'No. These messages, the photos, we've still no idea why he's been taking them, much less sending them to you. I don't want you anywhere near him. Go home.'

'There's no way I'm going home.' Bishop retorted. 'I want to be here to interview him at least.'
Kendrick folded his arms, every inch the immovable object.

'It's taken us long enough to find him and I don't want the investigation compromised by you arresting him or interviewing him. I don't want him to see you. Now, off you go. We'll let you know what happens, I promise you that. There's nothing to stop you coming in once he's here to watch the interview on the monitors, but there's no way you're conducting it. Do I make myself clear, Sergeant Bishop?'

Bishop muttered: 'Crystal.' and turned away. Without a word to her colleagues who were all watching sympathetically, she picked up her bag and pulled on her coat.

'Good luck, then.' she said over her shoulder and then she was gone, the door banging closed behind her.

62

Paul Hughes could no longer see, could no longer feel. His body was numb, senses overloaded, his will broken, his mind almost gone. His last conscious action was to offer a prayer to the God he had never believed in to end his life.

63

Bishop drove as quickly as she dared through the quiet streets. It was raining, more like fine mist than an actual downpour. The orange glow of the streetlights blurred in the drizzle, traffic lights changing to a fizzing red as she approached them.

'Typical.' Bishop muttered to herself, drumming her fingers on the steering wheel. She glanced around as she waited. An old warehouse had been converted into flats, the lights in the windows warm and welcoming. Bishop looked beyond them to the River Trent. It was wide at this point, just down the road from the only bridge that spanned its depths for miles. Bishop glanced at the icy blackness, the whirlpool currents and deceptive pace of the river well known by all who lived in Northolme. She thought of Richard, the brother she had never known who had died at the age of two. Her parents had always tried to make sure Catherine and her younger brother Thomas were aware of Richard. They celebrated his birthday, lit a candle on the anniversary of the day he died, spoke of him often and had lots of photographs on display. Against her will, she felt a link to Jamie Fletcher, having lost a brother in a similar way to herself. How much worse would have been for him though? His brother's death had not been an accident, but a result of the callous actions of four young men.

A car horn sounded sharply behind her and Bishop cursed, shoving the car into gear and moving off. Who knew how long the light had been on green. Her colleagues would be no doubt on their way to Jamie Fletcher's house now. Her fingers tightened on the steering wheel. Kendrick couldn't let her go with them, of course he couldn't, but she still felt hurt, dismissed, as if it were all her fault somehow. She drove on, concentrating only on the road ahead.

Jamie Fletcher was unlikely to be expecting them but Knight, Varcoe, Sullivan, Rogers and Lancaster were accompanied by a van full of uniformed officers as they made their way to his address.

Varcoe felt Sullivan shift in the seat beside her and glanced around at her colleagues. They all seemed apprehensive, nervous but excited. Only Knight sat still, preoccupied with his own thoughts. Varcoe had to smile; nothing new there then. Rogers caught her eye and smiled and she nodded back. They were about ten minutes drive away from Fletcher's address. Varcoe tried to relax, chewing on a fingernail. Sullivan grinned nervously at her.

'All right?' he asked softly.

'Yeah, fine. Hope Catherine is.'

'Oh, you know her. She knows it's for the best, however much she might sulk to begin with. She'll be there with bells on later, you watch.'

'No doubt.' Varcoe replied, gazing past Sullivan and out into the rain.

'Eight minutes.' called the driver.

Bishop aimed her car carelessly at a space in the hotel car park, grabbed her bag and ran through the now pouring rain. The wind was strong too, her hair immediately drenched to rat's tails, whipping around her face. She reached the main entrance, dragging her mobile from her bag.

Claire was waiting at the door to her room, a huge smile on her face. She slid an arm around Bishop's shoulders and guided her inside, rainwater dripping from her jacket onto the beige carpet.

'I'm making a mess.' Bishop protested.

'I don't care,' Claire said, closing the door and kissing Bishop softly. 'I didn't expect you this early. Oh, you're freezing. Why don't you have a shower? Are you staying?'

'I'd love to,' Bishop said, shrugging out of her soaking coat. 'Can we go and have a quick drink when I get myself sorted out?'

'Sounds good to me.' Claire smiled. 'How was your day?'
Bishop half closed the bathroom door.

'Ha. Not as long as it should have been, really.'

'How do you mean?' Claire called, draping Bishop's jacket over a chair.

'I'll tell you when I get out.' Bishop yelled back, turning and sighing as the hot water began to cascade over her. She hadn't realised how cold she was.

'Four minutes.'

The atmosphere in the van was tense, the excitement palpable. This was what they had been waiting for. Knight's mobile rang, making several of the officers jump. The display read DCI KENDRICK.

'Hello, guv?' Knight said.

'Knight,' Kendrick roared. 'Where are you?'

Knight glanced around.

'We're about four minutes away from Fletcher's house, I'm told. Why?'

'Turn around now and get your arses back here, quick as you can!'

'I don't understand, what's the problem?'

'The problem is that Jamie Fletcher was killed six months ago in a motorbike accident. He's not our man!' Kendrick's voice was loud enough for them all to hear. 'Get back here, Knight, and I'll show you something interesting, very interesting. That's if I don't decide to change the bloody locks and get rid of the lot of you – Jesus!' Kendrick hung up, cutting himself off mid rant.

Knight leaned forward to the driver, bemused. 'Well – you heard him.'

The driver clenched his jaw. 'The whole sodding town heard him, as usual.'

Bishop wrapped her wet hair in a towel, dried herself with another and slipped her clothes back on. Claire had thoughtfully put them to dry on the heated rail and they were hardly damp at all now.

In the main part of the bedroom Claire lounged on the bed, watching the news. She switched off the television as she saw Bishop and sat up, smiling.

'So what happened today? You seemed a bit . . . '

'Upset?' Bishop threw herself down onto the bed.

'Well, maybe.'

'We had a breakthrough, well, Anna Varcoe did. The whole lot of them, Knight, Chris Rogers, Anna and everyone are off to arrest our suspect, but I was told to come home.'

Claire frowned.

'But why? You've worked the whole case, haven't you? Since when do they send detectives home early on murder investigations?'

'Since . . . well, since there's a conflict of interest, you could say.'

Claire got up from the bed and went to stand by the window.

'What you mean, Catherine?'

'Oh, don't worry about it. I can go back in later anyway, so it might be a flying visit after all. Shall we go and have that drink?'

Claire moved again, over by the door this time.

'This suspect . . .' she said carefully.

'You know I can't talk about it.' Bishop said, sitting up on the bed and swinging her legs around so her feet were on the floor. 'What's wrong, Claire? Are you worried we've missed something?'

Claire shook her head slowly.

'What then? What's wrong?'

'Is your suspect called Jamie Fletcher, by any chance?'

Bishop gaped at her.

'How the hell do you know that? We only found out ourselves this evening and you weren't even at work today.'

Claire said, 'He was my brother.'

67

Kendrick's huge paw pointed at the monitor, his finger jabbing at the lines of text.

'Jamie Fletcher died earlier this year, he's not the one. Look. Look Knight, you bloody idiot. Look at his sister's name. The half sister, she's the one we want. Claire Fletcher, now masquerading as our own charming, smiley Intel officer – Claire bloody Weyton. HOLMES spat her name out straight away. Not quite as clever as she thought.'

Knight gawped at the screen. 'But how? She must have had background checks, the whole deal, same as we all have. Why the hell hasn't this been picked up before?'

Kendrick turned to him, furious as Knight had ever seen him.

'I've no idea but the Super's on her way in, no doubt the press are gathering outside and meanwhile we have one of our own picking off half the town. Where's she staying?'

Knight shook his head, trying to coax his brain into life through the shock.

'I don't . . . Oh, Christ.'

'What now?' Kendrick snarled, grabbing his phone and stabbing at the screen.

'Catherine Bishop.'

'What a-bloody-bout her?'

'The rumour is, she's been seeing Claire. She probably went straight to meet her after she left here.'

'You're joking. This gets worse by the fucking second. Phone her!'

Knight did as he was told.

68

Bishop was bemused, her stomach churning.

'Your brother? What do you mean, "was"?'

Claire took a step forward.

'He's dead. Everyone's dead, more or less. Just me left now.'

She smiled and Bishop shivered.

'But if he's dead, he can't have . . . '

'He didn't.'

'So . . . No. You?' The realisation hit Bishop like a punch.

'I'm afraid so.' Claire was matter of fact.

'You? You did this? Are you telling me you killed two people? Tried to kill another?'

'I would have had a go at Dave Bowles too, given the chance.' said Claire carelessly. 'Still, it doesn't matter now.'

Bishop shook her head, agonised.

'But Claire . . . Claire, I don't understand. I thought we . . . '

'I know, my lovely.' Claire took another step closer. Bishop shrank away from her on the bed. 'Don't be like that, Catherine.' She spread her arms wide, a pleading expression on her face. 'I thought you would understand, you more than anyone.'

Bishop's phone started ringing, making them both jump, the sound cutting through the strange, charged atmosphere in the room that had seemed so warm and welcoming to Bishop. Now she couldn't wait to escape.

'Where is it?' Claire asked softly. She bent forward, hauling a holdall from under the bed. The phone continued to ring.

'In my bag.' Bishop gulped.

Claire removed an object from the holdall and held it up. A cricket bat, stained with dark brown and chipped in places.

'I really wouldn't answer it, Catherine.'

Bishop sneered at her, nothing left to lose.

'You'd do that to me, would you? But I'm facing you, Claire, I can see you. You only usually batter people when they've no idea you're there, don't you? Can't run the risk of anyone fighting back.'

Claire snorted as the phone stopped ringing.

'Did my brother have a chance of fighting back when they taunted him? Did he? He was six, Catherine, six years old.'

'And you left him. It was you, wasn't it, on the moor that day? Not an older boy with his little brother at all but you, his big sister, supposedly looking after him. Some use you were.'

Claire passed the bat through the air a few times.

'I know that, I've lived with it ever since. Don't think you can make me feel any worse than I already do about it. Now, it's time I said goodbye.'

Bishop got slowly to her feet, her eyes never leaving Claire's. 'Claire Weyton, I'm arresting you . . . '

69

Knight listened to Bishop's cheery voicemail in dismay.

'No answer.'

'Right.' Kendrick ended the call he'd been on to headquarters in Lincoln.

'Weyton's staying at that hotel by the river. Let's go. Keep trying Catherine, but we'll be there in five minutes anyway. She'll be okay.'

Knight followed Kendrick out of the door, desperately hoping he was right.

70

Bishop's voice wobbled and broke. She tried again. 'Claire Weyton, I'm arresting you . . . ' She couldn't finish, her throat choked with tears. 'How could you, Claire?' she whispered. 'How could you work with us like you have, coming in every day knowing the person we were searching for was you? Letting me get close to you, letting me believe that you might feel something for me? And all the time it was pretence, just play acting so you could keep an eye on our progress.'

Claire gripped the cricket bat tightly.

'It wasn't like that, Catherine. In the beginning, I admit I planned to use you as much as possible, but then I felt . . . '

'What?' Bishop spat. 'You felt what?'

'Something I've never felt before.' Claire replied softly. Her blue eyes were dull, filmed with tears.

There was a silence. In the distance, they could hear sirens.

'I need to go.' Claire's head turned towards the sound.

'I can't let you, you know that. I'm a police officer.' Bishop said firmly.

'You have to, Catherine,' Claire pleaded, her voice tormented. 'I can't go to prison. Those men deserved it, you know they did.'

Bishop shook her head.

'That's not your decision, or mine. Why didn't you come forward before, or when your brother died?'

'My parents wouldn't talk about it, his death destroyed them. Jamie and I talked about revenge and then when he died too – well, what did I have left to lose?'

'So what, you got a job with the police and hunted them all down with your cricket bat?'

'Tommy's cricket bat. And yes, more or less. I didn't plan on meeting you though.'

Bishop shook her head again, vigorously this time.

'Stop it, Claire. It's over, you must see that.'

The sirens were nearer now. Claire held the bat tightly.

'I don't want to hurt you, Catherine, but I will if I have to. I can't stay, they're almost here. Let me go.'

'No chance.' Bishop snarled. In one movement, she leapt to her feet and sprang at Claire.

The police van screeched to a halt in the hotel car park, though Knight and Kendrick leapt out while it was still moving. They raced through the double doors and into the hotel, screaming at the terrified receptionist that they were police officers, wanting to know which room Claire Weyton was staying in. She searched frantically on her computer system, yelling the number out in panic, saying that Miss Weyton had a guest . . .

They thundered down the corridor, any thought of doing this subtly gone as soon as they had realised that Catherine Bishop could be in danger. They reached the right room and Knight pounded on the door. Terrified guests began appearing, wanting to know what the problem was. Kendrick yelled at them to close their doors.

No response from Claire Weyton's room.

'Open the door, Claire,' Kendrick bellowed. 'Right, we're coming in.' He took a couple of steps back and gave the door an almighty boot. It flew open and Kendrick staggered inside with Knight on his heels.

The curtains fluttered limply in the freezing gust that was blowing through the open window. In the centre of the floor lay a heavy cricket bat. Just beyond that was Catherine Bishop, face down, blood staining the carpet around her head. Of Claire Weyton, there was no sign. The rain continued to pour as Knight fell to his knees beside his sergeant and Kendrick sombrely took out his phone.

The body of Claire Weyton was recovered from the River Trent a few hours later, just before Catherine Bishop's first visitors were admitted. She lay in the hospital bed, her face mottled with bruising, her broken nose set. She had been crying, though Kendrick and Knight didn't mention that.

'Who'd have thought it, Sergeant?' boomed Kendrick, heaving himself into a green plastic chair and leaning forward to pat Bishop's hand clumsily. Bishop smiled ruefully, then winced in pain.

'Not me, guv, that's for sure.'

'We have some news.' Kendrick tried to arrange his face into an expression that conveyed regret, but couldn't quite manage it. 'I'm afraid Claire Weyton is dead. She threw herself straight into the river after she left you and drowned. Like her brother, I suppose.'

Knight winced and Bishop looked away for a second.

'She told me I'd have to let her go.' she said softly. 'I suppose she always planned to kill herself as well, I thought she just meant not arrest her.'

'About that . . .' Knight stepped forward. 'We'll have to take a formal statement, of course, when you're up to it, but . . . '

Bishop managed a smile.

'She didn't do this.' She raised a hand slowly, gesturing to her injured face. Kendrick snorted in disbelief.

'What are you on about? Looks just like her handiwork to me, apart from you've got a broken nose and a couple of shiners instead of a big hole at the back of your head.'

'She didn't do it, honestly. She'd already told me that she'd killed Pollard and Kent. I . . . I tried to arrest her, but I couldn't get the words out. We heard the sirens and she said I had to let her go. I told her I couldn't and went for her.'

With a gesture of impatience, Kendrick said, 'So she battered you with her trusty cricket bat.'

'No, I keep telling you, she didn't. I tripped over something on the floor, my bag I think, and I smashed into the corner of the bathroom wall where it juts out into the room. I must have knocked myself out cold.'

Kendrick stared then shook his head, muttering 'Jesus Christ Almighty, it's like bloody Police Academy.' He got to his feet. 'I know you're in pain and feeling sorry for yourself, so I'll leave you now. No doubt the Superintendent will be along for a chat.'

'Can't wait.' mumbled Bishop.

'Now now, Sergeant, that's no way to talk is it?' Kendrick grinned.

As he crossed the room, the ward sister strode in purposefully.

'I'm sorry, sir, I'm going to have to ask you to leave. You're upsetting the other patients.' she said firmly.

Kendrick gave an exaggerated glance around.

'What other patients? This is a private room.'

'The ones out there,' she gestured to the door, 'and on every other ward in the hospital. Your voice carries very well.'

Kendrick drew himself up. 'I should think so, I'm a detective chief inspector.'

'Congratulations, sir, now off you go.' She herded him to the door.

'Can I at least say goodbye?' Kendrick was enjoying this. She tutted.

'If you're quick.'

'Look after yourself, Sergeant. I'll call in again tomorrow.' Bishop waved. The sister rolled her eyes.

'We'll all look forward to it. Now, please . . .' she said.

'I'm going.'

The door closed behind them. Knight moved over to the bed, looking down at Bishop. Her cheeks flushed and she turned her face away.

'Don't.' said Knight gently. 'You weren't to know.'

'I just feel such a bloody idiot,' Bishop croaked, tears falling again. 'Some detective I am, falling for the prime suspect.'

'But she wasn't the prime suspect. None of us had any idea, so how could you have known?'

'Why didn't her name come up before?'

'Because we presumed the killer was a man? There was no reason it had to be of course, a young girl can easily be mistaken for a boy. Questions will be asked, no doubt.' Bishop grimaced. 'Honestly though, I don't see what more we could have done. Nothing pointed to her, nothing at all.'

They were silent for a while until eventually Knight said, 'Anna's waiting outside, wanting to see you. You need to get some rest too. They said you'll probably be able to come home tomorrow. You could stay with me again if you like? It's up to you, no rush to decide. I'll nip off and get a drink while Anna comes in, but I'll call back before I leave.'

'Thank you.' Bishop said. 'Thank you for . . . you know. At the hotel.'

Knight nodded, not trusting his voice. He'd held her in his arms until the ambulance arrived, then travelled in it with her to the hospital.

Anna Varcoe was sitting on a chair in the corridor and she jumped to her feet when she saw Knight.

'How is she?'

'Not a pretty sight, but she'll survive, that's the main thing.' said Knight. 'I'll see you in the morning, Anna.'

'Okay, boss. Goodnight.'

He began to walk away.

'Will she be in trouble?' Varcoe asked softly.

Knight turned back, meeting her eyes for once.

'I honestly don't know. Let's hope not.'

She nodded, then pushed the door open and walked inside.

'Hello, Anna. Here I am, detective of the year.' Bishop said, her voice hoarse.

'Rubbish. How were you to know? Stop that, Sarge, we all worked with her and none of us twigged.'

'Yes, but you didn't all sleep with her did you?'

There wasn't much Varcoe could say to that, so she stayed quiet. Bishop muttered, 'Sorry.'

Anna shook her head. 'Nothing to apologise for. Anyway,' she gestured to Bishop's face with its mess of blooming bruises, 'that colour's good on you.'

Bishop started to laugh and Varcoe touched her hand.

'You'll be fine, Sarge,' she said. 'Honest.'

73

When she was alone, all Bishop could think about was Claire. It had seemed so perfect. Had she missed the signs? Should she have realised? Knight and Varcoe said no, even Kendrick had in his gruff, clumsy way. She didn't believe them though, and couldn't imagine she ever would.

In time, Bishop closed her swollen eyes, exhausted but unable to sleep. Her bed was by the window and after a few hours, she saw an orange glow in the night sky – a fire, a big one. She tried to work out where it was, couldn't and eventually dozed.

Acknowledgements

This book has been a long time in the making, and there are a number of people who have helped me along. Huge thanks to my agent, Britt Pflüger of Hardy and Knox (hardyandknox.com) for her advice, hard work and encouragement.

Thank you also to my lovely friends Charlotte Sing and Debra Ramsdale who read the book and took the time and trouble to give me very valuable feedback and suggestions, along with lots of encouragement. Janet O'Kane also has been very encouraging and gave me some food for thought after reading one of the drafts. Thank you too to my Twitter friends for advice and lots of laughs.

Thank you to Christa Holland of Paper and Sage Design (paperandsage.com) for creating just the right cover.

Finally, a huge thank you to my wonderful family: my partner Tracy and our son and my Mum and Grandma for all of their support and encouragement and most of all for their unfailing belief in me. For Grandad too, who always encouraged me to do whatever I wanted to and who is greatly missed.

You can follow me on Twitter: @rainedonparade and my website is lisahartley.co.uk
Thank you for reading. DS Bishop and her colleagues will be back soon.